James Hadley Chase (born Re… born in London in 1906. H… which time he was inspire… and went on to write his own … also set in the United States. … with *No Orchids for Miss Blandish* w… …shed in 1939 and was one of the most success… …oks of the thirties, selling several million copies. George Orwell described it as 'a brilliant piece of writing with hardly a wasted word or a jarring note anywhere'. It was subsequently dramatised and performed on London's West End and also made into a film. Chase went on to gain popularity for his numerous other gangster stories, and by the end of the war he was one of Britain's most successful thriller writers. During his career he produced some ninety books, also writing under the names of James L Dochery, Ambrose Grant and Raymond Marshall. He travelled widely, though only visited the USA late in life. He died in 1985 whilst in Switzerland.

BY THE SAME AUTHOR
ALL PUBLISHED BY HOUSE OF STRATUS

An Ace Up My Sleeve
An Ear to the Ground
Goldfish Have No Hiding Place
The Guilty are Afraid
Hand Me a Fig-Leaf
Have a Change of Scene
Have This One On Me
Hit and Run
Hit Them Where it Hurts
Just a Matter of Time
Knock, Knock! Who's There?
Like a Hole in the Head
Make the Corpse Walk
More Deadly Than the Male
My Laugh Comes Last
Not My Thing
So What Happens to Me?
Tell it to the Birds
The Whiff of Money
You Have Yourself a Deal
You're Dead Without Money

JAMES HADLEY

CHASE

THE FAST BUCK

First published in 1952

This edition published in 2000 by The House of Stratus, an imprint of Stratus Books Ltd., 21 Beeching Park, Kelly Bray, Cornwall, PL17 8QS, UK..

www.houseofstratus.com

Typeset, printed and bound by The House of Stratus.

A catalogue record for this book is available from the British Library and the Library of Congress.

ISBN 1-84232-102-1

Cover design: Marc Burville-Riley
Cover image: Photonica

CONTENTS

PART ONE

Rico opened his office door and peered cautiously into the dimly lit restaurant. The long, narrow room with its tables already set for dinner, its small, rectangular dance floor, the band dais decorated with flowers, was empty and silent. He listened intently, then stepped back into the office and shut the door.

"Be another half-hour before anyone shows up," he said. "What are you nervous about?"

Seated by the flat, ornate desk in a red-leather lounging chair was a blond giant of a man, whose thick, lumpy shoulders dwarfed the back of the chair. His clothes were creased and dusty. His slouch hat had an oil stain on the front, and the ribbon was frayed. His big, granite-hard face was yellowish white, and his eyes were pale grey: the colour of ice.

Rico watched him with uneasy excitement. He was always nervous and unsure of himself when he was with Baird. He knew Baird was dangerous, and yet he was fascinated by him as some people are fascinated by a snake.

Baird pulled out a dirty, screwed-up handkerchief and tossed what it contained on the desk.

Rico peered intently at the emerald and diamond bracelet. A little pang of greed ran through him. He had never seen anything so beautiful. Then caution edged the greed out of his mind. The bracelet was beyond his class: to attempt to handle it would be as dangerous and futile as a midget attempting to fight Joe Louis.

"Don't I keep telling you to leave this kind of stuff alone?" he said furiously; furious because he was forced to recognize his own shortcomings. "It's no good to me. It's too dangerous. All these stones match. The value of the piece is as it is now. Break it up, and it ain't worth a goddam!"

"Don't feed me that crap," Baird said. His voice was surprisingly soft for a man of his size. "It's worth a couple of grand even if you have to break it up."

Rico shook his head. He wouldn't admit to Baird that he knew of no one to whom he could sell a piece of this value. Ever since he had first met Baird he had tried to impress the big man with his importance.

"I don't want it," he said. "It's too dangerous."

Baird looked at Rico, his pale eyes probing.

"All the same you've got to take it, Rico," he said. "I'm in a jam. The twist might die."

Rico stiffened. His heart skipped a beat and then began to race madly.

"What was that? What do you mean?"

Baird reached for a cigarette from a box on Rico's desk. He smiled jeeringly at Rico. The sudden fear in Rico's eyes amused him.

"The bitch tried to scream. There was a prowl car not more than ten yards away. I had to hit her."

Rico looked is if he were going to faint. He clung to the edge of the desk, his face turning white.

"Why, you crazy bastard!" he snarled furiously. "Get out of here! Don't you know this'll be the first place the cops will come to? They know you're always here. What are you thinking of? Get out and stay out!"

Baird eased his powerful muscles. All along he had known Rico was a cowardly little rat. He had chosen him because of his cowardice. There were plenty of other fences in town he could have gone to, but none of them would be so easy to handle as Rico in a crisis. He knew, too, he had a fatal fascination for Rico. He was everything Rico wanted to be: big, strong, ruthless, and a killer; he was the out-of-reach fantasy of Rico's private dreams.

"I want some dough," he said. He lit the cigarette and flicked the match across the room. "Give me five Cs."

Rico was frightened. Baird wouldn't have said the woman might die unless he had a good reason for saying so. Murder! This was something he hadn't bargained for when he had told Baird he could handle anything Baird brought to him.

He swept the bracelet across the desk towards Baird.

"Not a dime! Take it and get out! Think I want to be caught on an accessory rap? Maybe you're crazy, but I'm not!"

A muscle high up near Baird's right eye began to twitch. He opened his coat so Rico could see the butt of the .45 Colt he carried in a holster under his arm.

"Five Cs, Rico," he said, and Rico could read the threat in the pale eyes.

"No!" Rico said violently. His pockmarked face began to glisten with sweat. "You can't do this to me, Baird! You're not going to hold me up for something I don't want! You and me have worked together ..."

"Five Cs," Baird repeated, "and snap it up. I want to get out of town before the heat's on."

Rico snarled at him. He looked like a cornered rat as he crouched over the desk, his teeth showing and sweat running down his face.

"Get out!" he said. "Take that bracelet with you! I wouldn't touch it if you gave it to me!"

Baird's hand shot out and gripped Rico's shirt-front. He hauled him out of his chair, dragged him across the desk, sweeping papers, the cigarette box, the rack of fountain pens and the telephone to the floor. He stood up, lifting Rico off his feet. Rico hung in Baird's grip like a sawdust doll, staring with protruding eyes at Baird's expressionless face.

"I said five Cs," Baird said softly.

He slapped Rico's face with his left hand. He slapped it four times, very hard, knocking Rico's head from one side to the other. The sound of the slaps was like the bursting of a paper bag. Then he let go of Rico, who staggered against his desk, his knees buckling.

"Snap it up," Baird said, "or you'll get some more."

Rico staggered to his desk and sat down. His hand went to his cheek, which had puffed up and had turned the colour of port wine. He opened a drawer, took out a bundle of bills and counted out five of them. With a shaking hand he pushed the bills across the desk.

Baird picked them up, tossed the bracelet into Rico's lap and pocketed the bills.

"Why do you have to do it the hard way?" he asked. "When I want anything, I damn well get it. You should know that by now."

Rico didn't say anything. His fingers caressed his burning face, but he picked up the bracelet and dropped it into his pocket.

"I'll let you know where I get to," Baird went on as if nothing had happened. "I'll be back in a week if she doesn't croak. I've another little job lined up that might be something. If you hear of anything that'd fit me, keep it on ice until you hear from me? Okay?"

Rico licked his dry lips.

"Sure," he said hoarsely, his hand still on his cheek.

"Well, so long for now. Take a look outside. I don't want to walk into any trouble."

Rico made the effort and went to the door. He peered into the restaurant, listened, stepped back.

"Okay," he said. "Go through the kitchens. Don't let anyone see you."

"So long," Baird said again, and moved through the dimly lit restaurant, skirting the tables, moving softly, his hands in his pockets without looking back.

Rico returned to his office and straightened his desk. When he had picked up the various articles that had fallen to the floor, he sat down limply. He took out a mirror from a drawer and examined his reflection. His eyes were hot and intent as he stared at the livid bruise across the side of his face. He put the mirror away, got up and crossed over to a cellaret standing in a corner. He mixed himself a stiff whisky and soda, sat down again, and took the bracelet from his pocket. He studied it for some time. It was a beautiful piece. At a guess it'd be worth five or six grand. But who would buy it? He frowned at the bracelet. It was the best piece he had ever had through his hands; the best and the most dangerous.

He got up and locked the bracelet in a concealed wall safe. He would have to wait and see if the woman died. If she didn't die it might not be so difficult to find a buyer. But if she did ... He grimaced and took a long pull at his glass.

He went into the bathroom, leading off his office. He spent some time holding a sponge of cold water against his burning face, his eyes still hot and intent, his mind busy.

What a guy that Baird was, he thought. Not a nerve in his body! "If I want anything I damn well get it," he had said, and it was true. Working with a fella like Baird meant big-time, Rico told himself. It was dangerous, but look what he stood to gain! He gently patted his face dry. He felt no anger or animosity against Baird for hitting him. It was just another proof of his strength of purpose. Baird was like no other crook who came to Rico. No one else would have dared to touch Rico.

Rico adjusted his tie, smoothed down his thinning hair and went back to the office.

He came to a standstill just inside the door, fear clutching at his heart.

Seated in the red leather chair, chewing a dead cigar, was a short, thickset man with a red, freckled face, sandy hair and wide-set, cold, green eyes. He had on a grey suit, a little baggy at the knees and shiny at the elbows; a nigger brown hat rested far to the back of his head.

"Hello, Rico," he said, eyeing Rico's face with his bleak, green eyes. "Who's been knocking you around?"

Rico smiled stiffly; his mouth felt frozen.

"How did you get in here, Lieutenant?" he asked, coming to the desk. "I haven't seen you in weeks."

Lieutenant George Olin of the Homicide Bureau crossed one thick leg over the other, took the cigar out of his mouth and stared at it with an expression of disgust. He tossed it into Rico's trash basket, produced a cigar case, selected another cigar and put the case back in his pocket.

"I sneaked in," he said, staring at Rico. "I hoped to catch you on the wrong foot. Have I?"

Rico tried to laugh. The croaking sound he made deceived neither himself nor Olin.

"I'm very careful where I put my feet," he said, and sat down. "What's on your mind, Lieutenant?"

"Suppose you tell me," Olin said. "Had any visitors within the past half-hour?"

Rico poured himself another drink while his mind worked swiftly. Had there been a patrolman watching the club? He didn't want to admit Verne Baird had just left, but if the club was being watched, and Baird had been seen leaving, it would be awkward to be caught in a lie. But as lying came more naturally to him than telling the truth, he decided to lie.

"I haven't had anyone in here," he said carefully. "The club doesn't open until eight." He glanced at the desk clock. The time was twenty minutes past seven. "I've been working. Of course, anyone could have come into the restaurant without me knowing: like you did."

Olin grinned sourly. He knew all about Rico. He knew he was itching to move out of small-time into big-time. He had been watching Rico for months now, waiting for a false move.

"Still playing it close to your chest, Rico? One of these days you're going to lie yourself into the gas chamber. I hope I'm there to spit in your eye before they close the door."

Rico continued to smile, but his eyes shifted uneasily. Even when spoken about in jest, death had a horror for him.

"What's biting you, Lieutenant? You sound a little sour tonight. Have a drink?"

Olin shifted his squat figure to make himself more comfortable.

"I don't drink on duty," he said, rubbing his fleshy jaw. "Who hit you – Baird?"

Rico was expecting something like that, but although he was prepared he couldn't conceal a little start that told Olin all he wanted to know.

"One of the girls," Rico said, and lifted his shoulders. "I thought she was a pushover, but I made a mistake. The little devil hit me with a hairbrush."

"Good for her," Olin said. "Where is she? Maybe I could persuade her to make a charge against you."

Rico laughed.

"She went home. There was nothing to it, Lieutenant. It happens every day. But why bring Baird into this?"

"Has he been here tonight?"

"I haven't seen him," Rico said, shaking his head. "I haven't seen anyone but you tonight."

"And your pushover friend," Olin said.

"Well, yes ..."

Olin lit his cigar, puffed contentedly for a moment, took the cigar from between his teeth and blew gently at the glowing end.

"About a couple of hours ago," he said, looking at Rico "Jean Bruce, the actress, in case you don't know, left her house to attend some shindig at the Martineau Galleries. Between her house and the end of the drive, she was held up and robbed. An emerald and diamond bracelet worth five grand was stolen. From the way the stick-up was staged, it's my bet Baird did it. There was a prowl car within twenty yards of the robbery, and the officers didn't see or hear a thing in spite of the fact it was done in broad daylight. Baird specializes in that kind of recklessness. He's been hanging around this club for the past few months, so I thought I'd drop in and see if you and he were dividing the spoils."

Rico sipped his whisky, patted his thin lips with a stiff linen handkerchief and stared back at Olin, his eyes intent and sick looking. At this moment he wished he had never had anything to do with Baird.

"Couldn't she identify him?" he asked. "He's big enough. I don't like that last remark of yours, Lieutenant. You can't talk that way to me."

Olin tapped ash on to the carpet. He showed his teeth in a mirthless smile.

"Can't I? Who's going to stop me? The reason why she can't identify Baird is because he murdered her!"

Rico gulped, and his smile slipped. He thought with horror of the bracelet in the safe.

"Murdered her?" he croaked. "How do you know Baird did it? What proof have you got?"

"He's a killer," Olin said quietly. "I've rubbed around with crooks long enough to know who will kill and who won't. Ever since Baird blew into town I've been watching him. I knew sooner or later he'd break loose and kill someone. He's dangerous, Rico. Up to now you've played around with the little punks, but Baird isn't a little punk. He's a killer. Take my tip and keep clear of him. The guy who tries to pass that bracelet is booking himself a one-way ride to the gas-box."

Rico felt a cold chill run up his spine. He hurriedly gulped down the rest of the whisky.

"I've never been in trouble," he said, his face twitching. "You've nothing on me. You never have, and you never will have."

Olin made a weary gesture.

"Don't be a sucker, Rico. You haven't a bad little club here. You're making nice money. Keep clear of guys like Baird. If you know anything about the bracelet, now's the time to spill it. Why do you think I came here? Ask yourself why I didn't send a couple of my boys to pull you in and push you around just for the hell of it. I'll tell you why. I'm ready to do a deal with you, Rico. There's going to be a hell of a stink when the press hears this Bruce woman's been knocked off. I want it cleaned up quick. If you know anything about it, spill it, and I'll keep you out of it. That's a promise. I don't want you: I want Baird!"

Rico felt a sweat trickle down the back of his neck. He knew he could trust Olin, but if he fingered Baird, and Baird heard about it before Olin could reach him, Rico's life wouldn't be worth a damn.

Olin, who had been watching him closely, guessed what was going on in his mind.

"We'll pick him up in a few days. In the meantime, if you'd feel happier, I could tuck you away in a nice safe cell. Come on, Rico, get smart. It was Baird, wasn't it?"

Rico made up his mind. For the past year now he had dealt with petty crooks, making a nice sideline in stolen property. Baird was his first big client. He had made a lot of money out of his transactions with Baird during the past months. Besides, if he fingered Baird the rest of them would drop him like a hot brick. He wasn't going to be stampeded just when he was moving into big money.

"If I knew, Lieutenant, I'd tell you," he said with an ingratiating smile. "But I don't know. I don't know nothing about Miss Bruce or her bracelet ... not a thing."

Olin sat for a moment staring at Rico, his face slowly tightening with rage.

"Sure, Rico?" he said, leaning across the desk. "And, by God! you'd better be sure!"

Rico flinched back.

"I'm sorry, Lieutenant," he stammered, "but I can't tell you what I don't know. I haven't seen Baird since the day before yesterday. I don't know nothing about the bracelet ..."

Olin got up.

"I'll get Baird," he said, his face set and menacing. "Make no mistake about it. Don't kid yourself he won't talk. He won't go to the chamber alone. If you're hooked up with him, you'll go too! I'll give you one more chance, and you'd better take it. Have you got that bracelet?"

"I tell you I don't know a thing about it!" Rico said, through clenched teeth.

Olin reached across the desk and grabbed hold of Rico's coat front, pulling him out of his chair. He shook him savagely.

"God help you if I find out you're lying, you little creep!" he snarled, and flung Rico back into his chair so violently the chair went over backwards and Rico sprawled on the floor. "And don't think you've seen the last of me!" Olin went on. "I'll be back."

For a long time after Olin had gone, Rico sat at his desk, staring with empty eyes at his twitching hands, and sweating.

II

Ed Dallas steered his tall, lanky frame into a pay booth. While he waited for a connection, he surveyed the busy hotel scene through the glass panel of the booth door, his eyes shifting from one beautiful woman to another, trying to make up his mind which of them he would take out for the night should a miracle happen and give him a choice.

A girl's voice said in his ear, "International Detective Agency. Good evening."

"This is Ed," Dallas said. "Gimme the old man, will you, honey?"

"Hold a moment, please," the girl said, and proceeded to make violent crackling noises in Dallas' ear.

"Must you knock my brains out?" Dallas complained, holding the receiver at arm's length. "Why don't you use your hands instead of your feet?"

"I would if I thought you had any brains," the girl said pertly, and completed the connection with a loud whistle on the line.

Harmon Purvis, head of the agency, said in his dry, flat voice, "What is it, Dallas?"

"The Shine's just had callers," Dallas said, speaking rapidly, the glowing end of his cigarette bobbing up and down within an inch of the telephone mouthpiece. "A man and woman. The man's a well-nourished bird, pushing fifty, and looks made of money. The woman's a nifty; young, blonde, with a shape that's knocked my right eye out. The Shine was expecting them. They bypassed the desk and went right up. Want me to do anything about them?"

"Don't call the Rajah a Shine," Purvis said coldly. "He's a high-class Hindu. He may be coloured ..."

"Okay, okay," Dallas said impatiently. "I wouldn't know the difference. What about these two? Want me to cover them?"

"Better find out who they are," Purvis said. "We can't afford to take chances. They're his first callers, aren't they?"

"If you don't count the two rubes from the Embassy, and the floozy he had up there last night to fix his insomnia."

Purvis said he didn't count them.

"Well, okay. I'll see what I can do. I'll buzz you on the next move. So long for now."

Dallas replaced the receiver, pushed open the booth door and walked fast across the lobby of the Hotel Cosmopolitan to where Jack Burns was reading a racing sheet, with one eye on the reception desk.

Dallas leaned over his shoulder.

"The old man wants me to find out who those two are," he said. "Stick around and try to earn your money. If anyone shows up, give the old man a buzz."

Burns groaned.

"If I have to sit in this goddamn lobby much longer, I'll go nuts," he grumbled. "I wouldn't mind trailing that blonde myself. Get her telephone number, Ed. She might make blind dates."

"Not with you, she wouldn't," Dallas said. "A nifty like her needs the velvet touch. I could rock her dreamboat myself."

"You'd have to knock over a bank before you got within a mile of her," Burns said, mopping his round fat face. "A frill with that shape doesn't have to give anything away. It'd cost you plenty."

"You could be right at that." Dallas straightened. "Don't fall asleep on the job. The old man thinks this's important."

"I wish I did," Burns said, yawning.

Dallas made his way through the crowded lobby to the main entrance. He sat down in a basket chair, shifted it around so he could watch the elevators and waited.

He had a long wait. It was over an hour before the Rajah's visitors appeared. The girl came first: an elegantly dressed blonde with big blue eyes and a cold, sophisticated expression that intrigued Dallas. She moved gracefully, swaying her hips in a way that made all the men in the lobby look back at her, aware she was creating a sensation as she passed, and accepting it as her due.

Her companion was a tall, darkly tanned man, a little heavy around the waistline, but very upright. His sleek grey hair was taken straight back, and his military moustache bristled. In his immaculate clothes he had an arrogant air of confidence and authority that impressed Dallas, who wasn't easily impressed.

They passed Dallas without noticing him, and went down the hotel steps to the street. Dallas slid out of his chair and went after them. He was in time to see them get into a big black LaSalle, driven by a smartly uniformed Filipino chauffeur, and which moved away so quickly that Dallas saw he hadn't a hope of following it.

He memorized the licence number and signalled to a passing taxi.

"Police Headquarters," he said urgently, "and imagine you're driving to a fire!"

Three minutes later, the taxi pulled up outside the concrete and steel building that housed the city's police. As Dallas paid off the driver he saw Lieutenant Olin get out of a police car and start up the stone steps leading to the main entrance of the building. He ran after him.

"Hi, George," he said, joining Olin. "Too busy to do me a favour?"

Olin frowned at him.

"I'm pretty busy," he said reluctantly, "but I guess I can spare you a minute. Come on in. Have you heard Jean Bruce has been knocked off?"

Dallas' eyes popped.

"You mean she's been murdered?"

"That's what I mean." Olin walked quickly along the passage to his small office, kicked open the door, entered and sat down behind a small battered desk. "A stick-up job with a couple of my boys sunning themselves within yards of it. The guy got away with an emerald and diamond bracelet worth five grand. He hit the girl on the side of her jaw – broke her goddamn neck."

"Jeepers!" Dallas whistled. "Any idea who?"

Olin nodded.

"Yeah, but never mind that. What do you want?"

"Checking up on a black LaSalle, licence number AO 67. I want to know who owns it."

Olin accepted the cigarette Dallas pushed at him, and then a light.

"Working on something?"

"A fifteen-year-old robbery," Dallas said. "Want to hear about it? It's a good story."

Olin shook his head.

"Robbery isn't my line. Besides, who cares about a fifteen-year-old robbery?"

"The insurance companies – when the amount involved is four million," Dallas said seriously.

Olin looked startled.

"Is that right? Four million?"

"Yeah. The insurance companies were caught for the lot. They paid up, but they are still trying to find the jewellery."

Olin squinted at his cigarette end.

"I think I remember something about that job: wasn't it a Rajah's collection?"

"That's right. The Maharajah of Chittabad. He lent the whole of his family heirlooms to the Purbright Museum. That was fifteen years ago. The museum was staging an exhibition of the world's most famous gems. The Maharajah had his collection flown to New York. They never arrived, and they've never been seen since. A year later a fence in Holland was approached by Paul Hater with some of the stuff. Remember Hater? He was the smartest jewel thief of them all. The fence shopped Hater because Hater wouldn't agree to his price. Hater was arrested, but he wouldn't tell where he had cached the collection. He got twenty years: he's still serving his sentence, and is due out in a couple of years time. Old man Purvis is representing the insurance companies, and we've been trying to find the stuff ever since. Our one hope now is to wait until Hater comes out and then stick to him like leeches in the hope he'll lead us to the hiding place. There's four hundred grand in it for us if we get the stuff back, as well as a yearly retainer."

Olin blew smoke down on to his grubby blotter, then waved it away irritably.

"Did Hater do the job alone?"

Dallas shrugged.

"No one knows. The pilot and the crew of the plane were never found: nor was the plane, for that matter. We figure they must have been working with Hater, but he wouldn't finger them. We're pretty certain the stuff's never come on the market. Hater's the only one, as far as we know, who knows where it's hidden."

Olin pushed out his aggressive jaw.

"I guess my boys would have made him talk," he said sourly.

"Don't kid yourself. They worked over him until he looked as if he had been fed through a mincer. Nothing anyone did to him – and they did plenty – could make him open his trap."

"Aw, the hell with this!" Olin said impatiently. "I've got me a murder to solve. What do you want this car owner for?"

"A couple of years back, the Maharajah died," Dallas explained. "His son came into the estate. This guy has his own ideas of how to live, and he's been throwing his father's money around like a drunken sailor. Rumour has it he's run through half the old man's fortune already. Without warning he suddenly turns up here. The insurance companies have the idea he's over here to contact Hater. They think he's going to do a deal with Hater somehow or other."

Olin stared.

"What sort of deal?"

"They think Hater would be glad to sell the stuff back to the Rajah at a price. They argue the Rajah could get rid of it far easier than Hater could. From what they hear about the Rajah they think he's quite capable of sticking to both the jewels and the insurance money. Personally, I think it's a lot of phooey, but you can't tell these insurance birds anything. They've hired us to watch the Rajah, and report to them who he's seeing while he's here. Up to now the only two he has seen are the man and woman who left his hotel in this LaSalle. I want to know who they are."

"Well, I guess I'd better do something about it," Olin said, reaching for his phone. "Purvis has done me a lot of good in the past. How is the lug, anyway?"

"Just the same," Dallas said gloomily. "Doesn't spend a nickel more than he can help, and still thinks a woman's place is in the kitchen, and no place else."

"That's Purvis all right. He gave me a box of cigars last Christmas I swear he made himself."

"You can consider yourself lucky," Dallas said, grinning. "He didn't give me a thing. How about a little action on that car number? I haven't got all night."

Olin spoke into the phone, listened, waited, grunted and hung up.

"The car belongs to a bird named Preston Kile. He has a house on Roosevelt Boulevard which puts him in the money. Does that help you?"

"Not much. You wouldn't like to ask Records if they've anything on him?"

Olin sighed, dialled, spoke again into the phone. While he waited, Dallas crossed over to the window and stared down at the two-way stream of traffic flooding the main street. He spotted the *Herald* truck unloading a pile of newspapers at the corner. The boy snatched them from the driver and began running along the sidewalk, yelling excitedly.

"Looks like your murder's hit the headlines," he said.

"It's going to make a sweet stink," Olin said, grimacing. He spoke into the telephone again, then hung up. "We've got nothing on Kile. We don't know him."

"Well, okay and thanks," Dallas said. "I guess I'll have to do a little more leg work. This job gives me the hives. So long, George. Hope you find your killer."

"I will," Olin said, scowling. "The dragnet's out for him now. It's just a matter of time. If your job gives you the hives, my job gives me ulcers. So long. Drop in when I'm too busy to see you."

Dallas grinned and walked quickly along the corridor, down the stairs to the street. He took another taxi to the *Herald* offices, made his way through a maze of corridors to Huntley Favell's office, rapped and pushed open the door.

Favell was the *Herald's* gossip column writer. He made it his business to know everything about anyone in town whose income ran into four figures.

Dallas was a little startled to find Favell and a pretty red-haired girl wrapped together in an embrace worthy of the best traditions of Hollywood. They sprang apart on seeing Dallas, and the girl slid past him, her face scarlet, and fled from the office.

Favell, completely unruffled, eyed Dallas coldly. He was a tall, thin Adonis, with a Barrymore profile, who lived well above his income and was glad to augment his earnings by selling information to the International whenever the opportunity arose.

"Don't you know better than to burst into a private office like that?" he asked tartly as he sat down behind his desk.

"I wasn't thinking," Dallas said, grinning. "Accept my apologies. The next time I'll let off my gun before coming in."

"There's no need to be facetious," Favell said, wiping his mouth carefully with a handkerchief. He eyed the smear of lipstick that appeared on the handkerchief with a grimace of displeasure and tucked the handkerchief away. "And don't go getting any wrong ideas," he went on, distantly. "She had something in her eye."

"Sure. I always get things out of a girl's eye in the same way." Dallas sat on the edge of the desk and offered Favell his cigarette case. "I dropped in for a little information."

Favell's acid face brightened, but he didn't say anything. He lit the cigarette, leaned back in his chair and waited.

"Know anything about a guy named Preston Kile?" Dallas asked.

Favell seemed surprised.

"Why? Is he in trouble?"

"Not to my knowledge. I spotted him with a blonde who interested me. Is he likely to be in trouble?"

"He's seldom out of it," Favell said. "I haven't time to waste talking to you, Dallas. I've got my column to polish up."

Dallas took out his wallet, selected two tens and dropped them on the desk.

"That should cover five minutes of your precious time," he said. "I want to know as much about Kile as you can tell me."

Favell hurriedly pocketed the bills.

"I don't know a great deal," he said, relaxing. "By the way, you can keep your trap shut about that redhead. She has a husband in the wrestling racket, and he's been waiting to pick on me."

"Never mind about her: tell me about Kile."

"He comes from San Francisco. Hasn't been here more than a couple of months. He's bought a big house on Roosevelt Boulevard which he hasn't paid for yet, and probably never will. Three years ago he was a successful market manipulator and cleaned up a packet, but since then he seems to have dropped out of business. He spends a lot of his time on the racetracks. He must win more than he loses, as he doesn't seem to have any other means of making a living."

"What's this about trouble?"

Favell stubbed out his cigarette, and helped himself to another from Dallas' case.

"Scandal more than trouble. The guy's never grown up. His theme song's wine, women and irate husbands. He specializes in married women, and a couple of husbands have taken shots at him in the past. One of them winged him. It was hushed up, but it didn't teach him a lesson. He gets into brawls as easily as you get into bed. He drinks too much, and when he's lit up, he gets tough. For a man of his age he should know better, but he just won't learn."

"Who's the blonde he's going around with?"

"Eve Gillis. Quite a dish, isn't she? He took her out of the Follies about a month ago and set her up in an apartment on Roxburgh Avenue. It can't last long. He's a love 'em and leave 'em Joe, but from the look of her she'll get what she can out of him before he gives her the gate."

"They called on the Rajah of Chittabad about an hour ago," Dallas said thoughtfully. "From what you tell me they don't sound like people a Rajah would entertain."

Favell looked interested.

"They're not. Are you sure?"

"Yeah; I saw them go to his suite."

"You still working on that jewel robbery?"

"Sure; it's Purvis' main source of income."

Favell thought for a moment, his polished nails tapping on his blotter.

"You may be on to something here," he said at length. "I've heard rumours that Kile is in contact with the underworld. Just rumours, mind you; nothing concrete. I've never been able to get any proof. He spends a lot of his time at the Frou-Frou Club. It's run by a wop named Ralph Rico, a small-time fence. Rico's slowly moving up in the world. It wouldn't startle me to hear Kile's behind him. It might pay off to keep an eye on Rico."

"The police haven't anything on Kile," Dallas said, frowning.

"I know that. I tell you at one time Kile was in the money in a big way. Some of his deals were a little questionable, but then most big-shot financiers do edge over the line sometimes. What puzzles me is he's been out of business now for two years. Admittedly he's probably worth a lot still, but he certainly knows how to spend his money. You could do worse than to look into his association with Rico. He may be planning something."

"Okay, I will." Dallas slid off the desk. "If you hear anything you think'd interest me, give me a buzz."

"Don't blame me if there's nothing to it," Favell said, reaching for a pile of copy in his in-tray. "These rumours about Kile may be a lot of phooey."

"I know. Half the tips I get lead nowhere," Dallas said gloomily. "That's the hell of this job. Well, so long. Next time you stage an eye operation, better lock the door."

He went out, tipped his hat to the redhead who was busily typing in the outer office, grinned to himself when she tossed her head at him, and made his way rapidly down to the street.

III

So she was dead!

Verne Baird crushed the newspaper between his big, powerful hands. His pale eyes ranged over the noisy saloon, packed with people, cloudy with cigarette smoke and strident with voices, laughter and the jangle of a jukebox. No one was looking his way, and he dropped the newspaper on the floor, kicking it out of sight under the booth seat.

Damn her! he thought savagely. To have died like that! It wasn't as if he had hit her more than once. A broken neck! It was unbelievable!

He would have to get out of town now. Olin would be certain to pick on him. What a fool he had been to waste a precious hour in this saloon! He should have gone as soon as he had got his getaway stake from Rico. Now it wasn't going to be easy to get out. Every cop in town would be looking for him.

He signalled to the negro bartender, who came over, his face glistening with sweat.

"Another beer with a shot of rye," Baird said, "and snap it up."

While the negro went back to the bar, Baird lit a cigarette. He had no qualms about killing this woman. This wasn't the first time he had killed. The act of taking a life was of no consequence to him. If someone got in his way, he killed them. Even his own life was of no value to him. He knew, sooner or later, the police would corner him, and it would be his turn to die. But so long as he had life in him, he would rage against any interference, any break in his planned routine, and this woman's death was going to upset his plans. He wouldn't be free to wander the streets or sit in a saloon or drive the battered Ford along the highway when the mood was in him to escape from the noise and the congestion of the city's streets. He would have to watch his step. He couldn't walk into a saloon now until he had carefully checked what exits there were, if a copper was lurking inside, if someone was planning to reach for a telephone the moment he was seen.

He drew his thin lips off his teeth in an angry snarl. Damn her! To have a neck as brittle as that!

He became aware that the negro was whispering to the barman as he levered beer into a pint glass. Baird slid his hand inside his coat. The touch of the Colt was reassuring. He watched the negro carry the drinks across the room, and he could see the excitement of unexpected news in the negro's rolling eyes.

The negro set the drinks on the table. As he did so, he whispered, "A couple of dicks coming down the street, boss. They're looking in every saloon."

Baird drank the rye down in a hungry gulp, pushed the beer towards the negro.

"Got a back exit?" he asked, without moving his lips.

The negro nodded. Baird could see the sweat of excitement running down the ruts in the negro's black skin.

"Through the far door, down the passage," the negro said, and grinned delightedly as Baird flicked a dollar over to him.

"Take care of the beer," Baird said, got up and walked without hurrying across the smoke-filled room to the door the negro had indicated.

As he pushed open the door someone shouted, "Hey! Not that way, mister. That's private."

Baird felt a vicious spurt of rage run through him, and he had to restrain himself not to turn and go back to smash the face of the man who had called out. He didn't look around, but stepped into a dimly lit corridor and walked quickly to the door at the far end.

A fat little wop in an undervest, his trousers held up by a piece of string, appeared from a room near by. He was sleepily scratching his bare, hairy arms, and his red, unshaven face was still puffed by sleep.

"Can't come this way," he said, waving a hand at Baird. "The other way, please."

Baird looked at him, without pausing. The wop stepped back hurriedly, his mouth falling open. He stood stiffly still, watching Baird as he opened the door and peered into the dark alley beyond.

Baird didn't like the look of the alley. It had only one exit, and that into the main street. At the other end of the alley was an eight-foot wall; above the wall he could see the outlines of a tall, dark building.

He loosened the .45 in its holster, then stepped into the alley, closing the door quietly behind him. He stood for a moment listening to the roar of the traffic on the main street, then he walked quietly to the wall, reached up, hooked his fingers to the top row of bricks and pulled himself up. He hung for a moment looking down at a dark, deserted courtyard. Then he swung himself over the wall and dropped.

Across the courtyard he spotted the swing-up end of an iron fire escape. He decided it would be safer to go up the escape and over the roofs rather than risk the main street.

He just managed to touch the swing-up on the escape and hook his fingers in it. The escape came down slowly, creaking a little, and bumped gently to the ground.

He went up it, swiftly and silently, pausing at each platform to make certain no one was concealed behind the darkened window, overlooking the platform. He finally reached the roof without seeing anyone or hearing any sounds below. He crossed the roof, bending low to avoid being seen against the night sky, dropped on to a lower roof, climbed down a steel ladder to a garage roof, and from there, he scrambled down to a dark street that ran parallel with the main street.

He paused in a doorway to look right and left. He saw nothing to raise his suspicions, and walking quickly, he crossed the street and dodged down an alley that brought him to within a hundred yards of the walk-up apartment house where he had a couple of rooms.

He paused again at the end of the alley. Keeping in the shadows, he looked over at the apartment house. There were a few personal things in the apartment he wanted: a book of photographs, a suitcase of clothes, another gun. He was prepared to take the risk of returning to his rooms for the photographs alone. To anyone else the photographs were valueless; snaps he had taken when he was a kid of his home, his mother, his brother, his sister and his dog. They were the only links in a past long blotted out. His mother had been killed by a police bullet in a battle between G-men and his father. His sister was walking the streets in Chicago, and at this moment was probably inveigling some drunk into her apartment. His brother was serving a twelve-year stretch at Fort Leavenworth for robbery with violence. His dog had run out of the house when the G-men had come and had never been seen since.

Baird didn't want to remember them as they were now. He wanted to remember them as they were before his father hooked up with Dillinger, when the farm was a happy place, and his mother was always laughing, in spite of the endless hours of work.

But if Olin suspected him, he would have the house covered by now, and he wasn't going to walk into a trap, no matter how much he wanted that book of photographs.

He remained in the shadows, watching the house. There was no one in sight, and there was nothing suspicious about the house. His two windows, overlooking the street, were in darkness, but for all that, instinct warned him to take no chances.

After five long minutes of standing motionless, he decided it would be safe to cross the street. He pulled the Colt from its holster and held it down by his side. As he was about to step into the light of a street standard, he saw a movement from a dark doorway opposite him.

He froze, his pale eyes searching the doorway. It was several minutes before he made out the dim outlines of a man, standing against the wall.

Baird showed his teeth in a bitter, mirthless smile. So Olin was on to him, and he had nearly walked into a trap. Very possibly there were coppers in his apartment waiting to put the blast on him as he opened his front door. Cautiously he edged back, then when he was out of sight of the house, he turned and walked quickly back the way he had come.

At the other end of the alley was a drug store. He pushed open the door and crossed over to a row of pay booths. There was no one in the store except a young girl in a white coat, reading a paper-backed book, behind a soda fountain. She glanced up to give Baird an indifferent glance, then went on reading.

Baird shut himself in the booth and dialled Rico's number. He had to be sure Olin was covering the house. It would be infuriating to be stampeded by some loafer waiting for his girl. He would never forgive himself if he were panicked into leaving those photographs when it would be so simple to cross the street and get them.

Rico came on the line.

"Are they looking for me?" Baird whispered, his lips close to the mouthpiece. He heard Rico catch his breath in a startled gasp.

"Who's that?" Rico asked feverishly. "Who's talking?"

"Did Olin call on you?" Baird said, still keeping his voice low.

"Yes," Rico said. "Get off the line, you fool! They may be listening in! They're after you! Olin says he knows you did it! Don't come near me! He's after me too!"

"Don't lose your head," Baird said, seeing in his mind's eye Rico's twitching, terrified face. "They can't prove anything. They've got to have proof ..."

But he found himself speaking over a dead line. Rico had hung up.

Baird replaced the receiver. The muscle under his right eye was twitching. As he turned to leave the booth his quick, suspicious eyes spotted a movement at the drugstore entrance. He ducked down out of sight behind the panel of the booth door, his Colt jumping into his hand. He heard the drugstore door open and heavy feet walk over to the counter.

"Police, Miss," a curt voice said. "Anyone been in here within the last few minutes?"

Baird eased back the safety catch. They must have spotted him while he was retreating down the alley. He wondered if there were any more of them outside.

He heard the girl say, "There was a big fella in here about three minutes ago. He must have gone."

"In a brown suit?" the detective asked. "A tall, broad-shouldered guy with a white, hard face?"

"That's right. He used the phone over there."

"Which way did he go?"

"I don't know. I didn't see him leave."

There was a sudden sharp silence. Baird knew in a split second the detective would guess he was still in the pay booth. He didn't hesitate. Reaching up, he took hold of the door handle, turned it gently and flung the door open.

He had a glimpse of a short, stocky man facing him, whose hand was flying to the inside of his coat. He saw the girl in the white coat, jumping off her stool, her mouth opening, her eyes sick with terror.

The Colt boomed once as the detective got his gun out. The heavy slug smashed a hole in the detective's face, hurling him violently back against the counter.

Baird shifted the gun to cover the girl as she screamed wildly. The fear of death wiped the pert sophistication, the undisciplined sensuality and the old-young worldliness from her face. She looked suddenly pathetically childlike as she huddled into the corner formed by the wall and the counter with no hope of escape. The rouge on her cheeks and the lipstick on her mouth brought a sharp picture into Baird's mind of his sister when she was seven, plastering her face with a stolen lipstick, and laughing at his uneasy disapproval.

It was partly because of this sudden, bitter vision of his sister, and partly because he knew this girl mustn't be allowed to give the police a description of him that he shot her.

He was able to watch without a qualm the girl arch her body in agony as the bullet hit her. She slithered along the wall, her eyes rolling back, her outstretched arm knocking over a row of Coke bottles that fell with a crash of breaking glass to the floor. As she disappeared behind the counter her breath came through her clenched teeth the way the breath leaves the body of a rabbit when its neck is broken.

Baird left the booth, looked swiftly around the drugstore, spotted a door behind the counter, jumped over the counter and wrenched open the door.

Outside, not far away, he heard the shrill blast of a police whistle. He ran down a dimly lit passage and up more stairs. He was cold and unflurried, and his one thought was not to be seen. So long as no one saw him, Olin couldn't pin the killings on him. Already his calculating brain was at work on an alibi that would fox Olin. As soon as he could safely do it, he must get rid of his gun. That, and that alone, so far, could take him into the gas chamber.

Ahead of him he saw a glass panelled door that led to the roof of the building. As he opened it, he heard a sudden clamour of police sirens outside the building. He ran to the edge of the roof, and peered cautiously over it into the street below. It was alive with running police. Prowl cars were skidding to a standstill, and from them poured more police, guns in hand. Rushing around the corner came a truck, carrying a searchlight which went on before the truck came to a standstill. The great white beam of light flashed up the side of the building and lit up the roof with blinding intensity.

Baird didn't hesitate. He swung up his Colt and fired down the long beam. There was a crash of glass and the light went out. The darkness that followed was as blinding as the previous intense light. Someone down below let off with a sub-machine gun, but Baird was already running across the roof to the shelter of some chimney stacks. He ducked behind them, looked right and left, decided to go for a higher roof, and bending double, ran swiftly to a steel ladder, swarmed up it and reached fresh shelter as the first of the police came bursting on to the lower roof.

Still unruffled, Baird made his way silently across the roof, keeping the chimney stacks between himself and the police. He could hear them whispering together, unwilling to show themselves, not sure if he was waiting for them or getting away.

"Well, get on with it!" a voice bawled up from the street.

Looking down, Baird spotted Olin standing up in the middle of the street, gun in hand. He was glaring up at where his men were sheltering.

Baird was tempted to shoot Olin as he stood there, but realizing his chance of escape depended on keeping the police foxed as to where he was, he resisted the temptation, and made his way across the roof to look below on the far side of the building.

Another roof, fifteen feet or so below him, stretched out in a gentle slope, terminating in a low wall. There was no escape that way. He looked to his left. A higher roof seemed more inviting, and he could see a ladder that would take him up there.

Bending double he ran towards the ladder. Halfway up it, he heard running footsteps, and looking back over his shoulder he caught a glimpse of the silhouette of a policeman's flat cap against the night sky. The policeman was going to the lower roof, and apparently hadn't seen Baird on the ladder.

Baird swarmed up the remaining rungs of the ladder. In his haste to get under cover, he forgot to keep low, and for a second or so he was outlined against the sky as he reached the top of the ladder.

From the opposite roof came a crack of a rifle. Baird felt a violent blow against his right side a split second before he heard the shot. He staggered, went down on one knee, got up again, and swerving to right and left, ran blindly across the roof to the shelter of more chimney stacks.

The rifle cracked again, and he heard the slug whine past his head.

"He's up on the upper roof," a voice bawled from the opposite building. "I've winged him."

Baird felt blood running down his leg, inside his trousers. Jagged wires of pain bit into his side as he moved unsteadily across the roof to the far edge. Below was a flat roof with a skylight.

He swung his legs over the edge, dropped heavily on the lower roof. He caught his breath in a gasp as the pain in his side grabbed at him.

He put his hand to his side, feeling the wet stickiness of his bleeding. He was losing a lot of blood, and he began to be worried.

They were close behind him. He couldn't go on like this, running from roof to roof. If he didn't stop the bleeding he was going to pass out.

He went over to the skylight, hooked his fingers under it and pulled. It came up soundlessly, and he peered down into a dimly lit passage.

He lowered himself awkwardly down into the passage. It was as much as he could do to reach up and close the skylight. Sweat was running down his face. He leaned against the wall, the .45 heavy in his hand, while he struggled against the feeling of faintness that gripped him.

Making the effort, he began to move slowly along the passage, aware he was leaving a trail of blood behind him. It came to him with a sour bitterness that this was the end of him. Even if he hid somewhere in this building, they'd search him out. They knew they had winged him, and the blood would give him away. He would be cornered and shot down like a mad dog.

Well, he wouldn't go alone, he told himself. If only he could stop this damned bleeding, he might still give an account of himself. He wasn't afraid; only bitter at the thought of ending it this way. He wouldn't have cared if he hadn't been wounded. If he could have shot it out with them, knowing his aim was straight and he was taking some of them with him, he would have rather glorified in such an end. But as it was, his gun was now growing so heavy it was as much as he could do to keep it level, let alone shoot with it.

He approached a door. His hand, creeping along the face of the wall, guiding and supporting him, touched the door which swung open.

He paused, drawing back his lips off his teeth as a bright light came from the roof into the passage. He leaned against the doorway, staring into a bright but sparsely furnished room. His eyes took in the divan bed, the threadbare rug on the stained boards, a sagging armchair covered with a cheap but gay chintz, the cream-painted walls and the screen that probably hid the toilet basin.

He wedged his shoulder against the doorway, trying to give his buckling knees support. The shaded electric lamp hanging from the ceiling was beginning to spin around. He felt his fingers opened against his will, and heard a faraway thud of the Colt as it dropped on the floor.

This was how they would find him, he thought savagely. Helpless and unable to hit back. They would drag him down the stairs, handcuffed, into the street for the crowd to gape at: there was nothing now he could do about it.

As he began to fall into the black chasm of unconsciousness, he had a vague idea that a hand came out of the darkness and caught hold of his arm.

IV

As he poured whisky into a glass, Preston Kile noticed his hand was unsteady, and he frowned. He shouldn't be drinking this, he told himself. He was drinking too much these days. But what else could he do? A man must keep himself going somehow. He wasn't sleeping well. There was a woolliness in his brain that alarmed him. He had felt it coming on slowly like a deadly, creeping paralysis over the past year. It was blunting his mind. It made thought an effort. At one time he had been able to make lightning decisions, and the right decisions at that. He had also been willing to take any risk, no matter how dangerous it had seemed. He had had a shrewd recklessness, if you could put it that way, that had carried him from a poorly paid desk job in a bank to a position that had made him the most feared man on the Stock Market. But that was two years ago. He had gone to pieces. He wasn't the same man. His confidence had gone. He had lost his guts for a fight. Risks frightened him now. He found himself putting off making a decision until it was too late. And now, to worry him still more, there was this fantastic Rajah business.

He drank the whisky greedily, drained the glass and immediately refilled it. His heavy, bloodshot eyes moved to the mirror over the dressing table, and he stared at himself.

Well, at least he looked as strong, handsome and ruthless as he had ten years ago when he was at the height of his career. Of course his hair was grey at the temples now, and he was getting a little thick around the middle, but his figure wasn't bad for a man of his age. What was he thinking of? Age? Why, damn it, he wasn't fifty-six yet! But at this moment he felt like an old, feeble man instead of a man in his prime. There was this dull ache under his heart. That worried him. He was afraid to consult a doctor: no news was good news. If his heart was bad, he didn't want to know it. Probably indigestion, he told himself, his hand touching the smooth face of his evening dress shirt.

He took out a cigar case from his inside pocket, hesitated, then put it back. Perhaps not just now. He was smoking too much. He would wait until Eve came out of the bathroom. What an interminable time she spent in the bath!

He sat down amid the confusion of her clothes. She had thrown them off, leaving them scattered on the bed and floor, saying she wanted to think, and she thought best in a bath. A beautiful woman like her had no right to think!

He picked up the sheer silk stockings and pulled them slowly through his fingers, thinking of Eve.

He had known her for two months. At first, he had had thought of her merely as a woman to amuse him in his leisure moments. He had got rid of that dark girl – he had to think a moment to remember her name – Cora Hennessey.

Eve had moved into the apartment five days later. He was glad to be rid of Cora. She had demanded so much of him. He supposed she was too young for him, and he frowned uneasily at finding himself admitting such a thing. But how she had tired him! A week of her, and his nights became something to dread. There had been no satisfying her.

She hadn't been easy to get rid of, and it cost him much more than he could afford. She had gone eventually, taking his gold and diamond cuff links, his cigar cutter, and the little jade statue of a naked boy he had bought in a San Francisco brothel, an amusingly obscene bit of carving, and which he valued. He wanted these things back, but it would mean going to the police, and just now he was particularly anxious not to attract the attention of the police.

His mind shied away from this unpleasant channel, and he began to worry about Eve. What an extraordinary girl! How completely mistaken he had been about her! He had imagined she was an empty-headed little beauty whose only asset was her body. For the first six weeks he had no reason to believe otherwise. Then suddenly he realized she had been lulling him into a position of false security while she had been digging into his private affairs. Her apparently innocent questions about his past and present mode of life hadn't been, as he had thought, the idle chatter of an empty-headed blonde. She had been building up a picture of him until she knew him almost as well as he knew himself. She had managed to find out about his financial position. How she had got the information he couldn't imagine. He supposed a girl with her looks could find out anything if she made the effort. Someone must have talked: someone possibly at his bank.

She had surprised him horribly one night by saying in her quiet, cool voice, "What's the matter with you, Preston? Why are you drifting like this? You could be making piles of money instead of loafing here with me. Have you lost your ambition, or what is it?"

Startled, he had told her abruptly he had no need to work.

"I have all the money I want," he had said sharply. "I've retired from business. Besides, so long as I give you what you want, I really can't see it's any business of yours what I do."

But that hadn't touched her. She had gone right on confounding him.

"Why do you lie to me?" she had asked, her big blue eyes seemed able to see right inside his mind. "You don't have to pretend with me. I want to help you."

"I don't know what you're talking about," he said irritably. "I don't need anyone's help."

"You're broke," she said calmly, and put her hand on his. "Already the tradesmen are talking about you. You owe thousands. Whatever money you did have, you've spent. Isn't it time you did something about it?"

He had been so shocked that he had said nothing for some moments. True, he had immediately begun to bluster, but the expression in her eyes told him she was sure of her ground, and the bluster died sourly in his mouth. Instead, he tried to defend himself, though why he should make excuses to her he couldn't imagine. After all, it was no business of hers. He could have told her to pack up and get out if she didn't like him as she found him. But deep down, tucked away in his innermost being, Kile was afraid. He knew he was slipping. He knew unless a miracle happened, the slip would turn into a slide, and he would go down and down to the final crash where a revolver bullet would be his only way out.

There was something about this girl – not yet twenty-five, very beautiful to look at, detached and quietly determined – that gave him a sudden feeling of hope: something he hadn't had for the past two years: not since they had told him to get out of the Stock Market or they'd prosecute.

He told her he hadn't been feeling well.

"It's not that I'm a young man," he said lamely. "Perhaps I've lived too hard. I'm burned out, Eve. Not for long, but right now, I'm tired and disillusioned. In a little while I'll begin again. I just want to rest."

He could see at once she didn't believe him, although she gave him a sympathetic smile.

"I think I can help you," she said. "Something I happened to overhear ..."

That was how he had been committed to this Rajah business. At first he had thought she was joking.

"My dear girl," he had said, patting her long, sleek leg as she lay across his lap, her head against his shoulder, "I've never heard of such a thing. It's fantastic, and there's nothing I could possibly do about it. Even if I could, I don't think I'd care to dabble in such a venture. It's quite out of the question. Besides, this Rajah wouldn't want me to interfere."

"He might," she had said thoughtfully. "I think I'll ask him."

Kile didn't believe for a moment she would approach the Rajah. He had dismissed the whole thing from his mind, and he was startled when she told him a few days later that the Rajah would see them at his hotel that evening.

Immediately he had refused to go, but she had persuaded him.

"At least let's hear what he has to say," she had said, her face against his, holding his hand over her breast. "He may not agree. He may not offer enough. Even if he does agree and offers something reasonable, we don't have to go through with it if we don't want to. We can always say it wasn't possible."

Reassured by this argument, and a little flattered to be received by a Rajah, Preston allowed himself to be persuaded. The meeting had turned out far easier than he had expected.

It was pretty obvious that Eve had already laid a solid foundation for the interview. The Rajah said he would be delighted if they could help him recover the jewels. They were, he said, heirlooms of the utmost value. If they found them and returned them to him he would pay the sum of half a million dollars and their expenses; the only condition being the deal must be secret.

Kile realized the Rajah was out to gyp the insurance companies, but that didn't worry him unduly. If he had the chance he wouldn't hesitate to gyp any insurance company himself. He considered them fair game. But five hundred thousand! Why, with such a sum he could make a new start; he could even get back on to the Stock Market.

Those were the immediate thoughts that had chased through his mind when the Rajah had casually mentioned the sum, but as the Rajah went on talking, Kile's latent shrewdness and caution asserted themselves. The undertaking was impossible. The Rajah was only offering this sum because he knew he would never be called upon to pay it. The whole thing was an absurd pipe dream that no one in his right mind could or would take seriously.

Eve had apparently convinced the Rajah that if anyone could get the jewels, Kile could. How she had done it, what arguments she had used, Kile couldn't think, but it was obvious the Rajah was impressed by him, even before they met.

"I don't expect miracles," the Rajah had said, holding Eve's hand and looking at Kile as they stood at the door at the end of the interview. "I'm afraid you are setting yourself a very difficult task. But I believe in supporting the long chance. I will pay up to five thousand to cover the expenses of – shall we say – an examination of the prospects. Naturally you will require help, and you will have to pay well. I think five thousand should be enough to start with. The amount will be paid into your bank tomorrow."

Kile had recoiled, like a man seeing the ground suddenly open before his feet. If once he accepted the money, he would be seriously committed to this fantastic plan. He wasn't fool enough to imagine the Rajah would give him such a sum without extracting full value for his money.

But Eve hadn't given him a chance to refuse. She had told the Rajah the name of Kile's bank, prevented Kile from breaking into the conversation, and got him out of the Rajah's suite before he could gather his startled wits together.

On his way down to the hotel lobby, he had protested, but again she had reassured him.

"We needn't spend it," she had said. "If we can't think of a plan we can return it to him. It won't do any harm, Preston, for your bank to get that money; even if it is only a loan."

When they had got back to Eve's apartment, Kile had patiently pointed out the impossibility of such a task.

"The jewels have been missing for fifteen years," he had said. "The trail's cold. Every detective in the country has been searching for them, and as far as I know, is still searching for them. What chance have we got?"

"That's something we have to think about," she had said briskly. "I'm going to take a bath. I think better lying in hot water. Sit down and think, too, Preston. It's worth five hundred thousand, and that's a lot of money."

He hadn't thought. The whole thing was absurd and fantastic. Admittedly the money would be a life-saver, but he couldn't search the whole country like a damned detective. He hadn't the faintest idea where the jewels might be.

He had finished his second whisky and was pouring a third when Eve came out of the bathroom. She was wearing a lilac-coloured silk wrap that suited her and emphasized the gold in her hair and the blue in her eyes. She went over to the dressing table and sat down.

"Is that your third or fourth?" she asked, beginning to brush her hair.

He was immediately furious with her. What right had she to say such a thing to him?

"Oh, be quiet!" he shouted, banging his fist on the table. "God damn it! I won't be questioned like this! I'll drink as much as I like!"

She went on brushing her hair, her face thoughtful, her eyes serious.

"We're going to talk to Rico tonight," she said. "It's important that you shouldn't be drunk, Preston."

Kile set down his glass, took hold of Eve by her arms and pulled her to her feet. He gave her a hard, little shake. His face was red and congested, and his bloodshot eyes gleamed furiously.

"I won't be spoken to like this!" he said in a loud, bullying voice. "I'm master here, and you'd better remember it! I'm not seeing Rico tonight. And if I want to get drunk, I'll get drunk!"

"You're hurting me, Preston," she said, and her steady, quiet look was like a douche of cold water in his face.

He released her with an impatient exclamation, turned and walked heavily across the room to stand with his back to her, his hands thrust deep in his trouser pockets.

"Don't be like this, Preston," she said patiently. "I only want to help you. You know as well as I do if you don't take yourself in hand the crash is bound to come. This is your chance. Five hundred thousand! It's a tremendous sum. Think what you could do with it!"

He turned.

"What's the use of talking like that?" he snapped. "It's impossible to find those jewels. It's ridiculous to think about it. Why do you imagine he offered such a sum? He knows perfectly well he won't have to pay out."

"He said it was a long chance. Well, he's not the only one who's willing to back a long chance. I know it won't be easy, but it's not impossible." While she was speaking, Eve had got up and walked over to sit on the bed. She began to pull on her stockings, and Kile watched her, fascinated by her beauty and her swift movements. "I have an idea. We must see Rico tonight. We've got to have someone to do the dangerous work. He might know of someone who would do it."

Kile came over and sat on the bed by her side. He was thinking that of all the women he had had in this apartment she was by far the most beautiful.

"Dangerous work?" he repeated, frowning. "What dangerous work?"

She stood up and undid her wrap.

"Let me get dressed, darling, and on the way to the club I'll tell you my idea. It's getting late, and we must talk to Rico."

She slipped out of the wrap and reached for a flimsy under-thing. Kile's eyes dwelt on her naked loveliness. He reached out and caught her arm, pulling her down beside him.

"You're too beautiful to bother your head about such things," he said, his heart beginning to beat violently and jerkily. "I'm not going out tonight: nor are you."

She made a quick, impatient movement to break free, but immediately checked it. Instead, she slipped her arms around his neck and hid her face against his silken lapel, so he couldn't see her expression of loathing and revulsion.

V

Although it was after nine-twenty, a light still showed through the glass panel of the door leading to the inner office of the International Detective Agency. That meant Harmon Purvis hadn't yet gone home.

Ed Dallas pushed open the door and looked into the large airy office.

Purvis, a tall stick of a man, sat behind a desk, busy with a pile of papers, a pencil held between his teeth. He glanced up, nodded briefly, laid down his papers and took the pencil out of his mouth.

"Come in," he said, waving to a chair by the desk. "I guessed you'd be in so I waited for you."

Dallas sat down, laid his hat on the floor, and ran his fingers through his crew-cut brown hair.

"I might have something with those two," he said. "The guy's Preston Kile. Ever heard of him?"

Purvis thought a moment, then nodded.

"That's the San Francisco market manipulator," he said, putting his fingertips together and staring up at the ceiling. "About two years ago he pulled a very shady deal. A bunch of brokers decided to chip in and cover him rather than scare the market with a scandal. They forced him to get out of the market and stay out. He came here ..."

"I know, I know," Dallas interrupted. "I thought I was going to tell you. I got the dope from Favell."

It never ceased to surprise him how much Purvis seemed to know. There wasn't anyone in town who was connected in some way or the other with shady deals or crime that Purvis didn't know the details about. He could trot out his information as easily as the most complicated card index system, and as fast.

"I hope you didn't pay Favell anything," Purvis said anxiously. "That vampire is sucking up all my profits."

"Well, I had to give him something. How was I to know you had the information?" Dallas said wearily. "Two tens won't break us."

Purvis winced.

"The trouble with you ..." he began, but Dallas broke in hurriedly, "I know, I know. My mother told me the same thing. Want to hear about the girl – Eve Gillis?"

"I know about her," Purvis said coldly. "She won a five-thousand-dollar beauty prize a couple of years ago. She persuaded the Follies to give her a chance, got top billing after a year, and has been a hit ever since. She has a brother – a twin if I remember rightly – who's been in India for the past three years. I believe he's back now. This Gillis girl suddenly chucked the Follies about a couple of months ago and became Kile's mistress. Why she should have done that I can't imagine. It's not as if Kile can do anything for her. He's going broke fast, and isn't expected to last the year. I should have thought she would have found that out before giving up the Follies. They were paying her pretty well from all accounts."

Dallas groaned.

"It beats me why you employ me when you know so much," he said a little irritably. "I've been walking my legs off ..."

Purvis looked smug. He was childishly pleased with his phenomenal memory, and was inclined to ram its efficiency down Dallas' throat.

"I don't pay you to find out about the past. I pay you to keep tabs on the present," he said. "We can't all keep facts in our minds. I just happen to be gifted that way. So these two have talked with the Rajah?"

"They have. They were with him about an hour."

Purvis slid lower in his chair. He placed his fingertips along the edge of the desk and began to play an imaginary piano; a trick of his that irritated Dallas almost beyond endurance. Dallas considered the habit to be the height of affectation.

"Now I wonder why," Purvis said, executing a trill. He then commenced a complicated movement that ended in a showy crossing of hands.

"Could you stop acting like Beethoven for a moment?" Dallas said, breathing heavily through his nose. "Or would you like me to stand up and conduct?"

Purvis placed his fingertips together again and stared at Dallas from over them. His eyes reminded Dallas of two sloes on white saucers; his face of an inverted pear. There was nothing attractive about Harmon Purvis, but he gave the impression that he would deliver the goods no matter how difficult the job.

"I've always thought I should have been a professional pianist instead of a private eye," he said gloomily. "One of these days I'll buy myself a piano."

"That'll be the day," Dallas said tartly. "Maybe it'll convince you you're better at blowing a trumpet."

Purvis waved this away with a chilling frown.

"We've got to watch our step," he said. "We might be within throwing distance of grabbing those jewels. I've always thought the Rajah could find them quicker than anyone. I'm surprised he hasn't tried before."

"How do you know he's after them?" Dallas said impatiently. "Just because the insurance companies are suspicious of him there's no reason why we should be – or is there?"

"They're suspicious of him because I told them to be," Purvis said quietly. "Knowing what I do about the man and his reckless spending, it's obvious that as soon as he realized he was getting through his money, and there wouldn't be any more, he'd think of the jewels. He's the type who wants his cake and wants to eat it as well. You mustn't forget that the jewels now belong to the insurance companies. They paid out the insurance, but the value of the jewels has enormously increased now. At a guess I'd say they were worth three times as much as the insurance companies paid for them, and that fact must stick in the Rajah's throat. It's my bet if he finds them he'll stick to them. He could get rid of them in India without questions being asked. Most of the stuff would be snapped up by Indian Princes, and no one would be any the wiser. He must lay his hands on some money soon. From what I hear he's down to his last million."

"You don't say!" Dallas said sarcastically. "Why, the poor fella must be starving!"

Purvis pursed his lips. He considered such comments about money in poor taste. Money was Purvis' god.

"Never mind that," he said. "If we handle this right we stand to pick up four grand." He played a scale up and down the edge of his desk. "It's my bet the Rajah will take us to the jewels if we're patient and don't tip our hand. MacAdam and Ainsworth are covering him at night. Burns is sticking with him during the day. I want you to watch Kile. The Rajah won't go for the jewels himself. He'll have someone to do the work for him. That someone might easily be Kile. Keep on his tail, but don't let him have an idea you're watching him. If he doesn't show signs of getting into the game by the end of the week, drop him, and we'll wait for someone else to show."

Dallas grunted. His lean brown face didn't show any enthusiasm.

"You could be barking up the wrong tree," he pointed out. "The easiest way to handle this is to sit tight and wait for Hater to come out of jail. He's the one who'll lead us to the jewels."

Purvis made a wry face.

"He won't be out for two years!" He leaned forward and rapped on his desk. "I can't afford to wait two years. We've got to produce something before then."

"What's the hurry?" Dallas said, yawning. "We've been at this off and on for fifteen years. Why not concentrate on other jobs and wait until Hater gets free?"

"Don't you realize how much we stand to pick up ...?"

"Yeah, you told me. I don't know if you're using the royal 'we', but I'm damned sure I'll never smell that four grand, or even a dollar of it."

"That remains to be seen," Purvis said hurriedly. "We haven't got it yet. The insurance companies have been paying us a retainer for the past fifteen years, and we've done precious little to earn it. We can't afford to wait until Hater comes out. We've got to get busy right now."

Dallas looked at him suspiciously.

"Have they been bellyaching?"

"They've been doing more than that. They've stopped the retainer. It was as much as I could do to persuade them to let us represent them for another three months. We've got to get things moving or some of us will have to look for another job."

Dallas unfolded his lanky frame out of the chair. He picked up his hat and slapped it on the back of his head.

"Don't kid yourself you're scaring me," he said. "I could get me a better job than this one any day of the week. The only reason why I stick with you is because you've become a bad habit. Okay. I'll watch Kile. Maybe he'll lead us to the jewels, but I very much doubt it. There's only one man who knows where they are, and that's Hater. So long as he's in prison they never will be found."

"That's defeatism," Purvis said severely. "We haven't two years to wait: we've only three months. Keep after Kile, and watch that girl. She may know something."

Dallas' face brightened.

"Watching her won't be hard work," he said, making for the door. "It's going to be a pleasure. If I didn't think you'd take me up on it, I'd say I'd do it for free."

As an eager look came into Purvis' eyes, Dallas ducked out of the office and hurriedly closed the door.

VI

At half-past ten, Rico left his office and walked across the restaurant to the bar. There were not more than twenty couples dining in the restaurant, but that didn't worry him. It was seldom the club got busy until after eleven o'clock.

Rico bowed when he thought he recognized a face, but he didn't stop to chat as he usually did. He noticed some of the diners were looking curiously at his bruised face, and he felt a little self-conscious. Besides, he didn't feel up to his usual suave, gossipy round of the tables. He was still horribly shaken by Baird's telephone call. Baird must have been crazy to have used the telephone: the kind of slip that put a man in the gas chamber!

With an uneasy grimace at the thought, Rico entered the bar. There were only a dozen or so people at the tables around the dimly lit room. Rico ordered a double whisky. He approved of the barman's good manners. He had taken a quick look at Rico's bruised face, and then had kept his eyes studiously away from it.

As Rico sipped the whisky he once more glanced at the people in the room. He noted with satisfaction that all but two of them were in evening dress. When the Frou-Frou Club had first opened, a year ago, you wouldn't have found anyone there in evening dress: even Rico hadn't worn it. Only the rougher element of the town patronized the club, but as soon as he could afford to take a risk, he raised his prices and gradually squeezed them out. Now, by careful advertising and recommendations he had attracted what he liked to call 'the carriage trade', and evening dress was the rule instead of the exception.

Among his numerous clients were wealthy businessmen who knew they could pick up a girl at the club without being involved in any awkward complications, a half a dozen or so not-so-well-known actors and actresses, several con men, crooks and prostitutes, and a small army of tough looking characters who didn't advertise what they did for a living, but who brought their women to the club regularly and had money to burn.

Rico glanced at the two men not in evening dress. One of them was sitting up at the bar; the other was alone at a corner table, reading a newspaper.

The one at the bar Rico knew by sight. He was tall, slightly built, fair and distinctly handsome. There were dark smudges under his blue eyes that gave him a worn, dissolute look. He was fine drawn as if he didn't get enough to eat, and his mouth drooped unhappily.

Looking at him, Rico thought sourly that women would be mad about him. He was just the shiftless, pathetic type women would insist on helping. He was not only shiftless, but completely untrustworthy, Rico decided.

He had seen him in the club on and off now for more than a month. His name was Adam Gillis; not what you could call a good customer, but more often than not he brought some girl with him who bought champagne.

Rico wondered how he managed to get hold of these girls: they were all very young, rich and stupid. He had seen them pass money to Gillis, when they thought the waiter wasn't looking, to pay for the champagne they invariably ordered.

At the moment Gillis wasn't drinking. He sat on the stool, staring bleakly at himself in the mirror, his charm switched off, and his years of shabby living plainly written on his face. He looked as if he needed a drink badly, and Rico assumed he was waiting for someone – probably another stupid girl – to buy him one.

With a shrug of contempt, Rico turned his attention to the man reading the newspaper. He hadn't seen him before, and Rico was a little puzzled by him. He wasn't the nightclub type. He was tall and lanky and deeply tanned. His eyes were bright and healthy looking. His crew haircut made Rico think of the tennis player, Budge Patty. This fella, Rico thought, had the same out-of-door look: probably a salesman passing through town on the lookout for some fun.

He finished his whisky and went into the entrance lobby to check the register, which was carefully kept by Schmidt, the doorman.

"Who's the guy with the crew haircut?" he asked, as Schmidt drew himself up and saluted. "I haven't seen him in here before."

"Name of Dallas," Schmidt told him. He was a giant of a man, with a red, cheerful face and enormous moustaches. "Had an introduction from Mr Rhineheart so I let him in."

Rico nodded.

"That's okay. Thought I'd check on him. First time he's been here, isn't it?"

"Yes, sir. He's a nice guy, but I don't reckon he's got much money."

"The nice guys never have," Rico said, shrugging. "Okay, Schmidt. Let me know when Mr Kile arrives. I want to see him tonight."

He wandered back to the bar and paused to look in. Dallas was talking to a redhead in a green evening dress: one of Rico's hostesses: a girl named Zoe Norton. Rico nodded his approval when he saw the half bottle of champagne on the table. Zoe wouldn't rest until she had had the other half: she was a keen saleswoman.

Adam Gillis watched Rico in the mirror. He wondered how he had bruised his face so badly. He wished he knew more about Rico: that Rico was coming up in the world was beyond doubt, but how far would he get? What were his nerves like? Had he the guts for a big job?

When Rico went away, Gillis looked at his wristwatch and frowned. What could be keeping Eve? She said she'd be here with Kile at ten o'clock. It was getting on for eleven now. He wondered if he should phone her, but decided it wouldn't be safe. Kile might answer. No point in making Kile suspicious at this stage of the same.

How he wanted a drink! He looked longingly at the row of bottles along the chromium shelves behind the bar. He hadn't two dollars to rub together! Looking thoughtfully at the barman he wondered if he could get credit. Reluctantly he decided not to try. He didn't want to attract any attention to himself. The barman was certain to consult Rico.

He felt in his hip pocket for his cigarette case, opened it and found it empty. Oh, damn Eve! Why couldn't she come? Angrily he replaced the case in his pocket and began to drum on the counter with his fingertips.

The barman came over to him and offered him a cigarette from a crumpled pack.

"I get caught myself like that some nights," he said amiably. "Makes me want to walk across the ceiling. Help yourself."

Gillis stiffened with mortification and rage. A damned lackey offering him a cigarette! The blasted cheek of the man!

"I don't smoke a barman's cigarettes," he said venomously. "Kindly mind your own business and let me mind mine!"

The barman flushed. He looked as if he wanted to hit Gillis, but he swallowed his anger with an effort and put the pack back in his pocket.

"If that's the way you feel about it," he said, "I'm sorry I spoke."

He walked to the other end of the bar and began to polish glasses, his flush deepening as he appreciated more fully the snub he had received.

Gillis got off the stool and walked out into the lobby.

"Mr Kile hasn't been in yet, has he?" he asked Schmidt casually. "I've been in the bar and I might have missed him."

"He hasn't been in yet, sir," Schmidt said coolly. He had had a lot of experience of the men and women who came to the club, and he prided himself on spotting the wrong one. He hadn't any use for Gillis: a sponger if ever there was one.

Gillis went into the gentlemen's retiring room. He washed his hands under the disapproving eyes of the negro attendant who knew from experience he wasn't going to be tipped, poured lavender water on a towel and touched his temples with it. While he was combing his blond hair, the door pushed open and Dallas wandered in.

He stood near Gillis and began to wash his hands. Their eyes met in the mirror and Dallas grinned.

"That redhead I'm with is trying to take me to the cleaners," he said breezily. "I guess you wouldn't know if I am wasting my time and money?"

Gillis switched on his charm. It was remarkable how his face changed when he smiled. He looked almost boyish; certainly not twenty-five, and the worn-out look of dissipation seemed to melt away.

"You're on to a good thing," he said. "Zoe rates a little high, but she doesn't shirk her responsibilities. If she asks you home, you go. Of her kind, she's unique."

Dallas, who had seen the byplay at the bar, took out his cigarette case and offered it.

"As good as that, is she? I'm obliged to you. This is my first visit here, and I didn't want to get off on the wrong foot. I'm in town for a couple of weeks on business, and this seemed the place to come to."

Gillis lit the cigarette and inhaled gratefully.

"It is," he said. "If you want a little fun and an accommodating girl you couldn't do better."

They stood talking for a few minutes about the club, then Dallas said, "Well, maybe I'll be seeing you again. My name's Ed Dallas."

"Mine's Adam Gillis. Sure, I'll look out for you, but don't let me keep you away from Zoe. You have a treat in store. She certainly knows how to please a guy when she feels that way," Gillis said. "I'm here three or four times a week. Maybe we can have a drink together some time."

"Glad to," Dallas said, sure now this blond man was Eve Gillis' brother. The likeness was remarkable. He had the same blue eyes, the same shaped face.

"Before you go, I wonder if I could possibly ask a favour of you," Gillis said, smiling. "If you hadn't been a member of the club I wouldn't dream of mentioning this, but I've stupidly forgotten my wallet, and until my friends arrive I'm stuck for money. I suppose you couldn't lend me ten dollars for an hour or so?"

"Why, sure," Dallas said, concealing his surprise. "I'd be glad to." He took out his wallet, extracted two fives and handed them to Gillis. "I'm in no hurry. Let me have it the next time we meet."

Gillis slipped the bills into his pocket.

"I can't thank you enough. As soon as my friends arrive I'll pay you back. Thanks a lot. It's really very kind of you."

"Forget it," Dallas said, moving towards the door. "I've forgotten my wallet myself before now. It's no joke to be stuck for money."

They walked back to the bar.

"Don't let me take you away from Zoe," Gillis said as they entered the bar. "I'll buy myself a drink and wait for my friends."

Dallas spotted Eve Gillis standing with Kile at the bar. She was wearing a sea-green backless evening gown, cut so low in front that he could see the deep furrow between her breasts.

He nudged Gillis.

"Some girl," he said under his breath. "Some dress she's nearly got on."

Gillis looked at Eve, who glanced at him and then looked away. Neither of them gave any sign of recognition.

"The club is noted for its beautiful women," Gillis said indifferently. "But you should remember, in the dark, one woman is very much the same as another." He gave Dallas' arm a friendly pat and walked over to the bar, where he climbed up on a stool within a few feet of Eve and Kile.

Dallas returned to where Zoe was waiting for him, and sat down.

"Sorry to have been so long," he said, smiling at Zoe, "but I got caught up with the blond profile. He has quite a way with him, hasn't he?"

Zoe's pert little face hardened.

"That cheap chiseller?" she said scornfully. "All he's got are his looks, and they won't last him much longer from the way they're wearing. Did he try to bite your ear?"

"He did more than that; he succeeded to the tune of ten dollars. At the moment he's buying a double whisky with the proceeds. How do you like that?"

Zoe stared at him.

"Well, you don't look a sucker," she said. "For heaven's sake, why did you give it to him?"

"Oh, I felt sorry for the guy. He was in a bad way for a drink, and I hadn't the heart to refuse him," Dallas said, shrugging. "Besides, he said some nice things about you."

"Did he?" Zoe said scornfully. "He once gypped me out of fifty bucks: the little rat!"

Dallas was eyeing Eve as she stood at the bar.

"That's a nice shape that girl's wearing, or maybe you wouldn't have noticed."

Zoe looked Eve over critically.

"She's good," she said grudgingly. "At least she doesn't have to wear falsies. In case you don't know, she's his sister, and it's my bet they're two of a kind. She was in the Follies for some time until she decided she could get along just as well in a bed."

"His sister?" Dallas said, pretending to be surprised. "They don't act that way."

"Maybe she doesn't want to introduce him to Kile," Zoe said indifferently. "She's Kile's mistress, and she's welcome to him. How about another bottle of champagne? I've a thirst that'd slay a camel."

"Sure," Dallas said, wondering what Purvis was going to say when he put in his expense sheet at the end of the week. "Everything I have is yours, honey."

Zoe gave him a suspicious glance.

"That sounds as if you haven't so much," she said, signalling to the barman. "How about buying me a dinner, if you're going to be all that generous?"

"Just a figure of speech," Dallas said hastily. "Maybe I'll buy you dinner tomorrow night, but I'll run to a sandwich if you're that hungry."

Zoe sighed.

"I'll settle for a sandwich." She looked at him and smiled. "Are you working up to come home with me tonight?"

Dallas wrestled with the temptation, decided reluctantly not to spend any more of Purvis' money, and shook his head.

"That's something I'll look forward to at a later date. I'll need to break into my kid sister's money box before I can go home with you."

Zoe giggled.

"You know, I like you," she said, and pressed her knee against his. "You leave your kid sister's money box alone. You won't need it."

Dallas was only half listening. He had seen Rico come into the bar.

Rico crossed over to where Kile and Eve were standing and said something to Kile in a low voice.

Kile's face was flushed as if he had been drinking heavily. He turned to speak to Eve, who nodded. Then he went out of the bar with Rico, leaving Eve alone.

Dallas saw Gillis raise his eyebrows at Eve and jerk his head to the door.

"I've got to run away," Dallas said quickly. He took out a twenty-dollar bill and dropped it in Zoe's lap. "Just remembered a pressing appointment. See you tomorrow night. Okay?"

"You leaving me flat?" Zoe asked, startled.

"Got to," Dallas said, getting to his feet. "Business. I'll dream of you tonight, sugar. So long for now."

He walked quickly out of the bar as Eve finished her drink. He went into the gentlemen's retiring room.

A moment or so later Eve came into the lobby. She collected her wrap and went out into the street. Dallas reappeared and sauntered after her. He saw her get into the LaSalle parked in the big parking lot at the side of the club. He concealed himself behind another car and waited.

Five minutes dragged by. He saw Eve light a cigarette. The flame of her lighter lit up her face for a brief moment. Dallas decided she was the most beautiful girl he had ever seen.

"And where does that get you, Dallas?" he said to himself. "She's way out of your class. If you're going to get those sort of ideas, you'd better stick to Zoe."

Then he spotted Gillis coming into the parking lot. He saw him look to right and left, then walk quickly over to the LaSalle, open the door and get in beside Eve.

Moving silently, Dallas left his hiding place and crept towards the LaSalle.

VII

For the first time in two years, Preston Kile felt confident and excited about his immediate future. Eve had convinced him that the plan she had thought of to find the Rajah's jewels might work. He hadn't been hard to convince because, once explained, it was obvious that it was the only possible way. It was daring and brilliant, and he felt drawn to it in spite of knowing that it could end in disaster if he made a false move. It was the kind of plan he would have given his whole-hearted support to ten years ago: a gamble against enormous odds, but with a tremendous prize if it succeeded.

What an extraordinary girl this Eve was! She had lain in his arms, her face against his, while she had outlined the plan. He couldn't think why he hadn't arrived at the solution himself. The more she talked the more he had realized that the Rajah's offer of half a million was not now entirely out of reach. With such a sum to play with, he was positive he could win back his old position in the Stock Market, and wouldn't he make them suffer for what they had done to him!

The plan depended on organization and nerve and the right man to do the job. He had agreed with Eve that Rico should be consulted. He might know of someone who would handle the dangerous part of the job. Rico might also be useful in the organization of the plan: it was too big and complicated for Kile to handle alone. It wasn't going to be easy to bring Rico into this, and at the same time keep from him the amount involved. He would have to be paid well, and the Rajah would have to foot the bill. Rico's money wasn't going to come out of the half a million. Kile intended to keep every nickel of that for himself.

He watched Rico make two highballs. When Rico came over to the desk and put one of the highballs near Kile, Kile said, "That's a nasty bruise you've got there. How did you get it?"

Rico sat down.

"I had an accident. It's nothing. It looks worse than it feels. I hoped you'd be in tonight, Mr Kile. I've something I wanted you to see. Unfortunately it's as hot as a stove at the moment, but in a year or two it'll fetch three or four grand; probably more."

Kile pursed his lips.

"I don't think I'd be interested," he said, "but let me see it."

Rico walked over to the office door and turned the key. Then he went to the wall safe, opened it and took out the bracelet. He put it on the desk in front of Kile.

Kile studied it without touching it. He glanced up at Rico's anxious face.

"How hot is it?"

"The woman who owned it was murdered," Rico said in a hushed voice.

Kile made a wry grimace.

"Jean Bruce?"

Rico nodded.

"I'm surprised you touched this," Kile said. "How did you get hold of it?"

"By accident," Rico lied glibly. "It wasn't until I saw tonight's paper I knew it belonged to the Bruce woman."

"Think the police would believe you?"

"I said it was hot," Rico pointed out. "I wouldn't give you a wrong impression, Mr Kile. I thought one of your rich friends might have it. It'd have to be reset, of course, but it's a beautiful piece."

Kile picked up the bracelet and studied it closely. "Yes; it's nice. What do you want for it?"

"Twenty-five hundred," Rico said promptly. "It's worth at least six grand."

"It's worth five," Kile said. "At the moment it isn't worth a dime. I'd have to keep it for some time: maybe a year. It's a dangerous thing to keep. I might give you a thousand for it, but not a dollar more."

"Make it two, and you can have it," Rico said hopefully, then as Kile pushed the bracelet back to him, he went on hastily, "Well, okay. I'm losing money, but I want it out of my place. I'll take a grand."

Kile nodded.

"You'll have to wait for the money, Rico. I'll let you have it in a week or two."

"That's okay," Rico said, sitting down. "I trust you, Mr Kile. Two weeks is okay with me."

Kile nodded again and put the bracelet in his inside pocket.

"There's something I want to talk to you about, Rico," he said, paused to take a long drink from his glass, stared across at Rico, trying to make up his mind how much to tell him. He decided to say as little as possible. "There may be a big job coming along in the near future," he went on. "If it comes off you could make yourself fifteen thousand. It's in the air at the moment, but I'm trying to get two or three good men together. Would you be interested?"

Fifteen thousand! Rico's eyes gleamed. This was big-time stuff!

"Why, sure," he said, leaning across the desk. "You know I want to work with you, Mr Kile. What would you want me to do?"

"I don't know yet," Kile said. "I haven't even started to organize the job, and it'll need a lot of organizing. I wanted to be sure I could rely on you."

Rico felt a twinge of uneasiness. He was too cautious to commit himself without knowing something of what Kile was planning.

"But can't you give me some idea, Mr Kile? For instance: is it dangerous?"

"Could be," Kile said mildly, thinking how horribly dangerous the whole idea was, "but you wouldn't be in on that end of it. You could get yourself a ten to fifteen year stretch if it turned sour. You see, you're not the only one who doesn't want to give a wrong impression."

Rico showed his teeth in a mirthless smile. Ten to fifteen years! He wasn't going to walk into that without knowing where he was going!

"What are the chances?" he asked. "I don't take unnecessary risks, Mr Kile. I'm not saying the pay isn't good – it is, but ten to fifteen years!"

"I can tell you about the risks better later on," Kile said. "It'll depend largely on the man who does the outside work. If he's a good man, has plenty of nerve and plays his cards right, there won't be any risk. But if he slips up, loses his head, then we're all sunk."

Rico nodded.

"Who's the man, Mr Kile? Anyone I know?"

"I haven't found him yet," Kile said, taking out his cigar case. He made motions of offering it to Rico, who shook his head. "It occurred to me you might know someone. He must have nerve. This isn't an easy job, Rico: it's damn near impossible, but I think the right man could pull it off. He'd have to be reliable, quick-witted, and a killer." He noticed Rico winced when he mentioned killing. He didn't blame

Rico for that. "Don't misunderstand me," he went on. "I dislike killing as much as you do, but we've got to face facts. If this man is to be of any use to me, he's got to have the qualities of a killer. That doesn't mean to say he has to kill anyone."

Rico looked relieved.

"I know the man," he said. "His name's Verne Baird. He's only been in town a couple of months. He and I've done jobs together. He's reliable, and he's got all the qualifications you mentioned." He lowered his voice as he said, "It's my bet he's responsible for the Bruce killing. I don't know for sure, but I think he is."

Kile rubbed his fleshy jaw.

"He's got to be right, Rico. I've already warned you. If he isn't, you and I will go to jail."

"I'd rather have him than anyone else I know," Rico said. "What has he to do?"

"That's something we'll talk about later," Kile said. "I want to see him first. Can you get him here tomorrow night?"

Rico shook his head.

"I'm afraid not. The police are looking for him. I think he's left town."

"Any idea where he is?"

"I haven't, but he'll let me know in a day or so. He said he would. As soon as I hear I'll make arrangements for him to meet you. Will that be all right?"

"It'll have to be," Kile said, frowning. He stood up. "You're sure this man's all right?"

"I'm positive," Rico said. "There isn't anyone else to touch him."

"All right. I'll go ahead with my part of the job. There's a lot to do yet. But the sooner I meet Baird the better."

"I'll fix it," Rico said eagerly. "You leave it to me." He hesitated, went on, "He'd want to know what the job is worth. Could I give him some idea?"

Kile tapped ash into Rico's tray.

"If he pulls the job off it'll be worth ten thousand to him," he said. "If he fails I'll give him five."

Rico's eyes opened.

"Ten thousand. This must be a pretty big job, Mr Kile."

"It is," Kile said.

VIII

As Adam Gillis got into the LaSalle, he said angrily, "You've kept me waiting over an hour! You said ten o'clock. Why can't you be punctual?"

"I'm sorry, darling," Eve said. She put her hand on his. "I couldn't help it. He was in one of his mauling moods. I didn't think I'd get him to come at all. Oh, Adam! I'm so sick of all this! How much longer have I to go on with it? You don't know what it means to live with him." She shivered. "I wish I'd never agreed to help you."

Gillis looked at her in alarm.

"Don't be difficult, for God's sake," he said, patting her hand. "I've enough on my mind without you sounding off. I know it isn't easy for you, but we've got to have Kile in on this. You and I couldn't swing it on our own."

"But the whole thing's dangerous and crazy," she said, twisting around to face him. "I must have been insane to let you talk me into it. We'll never get away with it!"

"Of course we will," Gillis said sharply. "It's just a matter of nerve. I don't see what you've got to worry about. I have all the responsibility. I'm the one who has to lie awake at night, making plans. All you have to do is to do what I tell you."

"I suppose you think it's nothing to me to have to let that old roué make love to me just whenever he feels like it?" Eve said hotly.

"I wish you'd concentrate on the big things instead of the little things," Gillis said. "Don't you realize this means a half a million? For heaven's sake, don't you think most girls would sleep with Kile for that money?"

"No, I don't!" Eve flared. "That's a beastly thing to say! We haven't even got the money, and I don't believe we ever will get it!"

Gillis studied her; a sudden venomous look in his eyes.

"All right," he said, "if that's the way you feel about it, there's no sense in going on with it. There's plenty of other girls who'll help me, and I dare say will make a better job of it than you. I'll make other arrangements. You'd better tell Kile you want to go back to the Follies."

Eve felt a little chill run through her.

"Don't be angry, darling," she said quickly.

"I'm not angry," he returned. "If you can't carry on, then you'd better chuck it before you make a mess of it."

"If I went back to the Follies," she said slowly, "would you come and live with me again?"

"If you go back to the Follies," Gillis said deliberately, "you've seen the last of me. I mean that, Eve. I'll have to find some other girl to help me. I'm not going to be cluttered up with two women. If you haven't the guts to go through with this, I'll be damned if I ever want to see you again."

He saw the fear jump into her eyes. Long experience of similar scenes in the past made him confident of his whip hand over her. Threats, arguments and made-up quarrels marked their lives like milestones along a dark, twisting road. He had only to threaten never to see her again for her to capitulate. The chain that bound her to him had been forged in the womb.

"Please, Adam, don't talk like that," she said, taking his hand. "Of course I'll go through with it. Forget what I said. I guess I'm feeling a little depressed tonight."

He was quick to meet her halfway, now he had won his point.

"I do understand, Eve," he said. "It won't be for much longer. I promise you that. If you'll only stick it for another month. After that you needn't ever see Kile again."

"I hope not," she sighed, acutely aware of her defeat.

He put his arm round her and pulled her to him.

"Snap out of it," he said lightly. "Everything's going to be fine and dandy. Think of the things I'm going to buy you when we get the money!" His sudden good humour didn't deceive her. She knew how untrustworthy, how shiftless and dishonest he was. There was nothing she could do about it. He was part of her: the Hyde to her Jekyll; something she was helpless to rid herself of. "You told Kile tonight? He knows now?"

"Yes. I told him."

"How did he take it?"

"Oh, he's enthusiastic." She felt the thin cloth of his suit. It had been pressed again and again. It was threadbare. Only he could have worn it and made it look something. On any other man it would have been a rag. "Didn't you buy the suit, darling?" she went on. "I was hoping you'd wear it tonight."

"Oh, yes, I bought it," he said glibly. "If I'd known you were going to be so late I'd have stopped to change."

She knew at once he was lying: that he hadn't used the money she had given him to buy a suit. She knew from past sordid experience that the money had been spent on some woman.

"But never mind the suit," he went on. "Is Kile going to approach Rico?"

"Yes, of course. I told him Rico should be consulted. That's what you wanted, isn't it?"

"Rico knows this chap Baird. If anyone can pull this off, Baird can. I've watched him for weeks now. He's terrific. Nothing will stop him once he's made up his mind. I wish I could say the same of Rico. Of course he may be all right, but I wish I was sure of him. Kile's not telling him the details, is he?"

"No. He's just asking Rico if he'd come in with him, but he's not telling him much."

"Did Kile say if he was going to give you anything for the idea?" Gillis asked.

Eve laughed bitterly.

"Of course not. It never entered his head. He's quite sure I'll be with him to spend it with him."

"Oh, well, he's due for an unpleasant surprise," Gillis said carelessly. He glanced at his wristwatch. "You'd better get back. For the moment there's no point in letting him know I'm in this. I'll drop in tomorrow night. I might be a little late; about half-past twelve. Leave the shade down if he's there."

"He won't be. He's going out to dinner. Can't you come earlier, Adam? I'll be alone from eight o'clock."

Immediately he became shifty.

"I don't know if I can. I'll try. I might get around by nine. Yes, I think I could manage nine."

Again she knew he was lying, but she hid her knowledge from him. It would be stupid and dangerous to warn him that his lies were so transparent to her. So long as he wasn't on his guard, she knew she could spot his lies, but if he took more trouble to deceive her, he might succeed. She told herself that one day he might tell her a serious lie; a lie that might affect them both. It was this lie she knew she had to recognize when it came.

"All right, darling," she said, trying to make her voice sound gay. "Then, if I don't see you at nine, I'll expect you at half-past twelve."

"You'll see me at nine," he said, deciding that half-past twelve was quite early enough. He had no wish to sit with her all the evening. There were times when she bored him to distraction. She would be so serious all the time: she would fuss over him.

She opened the car door.

"Oh, Eve ..."

Holding the door half open, she glanced quickly at him. She knew what was coming: every parting of theirs had this sordid little postscript.

"How much do you want?" she asked gently.

"Oh, damn it! You make it sound as if I were always sponging on you," he said irritably. "But you wait ... in another month I'll have all the money I need. I'll pay you back. I know exactly how much I owe you. I've written it down in a book."

"How much, Adam?" she asked again.

"Well, I owe a fella thirty dollars. I had to borrow off him tonight. You were so late I had to settle an account ..."

"Never mind the details, darling, just tell me how much."

"Would fifty ruin you?" he said sullenly. He liked to explain why he wanted the money. He justified himself in his own eyes when he gave her a fictitious list of debts.

She opened her bag and checked the amount of money she had in it.

"I've only forty."

"That would do. I'll be seeing you tomorrow night. Can't you squeeze something substantial out of Kile? I hate this continual asking. Three or four hundred would see me through to the end of the month. He should be good for that if you're nice to him."

"You mean if I behave more like a tart than I usually do?" she said quietly.

"There's no need to talk like that!" he snapped. "I didn't mean anything of the kind. You can persuade him your expenses ..."

"But don't you understand he hasn't any money?" she said impatiently. "It was you who told me he owes thousands."

"A man like Kile can always raise money. People trust him. That's why I picked on him. Hasn't he made a hit with the Rajah? A man with his looks and reputation can always get money."

She gave him four ten-dollar bills.

"You must try and manage with that," she said. "I can't ask him for any more just yet. I don't know how I'm going to manage myself: I'm cleaned out."

He touched the gold chain bracelet around her wrist. "I could hock that for you," he said, obviously pleased with the idea. "You must have a lot of junk you could raise money on. I could handle it for you. I know all the best places." There was a boast in his voice. He was proud of his knowledge of pawnshops. "We can get the stuff back when we've hit the jackpot."

"I'll think about it." The note of misery in her voice made him look sharply at her. "Have you forgotten this belonged to mother?" Her fingers touched the bracelet lovingly.

"Well, she wouldn't mind," Gillis said, scowling. "She hocked it herself, if I remember rightly, when the old man wouldn't give me a new suit."

"Goodnight, Adam."

"I wish you wouldn't look so damned miserable at times," he said crossly as he got out of the car. "I'll see you tomorrow night. You might look through your things. That fur coat he gave you ... you don't need it until the winter..."

"Goodnight, Adam," she repeated.

They stood facing each other for a moment. She was glad he couldn't meet her eyes. She leaned forward and kissed his cheek.

"Try and come early," she pleaded. "I want to talk to you, darling."

"About nine," he said, his voice flat and disinterested. Already he was thinking of more important things. He had forty dollars in his pocket. The night was still young. He might do worse than take Lois back to his room. He might persuade her to do that comic dance of hers again. She had wanted fifty dollars the last time: ridiculous! She might do it for twenty if he could convince her that was all she would get. Yet, he'd go along and pick her up. He felt in the mood for Lois' kind of fun.

He watched Eve as she moved back to the club. She was an odd girl. Sometimes he wondered about her. She didn't treat him as if he was her brother. There were times when she acted as if she were in love with him. He touched his pencil-lined moustache, frowning. Odd!

After he had left the parking lot, Dallas came out of the shadows and stood looking after him.

IX

Harmon Purvis had a small villa on East Boulevard: a modest, three-bedroom affair with a small garden crammed with roses and a *Clematis Jackmanii* over the front door.

A light showed in one of the downstairs rooms, and through the open window came the brittle notes of Chopin's *Etude* in E Flat.

Dallas got out of his car, pushed open the gate and walked up the path. The night was hot and still, and the perfume from the roses was a little overpowering.

He dug his thumb into the bell push, leaned forward to sniff at the purple flower of the clematis – as big as a breakfast plate.

Purvis came to the door and opened it. He was in his shirtsleeves and had changed his shoes for slippers.

"You're late," he said, giving Dallas a sharp look. "I was thinking of going to bed."

"You're lucky to have a bed," Dallas said, following him into the comfortable front room. It was lined with books and restfully lit by table lamps. Purvis was a bachelor, but he knew how to make himself comfortable. He had a Filipino boy to run the house and cook, and in his spare time he looked after the tiny garden himself. "I don't get any time for my bed," Dallas went on, lowering himself gratefully into a comfortable easy chair.

Purvis wasn't paying attention. He was listening to the concluding passages of the *Etude*.

"You should listen to this," he said, leaning against the radiogram and beating time with his finger. "It's the most difficult of any of Chopin's *Etudes*. Even Paderewski used to make some mistakes when he played it."

"Never mind Paderewski – he's dead," Dallas said, rubbing his eyes with his knuckles. "Turn it off for the love of Mike. I'm here on business."

Reluctantly Purvis turned off the disc and sat down opposite Dallas.

"Do you good to listen to some of the classics," he said, placing his fingertips together and staring at Dallas from over them. "You're losing your sense of culture."

"Never had one. Don't offer me a whisky: I'd accept it."

"I haven't any in the house," Purvis said happily. "I don't touch the stuff: wastes money, dulls your perception and rots your liver."

Dallas sighed.

"So that's what's the matter with me. Maybe I'd better switch to gin."

Purvis watched him light a cigarette.

"You've been to the Frou-Frou Club tonight?" he asked tentatively.

"Yeah," Dallas said, "and I'm willing to bet my eye-teeth Kile's getting set to grab the Chittabad collection."

"What makes you think that?" Purvis asked, sitting forward.

"He saw Rico tonight, but maybe I'd better start in at the beginning. Talk about a break! It fell into my lap," and he gave Purvis a detailed account of what he had seen and heard at the club, as well as the conversation he had overheard between Eve and Gillis as they sat in the car.

Purvis was enthralled. He just sat still, staring at Dallas, drinking in every word, and not interrupting. When Dallas had finished, he got up and began to pace up and down.

"What a break!" he said. "It's unbelievable! I've worked on this goddamn case for fifteen years, and never thought

I'd get anywhere with it, and then suddenly it's handed to us on a plate."

Dallas grinned.

"I made it sound too easy," he said, stretching out his long legs. "If it hadn't been for a hunch ..."

"Never mind that. These people must be after the collection," Purvis said, coming to stand over Dallas. "This morning Kile and the Gillis girl call on the Rajah. In the evening Gillis talks in terms of half a million. The connection's obvious. It looks as if the Rajah has offered Kile a half a million to get his jewels back, and Gillis plans to gyp him."

"The whole idea seems to have come from Gillis," Dallas pointed out. "Kile is being used as a stooge. But how is Kile going to get the jewels? Think he knows where they are?"

"I don't know," Purvis said, sitting down. "He must have some idea otherwise he wouldn't have seen the Rajah this morning."

"Who's this guy Baird, Gillis is so strung up about?"

"If it's Verne Baird," Purvis said, crossing his long, bony legs, "and I'd imagine it must be, he's suspect number one for Jean Bruce's killing."

"Is that right?" Dallas said, startled. "Is he the guy Olin's searching for?"

Purvis nodded.

"A pretty dangerous character, according to Olin. I ran into Olin on my way home tonight. He's had quite a night of it. As a routine precaution he put a couple of his men to watch Baird's apartment house. One of them spotted a big man watching the house and went after him. He cornered him in a drugstore, but wasn't fast enough with his gun. He and the girl in the store were shot to death, and the killer escaped by way of the roof. Olin got some boys down there in double quick time, and one of them spotted the killer as he was crossing the roof. He winged him, but he got away somehow. They've cordoned off the area and they're making a house-to-house search. Olin swears no one can get through the cordon, so with any luck, they'll catch him."

"Was it Baird?"

"Olin thinks so, but no one has identified him. The cop who shot at him said the man was Baird's build, but he couldn't swear it was Baird. Olin says there's no other hood in town who'd shoot it out with a cop, and then kill the girl so she couldn't identify him. I think he's right. We don't run to types so ruthless as that."

"Well, if it is Baird and they catch him, Gillis' plan may come unstuck."

Purvis didn't say anything. He was thinking, his hand covered his face. There was a long silence, then he looked up to say, "I'm going to put every man I have on this case, Ed. I don't think we need bother with the Rajah for the time being. The people who matter now are Kile, Eve Gillis, Rico, Baird and Adam Gillis. They're the ones who will lead us to the jewels if anyone's going to lead us to them. You've already made contact with Gillis, who's obviously the key man of the set-up. Keep close to him, Ed. That's your job from now on. Don't lose sight of him. Get friendly with him. Get his confidence if you can."

"That guy's as slippery as an eel," Dallas said, "and a first-class heel as well. The way he talked to his sister made me want to puke."

"Who'll I put on to Rico?" Purvis said, frowning. "Burns must cover Kile. Ainsworth can go after Baird, unless the cops get him first, but what about Rico?"

"There's a girl at the club; her name's Zoe Norton," Dallas said. "For some reason or other she seems to have taken a liking for me. I think I could persuade her to work for us. She would be in a much better position to report on Rico than anyone we could employ. That's what we want more than anything at this stage of the game: someone inside and working for us."

Purvis nodded.

"That's right. How do you persuade her?"

"I'd spread my charm before her and a purse of gold," Dallas said, grinning. "It'd cost you three or four hundred, but it'd pay dividends."

Purvis winced.

"Doesn't say much for your charm," he said tartly. "I wouldn't pay her more than a hundred. You seem to think I've money to burn."

"She wouldn't do it for that," Dallas said. "It'll have to be three at least. But don't let me persuade you to throw your money away – as if I could."

Purvis brooded. He realized he would be getting value for money, and this wasn't the time to cut corners.

"Well, talk to her," he said finally. "Get her as cheaply as you can, and not a dime more than three hundred."

Dallas said he'd see what he could do.

"Let's get this straightened out," Purvis went on. "Everyone of us has got to watch his step. You've got the toughest job, Ed, and you've got to handle it as if it were dynamite. We can't afford to let them have the slightest idea we're on to them. Our job is to find the jewels. We're not employed by the police. I want you to understand that. Whatever we find out, we keep to ourselves. If any of you find Baird you're not to report him to the police. We want

Baird to take us to the jewels, and he won't do that if he's in a cell."

"Isn't that making us accessories after the fact?" Dallas asked mildly.

"We stand to pick up four hundred grand," Purvis pointed out. "I'll split one per cent of that among you operators. That's a thousand bucks apiece. Would that make you forget such things as accessories after the fact?"

"A thousand isn't much," Dallas said, scarcely believing his ears, but quick to bargain. "As I've got the heaviest job, how about making it two for me and one for the rest of them?"

Purvis shook his head.

"No, that wouldn't be fair to the others, but I tell you what I'll do. I'll give a cheque for five thousand to the first one of you who walks into my office and tells me where the jewels are."

"Do the big thing," Dallas said, "and give the boys a little confidence. Make it cash."

X

The distant sound of an approaching police siren penetrated Baird's brain. It grew louder until it filled the inside of his head with a vibrating scream of warning.

With an effort he forced back his eyelids and looked into darkness. He felt weak and cold, and there was a stiff, tight feeling of pain down his right side.

He turned his head. There was an open window to his left. He could see the dark night sky, pinpointed with the white brilliance of the stars. The faint haze of reflected light from the street lamps climbed the wall of the building and outlined the cross-sections of the window.

Below, a car skidded with a squeal of tortured tyres to a

standstill. The siren died down in a slow and reluctant wail of sound. Car doors opened and slammed. Feet ran across the street.

Baird suddenly realized there was someone standing against the wall, looking cautiously out of the window into the street: a woman.

It was too dark in the room to see much of her: she seemed small, and her hair hung loose to her shoulders. She was pressing her hands to her breasts, and she stood very still.

More police sirens wailed in the distance. A car started up suddenly close by, and drove away with a noisy change of gears. A dog began to bark furiously.

Baird lifted his head, his hand groped for his gun holster, but it wasn't there. He felt light-headed and weak, but the sound of the approaching sirens was like a spur to him, and he made an effort to sit up.

The woman at the window heard him and looked quickly in his direction.

"Don't move," she said, her voice coming across the intervening space in a frightened whisper. "They're down there: hundreds of them."

Baird got one foot to the floor. The bed on which he was lying creaked under his weight. He raised himself on his elbow. Pain rode through him, bringing him out in a cold sweat. He struggled against it, but it proved too much for him, and he dropped back on to the pillow, his mind seething with vicious, frustrated rage.

He was bad all right, he thought. He remembered the last time he had been shot. It had been nothing to this. This time he was cooked. He must have bled like a pig. The great strength he had always relied on to see him through in a jam had deserted him: he couldn't have pulled the wings off a fly.

More cars squealed to a standstill; sirens died down, car doors opened and slammed. A murmur of voices came up from the street.

"What's going on?" he asked. His voice was so weak he didn't recognize it. It was almost as if some other person had spoken.

"They're searching the houses," she said, not moving from the window. "They are splitting into groups of five, and each group is taking a house."

Baird snarled into the darkness.

"Where's my gun? Where've you put it?"

"It's on the bed by your side." She didn't look in his direction, but continued to stare down into the street, as if what she saw there held her with an irresistible fascination.

Feverishly he groped over the crumpled coverlet. His fingers closed round the butt of the Colt. He managed to lift it, but the effort made him pant.

"You'd better get out," he said. "Go and tell them I'm here if you want to. They won't get me alive."

This time she turned her head and looked in his direction, although he knew she couldn't see him in the dark.

"They may not come here," she said. "If they do, I can tell them I haven't seen you. They wouldn't force their way in here, would they?"

For a moment he couldn't believe he had heard aright.

"Of course they would. They won't take your word. Besides, I left blood in the passage. They'll find that."

"I've cleaned it up," she said simply. "It didn't take long."

Again he had a feeling he was dreaming this, and he peered at her, trying to see through the darkness.

"You cleaned it up?" His voice revealed his suspicious surprise. "Why? What's your game? Don't you know you'll get into trouble if they find out?"

"Yes, I know," she said. "I was sorry for you."

He bit down on his lower lip. No one had ever said that to him before. Sorry for him! He didn't like that. He didn't want her damned pity!

"You'd better get out," he said furiously. "There'll be shooting."

She turned back to the window.

"They may not come," she said.

Cautiously, Baird touched his wounded side. He wondered if he was still bleeding. His fingers moved over a wad, bound tightly against his side. He realized she must have taken off his coat and shirt. He touched the pad wonderingly.

"Did you stop the bleeding?" he asked.

"Yes. You'd better not talk. You may be heard. The walls are very thin."

"Is it bad?" he said, lowering his voice to a whisper. "It feels bad."

"It's bad enough, but the bleeding's stopped. You mustn't move. It may start again."

"What are they doing now?" he asked after a long pause.

The street was suspiciously silent.

"They're standing about," she said, watching intently. "One of them is looking up here. They seem to be waiting for something. Some of them have machine-guns."

Baird grinned savagely. He remembered Chuck Fowler, who had been trapped in a house. He had been one of the crowd that time, watching the fun. He had seen the police shooting it out with Chuck. He remembered how they had sprayed the front of the house with their Thompsons. The stream of lead had smashed windows, broken window frames, brought down plaster. It had been hell while it lasted. Then they had tossed in their tear-gas bombs and had gone in, shooting like madmen the whole time; wrecking the house, smashing down the front door, shooting their way up the stairs; and Chuck had been dead long before the final assault.

"You'd better get out," Baird said. "I know what's coming. They'll cut this room to ribbons."

"There's nowhere for me to go," she began, then stopped, and he saw her stiffen, her hands going once more to her breasts.

"What is it?" he asked, knowing at once what it was.

"I think they're coming now," she said breathlessly.

Again he made the effort and raised himself on his elbow. This time he succeeded in getting both feet to the floor.

"Help me up," he gasped. "I don't stand a chance on the bed."

"You must stay there," she said, turning. "You must. You'll start the bleeding again."

"Help me up!" he snarled. "Goddamn it! Do you want me to shoot you?"

She came over to him.

"They'll hear you," she warned. "You must keep your voice down."

He caught hold of her shoulder. His fingers felt the thinness of her. Her skin was tight over the bones. He pulled himself upright and leaned heavily on her. He felt her wilt under his weight. She was only a tiny thing, he thought. Her head was just above his shoulder.

"Get me against the wall near the door," he panted, "and then get out."

A violent hammering sounded on the street door. A voice bawled, "Come on, open up!"

Baird felt a little trickle of sweat run down his face. Five minutes: no longer. Well, upright and on his feet, he wouldn't go alone.

She helped him across the room and against the wall. The Colt hung heavily from his hand, too heavy to raise. He set his shoulders against the wall. The pain in his side made his breath hiss through his clenched teeth.

"Get out!" he said, giving her a feeble push. "Tell them I'm here. They won't do anything to you if you tell them I'm here. Go on, get out."

She went to the door, unlocked it and opened it. A shaft of light came in from the passage, and he saw her plainly for the first time.

He had only a quick glimpse of her. He saw the long, sensitive face, the wide, dark eyes and the firm, bitter mouth of a girl who was good-looking rather than beautiful: a girl of about twenty-three or four, whose young-old face had a force of character that had come from a life of hardship, poverty and sorrow.

She was wearing a white slip that clung to her thin but beautifully proportioned body, no stockings, and her narrow, long feet were thrust into a shabby pair of heelless slippers.

He watched her go out on to the landing, leaving the door ajar. From where he stood he could see through the opening without being seen.

A buzz of voices drifted up from the ground floor: men's voices, and a woman's voice screaming hysterically.

More hammering sounded on the front door. Then a hard, loud voice bawled, "Okay, okay, break it up! Get back to your rooms and stay in them. Hey, you! Seen a big guy in a brown suit around? He'll be a stranger, and he's wounded. Come on, now! Open up! The guy's a killer!"

Baird ached to lie down on the bed again. The pain in his side was torturing him, and his legs began to sag. He pulled himself together, pressing his shoulders against the wall, his lips coming off his teeth in a snarl.

He watched the girl lean over the banister rail.

"Toni! Toni!" she called sharply. "What's happening?"

Baird stiffened. What was she up to? Why didn't she get downstairs? The cops wouldn't bother about her if there was any shooting.

"Some killer loose," a man's voice called up to her. "The cops think he might be hiding in this house. You got him under your bed, Anita?" He laughed excitedly as if he had made the best joke in the world.

"You bet," the girl said, and laughed. "I've got him right here. Want to come up and see him, Toni?"

"I will come up and see you, bambino."

"With the cops coming up, too?"

"No cop stops me loving a girl," the man said, and laughed. "Not even a cop with a gun."

"That's what you say," the girl said, and snapped her fingers. "You're all talk, Toni."

"Yeah? This time I don't talk. I come up."

"Better not," the girl jeered, "they'll take you away in their little black wagon."

Baird heard quick, heavy footsteps on the stairs. He saw a fat, powerfully built fellow, going bald, with a blue-black growth of beard, come bounding on to the landing. He was wearing a soiled singlet and black trousers, and his face was shiny with sweat.

Laughing, he rushed at the girl, who avoided him. They dodged about on the landing. She was very quick, but she hadn't much room to manoeuvre, and he finally trapped her in a corner.

"No, Toni! I was only fooling," she said, trying to push him back as he crowded her, holding her arms and grinning like a mischievous monkey as she wrestled with him. "Not now. Some other night. Stop it! They'll be coming up!"

"It's always some other night," the man said, giggling excitedly. "To hell with them! All talk, you say. I show you it's not all talk!"

He grabbed her around the waist and under the knees and swung her off her feet.

"Put me down, Toni!" the girl said, keeping her voice low. She struggled to break away, but not so violently that he couldn't handle her.

"Not even a cop with a gun is going to stop me this time," he said, and there was a sudden change in his voice that made Baird stiffen.

"No! Stop it, you fool!"

He ran with her across the landing, kicked open the door and blundered into the dark room. He kicked the door shut and stumbled over to the bed.

Invisible against the wall, Baird lifted the gun. He stood motionless, every nerve in his body tense, while he listened to the struggle going on on the bed.

"You devil!" he heard the girl gasp. "You mustn't!"

"Not even a cop with a gun!" the man panted as he struggled with her. "You asked for it this time, bambino. You get it."

Baird made a move towards the bed, then stiffened back as he heard a quick rush of feet on the stairs.

A voice shouted outside the door, "Open up!" The door was flung open, catching Baird and pinning him behind it. The white light of a flashlight swept into the room and lit up the bed.

The man on the bed twisted his head around and glared along the beam of light. There was a savage, animal expression on his round, sweaty face.

"Ain't there any privacy in this goddamn world?" he shouted violently. "Get the hell out of here!"

The two cops, one with a Thompson at his hip, the other with an automatic rifle, gaped at what they saw.

"For crying out loud!" one of them exclaimed, grinning. "If I'd known, mister, I'd've knocked."

"Get out!" Toni shouted furiously. "Leave us alone!" The two cops backed out of the room, laughing, pulled the door shut and Baird heard them clattering down the stairs.

"You see," Toni said, "not even two goddamn cops with two goddamn guns!"

"Let me go!" the girl gasped. "Get out!"

"Yeah?" Toni said. "I go in a little while."

Baird stood motionless, sweat running down his face, listening to the struggle going on in the darkness. He heard the girl catch her breath sharply. He slid the barrel of the gun into his hand, and took a step forward, but away from the support of the wall, his legs wouldn't hold him, and he slithered down on hands and knees.

As he struggled to get back on his feet, Toni gave a sudden yell of pain.

"You bitch!" he shouted. "You've blinded me!"

"Get out!" the girl said, her voice low. "Let me go!"

The bed creaked; feet struck the floor.

"I fix you for this!" Toni snarled. He pulled open the door.

In the light from the passage Baird saw blood running down Toni's face. Four deep scratches, just missing his eyes, were like deep red ruts in his face.

The girl crouched on the bed. She was naked to the waist. Some of Toni's blood was smeared on her shoulder. Her eyes smouldered as she glared at Toni.

"Get out and stay out!" she said, still keeping her voice low.

Toni snarled at her, his hand to his face. He went out and slammed the door.

"You all right?" Baird asked hoarsely, crawling over to the bed.

He heard the girl slide off the bed on the opposite side. "I'm all right," she said curtly. "Are you bleeding again?"

"I don't think so." Baird pulled himself up on to the bed and lay flat, his breath coming in long, painful gasps. "You didn't have to do that for me."

The girl didn't say anything. He could hear her groping in the darkness. After a delay, the light went on.

She was fastening a shabby coat about her, and she looked sharply at him. They stared at each other for several seconds.

"I'll look at your wound," she said, coming over to him. "Does it hurt?"

"A little," he said, watching her. "I don't think it's bleeding."

She bent over him. Together they inspected the pad on his side. There was no sign of blood.

"No. It's all right," she said, and as she straightened he caught hold of her wrist. She remained bending over him, looking down at him.

"Do you know what you're doing?" he asked. "They could put you in jail for this."

She pulled free. "I don't like coppers," she said, her face hard. "They won't get you now."

"I guess I owe you something," Baird said uneasily. "If it

hadn't been for you I'd be dead now."

She smiled cynically.

"I dare say you'd have been better off," she said, turning away. "And you don't owe me anything."

"What's your name?" he said, wiping his damp face with the back of his hand.

"Anita Jackson," she said. "You'd better try and get some sleep."

"I'm Verne Baird," he told her. "Those punks think I killed a copper."

She looked at him, but didn't say anything. "You'd better get some sleep," she said after a long pause.

"You're a knockout," he said, shutting his eyes. "What did the cops do to you to make you hate them like this?"

"That's not your business," she returned curtly.

"I guess that's right. Give me an hour, and I'll get out." He touched his side and winced. "I owe you something."

"You'll have to stay here until you're better," she said, sitting in the armchair. "You won't get far with that wound."

"What about you?" he said, opening his eyes and staring at her. "The longer I'm here the bigger risk you're running. Suppose that fat guy comes back?"

She shook her head. "He won't. I know Toni. He won't come here again. I'm out all day. It's only the nights. I don't care."

"You've got to have the bed," Baird said, a little surprised he was thinking more of her than himself. "I'll lie on the floor."

"Oh, shut up!" she said crossly. "Go to sleep and don't talk so much." She pulled another chair forward and put up her feet. "I'm all right here."

"Suit yourself," he said, shrugging. "I'll be okay by

tomorrow."

She reached out and turned off the light.

"Go to sleep," she said.

Baird lay in the darkness, staring at the night sky through the open window. Below, the police still went on with their search for him. The voices, the trampling of feet and the hammering on doors became fainter as they moved farther down the street.

He felt an odd stirring inside him as he thought of the girl. She had saved him. Why? It was something right out of a book. He owed her something, and the thought made him uneasy. Gratitude was a new sensation to him. He felt restricted. No one had ever done anything for him up to now. He tried to push this feeling of indebtedness out of his mind, but he couldn't. Sooner or later he knew he would have to do something about it. He felt in his hip pocket for the five hundred Rico had given him. He could always give her some of the money, he told himself. From the look of her, she could do with it. Yes, he'd do that. But at the back of his mind, he was aware that money wouldn't square himself with her. His mind recreated the struggle on the bed. That had been something no other woman he could imagine would have done, and she had done it for him. No, money wouldn't square that.

The sound of her quick, light breathing told him she was asleep. She had guts, he thought: guts and nerve.

Eventually he fell asleep himself. He dreamed the girl in the drugstore, with blood on her white coat, came and sat at the foot of the bed and looked at him. He wasn't afraid of her.

PART TWO

Rico put down his pen and sat back with a little grunt. His swarthy, pock-marked face plainly showed his dissatisfaction. Five hundred and twenty dollars up on last month's figures. Six months ago he would have been pleased, but now he knew it wasn't enough. A month's work for five hundred and twenty lousy dollars, he thought, pushing back his chair. He got to his feet and began to pace up and down. Not enough, he thought, scowling. Already he was overdrawn at the bank. His standard of living had gradually risen, and he was now living well beyond his income. Recently he had moved from his three-room apartment to a six-room one that cost him four times as much. His taste for tailored suits and silk shirts had given him a tailor's bill he couldn't settle without pinching himself for ready cash. He had bought himself a Roadmaster Buick, and that had to be paid for. The erotic pleasure he derived from several of his carefully selected hostesses was also a heavy drain on his income; and they had to be paid in cash.

Since the Bruce killing he had stopped dealing in illicit jewellery. He knew Olin was watching him, and until things cooled off a little, it would be unwise to tempt providence. He sadly missed the extra income from his activities as a fence.

He went over to the cellaret and mixed himself a whisky and soda. Three weeks had gone by since Kile had come to him with the mysterious proposition that might put fifteen grand in his pocket. For three weeks Rico had been hunting for Baird, but Baird seemed to have vanished off the face of the earth. No one had seen him: all Rico's spies were hunting for him, and so far had nothing to report.

Kile was fast losing patience. He had been in last night and had bluntly said he would give Rico three more days to find Baird, and if he wasn't successful the deal was off.

Fifteen grand! Rico sipped his drink and scowled down at his expensively shod feet. Where the hell was Baird? Why hadn't he got into touch with Rico as he had promised? Had it been Baird who had been chased across the roofs and shot at that night the cop and the girl in the drugstore had been murdered? How long ago was that? Rico thumbed back the leaves of his calendar. Twenty-three days. The papers had said the killer had been wounded. Maybe Baird had holed up somewhere and had died. Rico felt sweat start out on his forehead at the thought. If Baird was dead, then the hope of laying his hands on Kile's fifteen grand was dead, too.

He finished his whisky, went over to the cellaret and made another. Then he lit a cigar and sat down at his desk again. There was nothing more he could do. Every petty crook in town was searching for Baird. Rico had offered a reward for reliable news of Baird, but so far no one had claimed it.

After he had finished his second whisky he decided he would take a turn in the restaurant. It was getting on for midnight, and it was time he showed himself. He went over to a vase of carnations, selected one, stuck it in his buttonhole and surveyed himself in the mirror. In spite of his bald head, his pitted complexion and his bloodshot eyes,

Rico was quite pleased with his appearance. He adjusted his silk handkerchief, shot his cuffs and turned to the door.

For a moment he stood completely still, scarcely believing his eyes, then with a sharp exclamation, he darted forward, holding out his hand.

"Baird! Well, damn it! I was only just this moment thinking about you. Where the hell have you been?"

Baird closed the door and walked across to Rico. He shook hands without enthusiasm, looked Rico up and down and then went over and dropped into the red leather armchair.

"Get me a drink," he said curtly. "I need it."

Rico gave him a quick, anxious glance. Baird was thinner than when he had last seen him, and his face fine drawn. There were smudges under his eyes as if he had been sleeping badly, and he looked surly.

"I've been hunting all over for you," Rico said, hurriedly splashing whisky into a glass. "Where've you been?"

"Out of town."

"Olin's still looking for you," Rico said, remembering with an anxious pang that Baird was a wanted man. "Maybe you shouldn't have come here."

Baird made an impatient gesture.

"You don't have to get steamed up. I've seen Olin."

Rico stiffened.

"You mean you've talked to him? When?"

"Gimme that drink, can't you?" Baird snarled. "I've been at headquarters all the goddamn afternoon."

Rico put the whisky on the desk by Baird's hand and sat down.

"What happened?"

Baird drank half the whisky, put the glass down and drew in a slow, deep breath. He reached out and helped himself to a cigarette from Rico's box, lit it and stretched out his long legs.

"I got myself a cast-iron alibi," he said. "Olin couldn't bust it, so I walked out."

"You mean they haven't anything on you?" Rico asked eagerly.

"They never had anything on me," Baird said, and his hard mouth twisted into a jeering grin. "No one ever saw me. They tried to pin the Bruce killing on me, but they hadn't any proof. As soon as I could get around again I went up to New York and fixed myself an alibi. I've got a lot of friends in New York. Six of them swore I was with them the night Jean Bruce was knocked off. I and my lawyer took their statements to Olin. There was nothing he could do about it."

Rico drew in a deep breath of relief.

"That's fine!" he said, rubbing his hands. "That's terrific! You're free to operate again?"

"Sure," Baird said indifferently. "Did you get rid of that bracelet?"

Rico nodded.

"I didn't get much for it, but I was lucky to find a buyer."

"Don't talk crap," Baird said roughly. "If the stuff's good there are always buyers."

"What happened to you? There was some talk you were shot."

Baird stared across the desk at Rico.

"I was. I was laid low for a couple of weeks. I had a pretty close call."

"How did you get away from them?" Rico asked, his eyes popping.

"I holed up with a girl," Baird said, and rubbed his hand across his eyes. "She looked after me." He frowned down at the desk. "The damnedest thing that's ever happened to me."

"Who was she?" Rico asked. "Talk about luck! Was she pretty?"

The look Baird gave him was hard and menacing.

"Shut your dirty trap," he said. "Never mind who she was. She had more guts in her little finger than you've got in the whole of your rotten body. So shut up about her!"

Rico smiled ingratiatingly.

"Sure, sure," he said. "I didn't mean to talk out of turn."

"I'm running short of dough," Baird said. "Anything around for me?"

"Yes," Rico said, leaning forward. "Something big. You've arrived in time. Another three days, and it'd have been too late. This is a big job; worth ten grand to you."

Baird lifted his head sharply.

"Ten grand? You been drinking?"

Rico rubbed his hands together excitedly.

"The guy who's behind this is Preston Kile, the financier. He's offering ten grand for a guy who'll do a job for him. I told him you were the only one I'd trust to handle it."

"What's the job?" Baird asked suspiciously.

"I don't know. Kile wants to see you first. He's acting awful cagey. Says he wants to talk to you before he spills any details, but it's okay, Baird. Kile's a big-shot. He's got a front that'll knock your eye out, and you want to see his girl. Used to be with the Follies. Everything about Kile is big. Getting in with him is the best thing that's ever happened to me."

Baird didn't seem impressed.

"You're sure about the ten grand?"

"Yeah. If you pull the job off it rates ten, if you fail he'll pay five. There's nothing small about Kile. You wait until you meet him."

Baird started to say something, but broke off as the door opened and a red-headed girl wandered in. She was wearing a low-cut evening gown of lemon yellow, and her green eyes looked Baird over sharply.

Rico said, "What do you want, Zoe? I'm busy."

"That guy Dallas asked me if he could cash a cheque," Zoe said, coming over to the desk. She tossed a slip of paper on Rico's blotter. "It's only for thirty bucks. He wants to buy me champagne."

Frowning, Rico picked up the cheque, scrutinized it, opened a drawer and dropped it in. He took out a cash box and began to count five-dollar bills on to the blotter.

"He's getting quite a regular customer," he said. "What's he do with himself?"

Zoe rested an elegant hip on the desk and swung her leg, her eyes roaming over Baird.

"I guess he's got ideas about me," she said, smiled and winked at Baird, who stared at her stonily. "He's spending a lot of dough here, so why should you worry?"

"I didn't say I was worrying," Rico said, and pushed the money over to her. "Next time you come in here, Zoe, please knock."

Zoe lifted her eyebrows.

"Why, sure, I didn't think. Aren't you going to introduce me to your boyfriend?"

Baird made an impatient movement.

"Run along, Zoe," Rico said, waving her away. "I'm busy."

She slid off the desk with an indifferent shrug.

"Well, I can console myself I'm not missing much," she said, making a little face at Baird. She crossed to the door with an elaborate sway of her hips, opened it and went out.

"Who's that?" Baird asked, when the door had closed.

"She's okay. She's one of my girls: Zoe Morton," Rico said. "Maybe I could fix it for you to see Kile tonight. Okay with you?"

Baird nodded.

Rico picked up the phone, dialled and waited.

"Put me through to Mr Kile," he said, when a voice came on the line. He listened, frowning, then said, "I gotta get in touch with him. Know where he is?" He scribbled down a telephone number and hung up. "He's with his girlfriend," he told Baird and grinned. "Hope I don't interrupt anything important."

Baird continued to stare at him stonily, and a little flustered under the hard look, Rico hurriedly dialled the new number.

"This is Rico," he said, when Eve Gillis answered. "Could I speak to Mr Kile?"

"Hold on a moment," she said, and he heard her calling Kile.

"What is it?" Kile snapped, coming on the line. "Who told you you could call me here?"

"The guy we've been looking for has shown up," Rico said quickly. "I've got him here now."

"You have?" The sharpness went out of Kile's voice. "Can you bring him over right away, Rico?"

"Sure. I told him you wanted to see him."

"Now look, he may not be the man I'm looking for. I can't tell until I've seen him. Warn him there may be nothing in it for him. I'll only see him on that understanding."

Rico laughed excitedly. He looked across at Baird and winked. Baird's face remained dour, and his look was still stony.

"You'll want him all right, Mr Kile, but I'll tell him."

"Be over as soon as you can," Kile said. "Apartment 200, Roxburgh House. You know where it is?"

"Sure, Mr Kile, I know it."

Kile grunted and hung up.

"He wants to see you right away. He's at Miss Gillis' place on Roxburgh Avenue. Maybe I'd better come with you.'

Baird got to his feet. He finished his whisky, mashed out his cigarette as he said, "Suit yourself."

Rico took his black slouch hat from a hanging cupboard, slapped it on his head and jerked it so it rested at a jaunty angle over his right eye.

"Let's go," he said. "Be careful how you handle Kile. He likes respect."

Baird sneered.

"For ten grand he'll get it," he said, opened the door and walked out into the passage leading to the kitchens and rear exit.

Neither of them saw Zoe watching them through a half-open door at the far end of the passage. As soon as they were out of sight she signalled to Dallas, who reached for the telephone on her dressing table and dialled Harmon Purvis' number.

II

Kile sat in Eve's morning room: a feminine room he liked, and which, up to now, had been restful to his nerves to sit in. The big windows overlooked the river, and from where he sat he could see the lights of the shipping, and on the far bank the headlights of the stream of cars heading up town.

It was a hot, close night, and the windows were wide open. Kile was sweating a little. He cradled a highball in his hand; a smouldering cigar rested in a deep ashtray on the arm of his chair.

Eve sat on the broad window seat, her back half turned to him while she stared down at the river. She looked pale, and the scarlet evening dress she wore seemed too gay for her mood.

Neither of them had spoken since Kile had told her Baird was on his way over. Both were preoccupied with their thoughts. Kile had an uneasy feeling that Baird was going to be the right man for this fantastic job. If he was then it would mean Kile would have to go ahead with the plan. Since his first enthusiasm had waned, he had begun to wonder if anyone in his right mind would have even contemplated such a plan, let alone waste time investigating the possibilities. He had to admit he hadn't done much himself so far. Eve had done all the necessary work. It was extraordinary how she managed to obtain her information. Admittedly, she was in a position to know many people, but how she had got together all the minute details and information with which she had presented him, defeated him.

The plan couldn't succeed, he told himself again and again, but Eve wouldn't admit defeat.

"What have we got to lose?" she had asked patiently. "If this man says it won't work, then we can drop the idea, but if he has the nerve to go through with it, and if he pulls it off, it's a half a million in your pocket."

That was the only argument that kept Kile in the running. A half a million! But if Baird turned the plan down, Kile would be relieved. Of course he would hate to let such a sum slip through his fingers, but the danger and the risks he would be involved in if Baird went ahead frightened him.

Up to now he had managed to concentrate on the prize, but now that Baird would be here at any minute, he could think of nothing but the risks.

"This fella won't do it," he jerked out suddenly, speaking what was in his mind before he could stop himself. "I've been considering your plan, Eve. It – it won't work. It can't work!"

She turned her head and looked at him. She looked tired and uneasy. She didn't think the plan would work, either. She thought it was the craziest, the most dangerous idea Adam had yet thought of, but he had said it would work, and she knew from past experience that once Adam had made up his mind about anything, no one or nothing would stop him. If she backed out now, or even encouraged Kile to back out, she knew instinctively that she had seen the last of her brother. In her more rational moments she knew it would be the best thing that could happen to her, but she also knew she was fooling herself: life without Adam would be no life at all.

"Let him judge," she said. "To hear you talk, Preston, I'm beginning to think you don't want the money."

Kile drank some of his highball.

"The risk will be frightful," he muttered. "Of course I want the money, but ..."

"I don't see what risk you run. This man Baird will shoulder the risk."

"He won't!" Kile said excitedly. "He wouldn't be such a fool!"

"Ten thousand is a lot of money," Eve said listlessly. She was speaking the words Adam had put into her mouth. "We can but ask him."

The front door bell rang.

Kile started so violently he spilled some of his highball on his trousers. Swearing softly, he wiped the wet patch with his handkerchief as he stood up.

The Filipino boy who looked after Eve's apartment came in.

"Mr Rico is here," he said, and Eve could tell he didn't approve of Rico.

"Show him in," Kile said, trying to steady his voice. He moved over to the fireplace and stood facing the door, a scowl on his heavy features. The pain under his heart had sharpened.

Eve didn't move. She felt frightened. She, too, had a feeling that once Baird was told of the plan there would be no drawing back.

Rico came in, followed by Baird, who hadn't taken off his hat. Baird's eyes went quickly and suspiciously around the room. He gave Eve a quick glance, then stared directly at Kile.

In his turn, Kile was looking at him. He saw at once this tall, powerfully built man in his creased brown suit, the shabby hat tilted to the back of his head, was dangerous, and he felt a little prickle run up his spine as he met Baird's ice-cold eyes.

"This is Baird," Rico said, coming forward. His smile was ingratiating, and he gave Kile a little bow. "I told him you wanted to see him, and that you might have something you could put in his way."

Kile nodded curtly to Baird, who continued to stare with cold, unfriendly eyes. He wasn't impressed with Kile. A rich, well-fed sonofabitch, he decided, soft at the core and jumpy. Not anyone you'd want to trust further than you could throw him.

"Sit down," Kile said, waving to two armchairs. He was aware that he hadn't made an impression, and that irritated him. "Whiskies, Philip," be said to the Filipino boy, "and then get out."

The boy put a tray containing whisky, charge water and ice on the table.

"I'll mix them," Rico said. "Baird?"

Baird shook his head. He dug out a crumpled pack of cigarettes, fished one out, stuck it on his lower lip and sat down in an armchair. He glanced across at Eve, who was still looking out of the window, her back turned to him. He allowed his eyes to run over her figure, paused for a moment or so on her neatly turned ankles, and then struck a match with his thumbnail and lit the cigarette.

As soon as the Filipino boy had left the room, Kile said, "Miss Gillis is interested in this proposition I want to talk to you about." He hadn't missed the searching look Baird had given Eve. "Eve, won't you come over here and join us?"

She turned and looked at Baird. What she saw in the brooding eyes chilled her. She left the window seat and came over to stand near Kile.

Rico bowed elaborately.

"I haven't seen you at the club for several nights, Miss Gillis," he said. "I hope you won't neglect us."

"Suppose we get down to business," Baird broke in in his cold, soft voice. "I've got a date in half an hour."

Kile looked at him sharply. The soft voice had startled him. He sat down, pulled at his cigar and said, "I want you to understand there is nothing definite yet arranged. I am sounding the ground, as you might say. It is probable that nothing will come of it."

Rico winced as he poured himself a whisky.

"But, Mr Kile ..." he began.

"Shut up!" Baird growled. He leaned forward to stare at Kile. "Rico told me you wanted a job done that paid ten grand. What's the job?"

Kile flushed, and his bloodshot eyes watered. For a moment he looked as if he were going to fly into a rage, but the cold eyes that stared at him warned him that bluster wouldn't get him anywhere.

"A certain man is in a certain prison. I want this man out."

He felt, rather than saw, Rico stiffen, but Baird showed no surprise.

"Go on," he said, "what's the rest of it?"

Kile licked his dry lips.

"I will pay ten thousand to anyone who can get this man out of prison and bring him to me," he went on. "That's the proposition. It won't be easy, and I don't want to know how it is to be done. When the man is brought to me, I will pay the ten thousand in cash."

Baird flicked ash on to the floor. He didn't show his surprise, but he was surprised. This was something he hadn't expected, and his shrewd brain looked for snags.

"That's a lot of dough," he said, studying Kile. "You could get the job done for a lot less than that. What's the idea?"

Kile touched his sweating temples with his handkerchief.

"It's very probable," he said, his voice thickening, "this man won't want to leave jail, and that makes it doubly difficult. Apart from that, the prison is extremely well guarded, and the territory is bad."

Rico was listening now, dumbfounded. He had been expecting Kile to propose a big jewel robbery. This business about getting a man out of prison made him uneasy.

"What you're trying to say is you want this man kidnapped from prison?" Baird said.

"Call it what you like," Kile said sullenly. "He may resist. Whatever happens he must not be hurt in any way."

Baird blew smoke to the ceiling.

"Why do you want this man?"

"That's my business!" Kile said sharply. "Your job is to get hold of him, not to question my motives."

Baird's eyes shifted to Eve. She was watching him intently. She was pale, and her breasts rose and fell quickly under the scarlet chiffon of her gown.

"It isn't easy," Kile went on, seeing Baird's apparent hesitation. "In fact, it may be impossible. But if you produce this man it'll be worth ten thousand to you. If you can convince me you have made a good attempt, but have failed, I'll pay you half the money."

"Where is he?" Baird asked.

"Bellmore State Prison Farm. It is situated about three miles from Red River Falls, and is in the swamps."

"Who's the man?"

"That I'll tell you when you've decided if you'll do the job, and when you've convinced me you have a workable plan," Kile said. "I can supply you with maps, the man's photograph and his prison number. At present he's working with other convicts on dredging operations at Red River basin, a mile outside the prison. The convicts arrive at the basin in trucks at eight o'clock in the morning and return to the prison at six. While they are at work there are four guards ..."

"Five," Eve put in quickly.

Kile frowned.

"Four or five," he said. "There are dogs, too."

Baird shifted lower in his chair. He looked down at his scuffed shoes, his face expressionless.

"I'll have to take a look at the territory," he said. "But it sounds as if it could be done."

He saw Eve give a little start and nervously clench her hands. Kile hurriedly put down his glass and sat forward.

"Don't forget this man may resist," he said, his voice unsteady.

Baird looked up sharply.

"So what? Don't you want the job done?"

"I wouldn't be offering you ten thousand unless I did," Kile snapped, flushing. "But it's only fair to you to know what you're up against."

Baird stood up.

"You don't have to worry about me," he said. "I can do that better than anyone. This time next week I'll tell you if I'll do it or not. I'll want a hundred to cover expenses, and I'll want it now."

Rico put in smoothly as he saw Kile hesitate.

"As I know Baird, and you don't, Mr Kile, perhaps you would let me take care of his expenses, and if he proves satisfactory, you could settle with me direct."

Kile nodded.

"Very well," he said, getting to his feet, "we'll leave it like that. If you're in no hurry, Rico, perhaps you'll remain behind. I know our friend here is anxious to get away."

Baird smiled jeeringly.

"If I do the job," he said, looking at Kile, "I'll expect proof that the money's there to pay me."

"That's okay," Rico said quickly. "Mr Kile and me have worked together before. You don't have to worry about your end, Baird."

"All the same I'm going to worry about it until I get it," Baird said. He nodded to Kile, glanced over at Eve and gave her an insolent little smile. She turned away and went back to the window. "Be seeing you in a week's time," he went on to Kile, walked across the room, opened the door and went out.

There was a long pause while Kile freshened his drink, and Rico stood staring uneasily at his feet.

"Your friend's quite a character," Kile said at last as he came back to his chair. "I can't say I like his manner."

Rico laughed uneasily.

"Baird's a hard man," he said apologetically, "but he's a man who gets things done. If the job can be done, he'll do it." He fidgeted uneasily while he studied Kile. "Where exactly do I fit in in this, Mr Kile. If you remember, you said ..."

"Once Baird agrees to do the job I'm dropping out of the picture," Kile said. "I intend to leave the whole thing in your hands. I don't wish to know how you are going to get this man out of prison or any of the details. I don't even wish to be consulted. You and Baird must handle the whole thing independently of me. If you think you'll need more help, that's up to you to arrange and pay for. Do the job and hand the man over to me, and you will receive fifteen and Baird ten thousand. Now do you see where you fit in?"

Rico nodded. He also saw how he could run into a fifteen to twenty years' sentence. He didn't like the proposition, but the money drew him like a magnet.

"This man's important to you, Mr Kile?"

Kile gave him a hostile look.

"I'd scarcely pay out twenty-five thousand unless he was," he said curtly. "I can understand you are wondering why I want him, but I have no intentions of telling you, so don't ask."

"That's all right," Rico said hurriedly. "But to kidnap a man from prison! It was something I wasn't expecting."

Kile didn't seem to think that called for a remark. He sipped his highball and looked away.

After an awkward pause, Rico said, "It depends on Baird, then. If he says he'll do the job, I take it you're satisfied for him to try?"

Kile glanced across at Eve, who nodded silently.

"Yes," he said, "but I don't think I need meet him again. Frankly, I don't like him. The less I have to do with him the better. If, after he has looked over the ground, he thinks he can succeed, then let him give you his plan, and you can pass it on to me. If I'm satisfied the plan will succeed, I will tell you to go ahead, and until the man is brought to me, I don't want to hear anything more of what you are doing. Have I made myself quite clear on that point?"

Rico nodded.

"Before he makes the attempt, Mr Kile, I expect he'll want an advance of some kind: say three or four thousand?" Rico smiled apologetically. "That could be arranged?"

"Yes," Kile said impatiently. "The best thing to do would be for me to give you five thousand, and for you to keep what you think for yourself, and the rest can go to Baird. Then if the job is successful, I'll pay the balance."

Rico relaxed.

"That's fine, Mr Kile. That'd suit me well. In the meantime I will finance Baird and keep an account."

Kile got to his feet.

"Then this time next week?"

"Yes," Rico said, bowing.

When he had gone, Kile joined Eve at the window. He stood near her, his hand resting on the sill. For some time they stood silent, looking down at the lights of the shipping, then abruptly Kile said, "Well, I hope to God you're satisfied."

Eve didn't say anything. Out of the corner of his eye he saw her shiver slightly.

Kile had a sick feeling in the pit of his stomach, and the pain under his heart nagged at his frayed nerves. He had a feeling that he was being dragged down into a nightmare situation like a swimmer helplessly caught in a whirlpool.

He felt he must get back to the quiet of his own home, where he could rest and try to forget that in a week's time this crazy plan might materialize.

"I'm going home now, Eve," he said. "I'm feeling tired. There's nothing more we can do until this fella reports back. Do you think he'll do it?"

Without turning her head, she said in a quiet, flat voice, "Yes, he'll do it. A man like that would do anything."

III

During his week in New York, Baird had thought a lot about Anita Jackson. Up to now he had never been interested in a girl. He had regarded women as a tiresome necessity, using them as a physical convenience and promptly forgetting them as soon as his infrequent desires were satisfied.

But this girl was different. He had spent thirteen days in her room, living in the closest contact with her, watching her prepare meals, seeing her dress and undress, go out to work at half-past seven in the morning and come in again late at night. He had watched her mend and iron her shabby wardrobe. He had lain in bed while she had shampooed her hair or cleaned her teeth or washed her stockings in the small toilet basin, seeing all the small activities that go on in hundreds of rooms rented by hundreds of girls like Anita Jackson, and which no other man was likely to see. It was this intimacy that created in him an interest he had never known with other women. It puzzled him that even though they had lived like this for thirteen days, he hadn't thought of her in the way he thought of other women. What she had done for him and was doing for him protected her from the brutal urge he felt sometimes towards women. There was something about her that he couldn't understand that made her untouchable to him.

She had saved his life by letting that fat wop maul her on the bed. That was something he just couldn't get over. She had changed the dressings on his wound day and night, and it was due to her care and attention that he was able to get on his feet ten days after the shooting. She wouldn't explain why she had given him sanctuary, and when he pressed her she had turned on him angrily, saying, "Oh, do stop talking about it! I'm doing this to please myself. I don't want your gratitude or your thanks. I'm not going to discuss it any more!"

It had worried Baird. He couldn't understand anyone doing what she had done for a stranger. By letting him stay in the room, she was also risking a prison sentence. It baffled him. When he was well enough to think of leaving he had put three hundred dollars on the table, saying, "I guess I owe you something. Take this: I've got enough for myself. I'm not going to forget what you did for me. Go on, take it. You've earned it."

He wasn't used to expressing himself, and this speech had embarrassed him. At the back of his mind he thought he must be crazy to give her so much, and yet there was something in him that drove him to be generous: something he had never known before.

And when she had refused the money it was like a slap in the face to him. She had refused it curtly, as if money meant nothing to her, and his savage temper got the better of his intentions.

"Then don't have it!" he snarled, putting the money back in his pocket. "To hell with you! I'm not going to beg you to take it. If you're going to be such a goddamn sucker you deserve what you get. I must be going soft in the head even to offer you anything!"

She had gone on preparing supper while he talked, and he had an uncomfortable feeling that she wasn't even listening. This had so enraged him he had caught hold of her and jerked her around, pulling her close to him.

"Do you hear what I'm saying?" he demanded, glaring down at her. "Three hundred bucks!" He gave her a little shake. "Why, you stupid bitch, it's a fortune to you! What do you think you're playing at – turning it down?"

"Take your hands off me!" she had said, with a fury that matched his own. "I don't want your money! Do you imagine kindness can be bought like something out of a grocery store? I helped you because I was sorry for you, as I would help anyone who was one against many. Let go of me!"

For a moment they had stood staring at each other, then he had released her and had moved away to sit on the bed. No other girl he had known had ever dared look at him the way she had looked at him. He hadn't frightened her as he had meant to frighten her. He might have been just any other man, instead of a killer who was mauling her, and the discovery that she wasn't afraid of him had given him a strange and intense pleasure.

Ever since he could remember people had been afraid of him. Even his mother had been afraid of him when he was in one of his savage tempers. His brother and sister seemed to know instinctively that he was dangerous, for they didn't kid him as they kidded each other, and they were never at ease when they played with him. The children at school had been wary of him, and as he grew older, he came to recognize the quick fear that jumped into people's eyes when they met him. Even Rico was afraid of him, although he fawned over him. Kile had been afraid of him, and that doll-faced blonde. They all seemed to sense the savage killer instinct that was in him.

This knowledge forced him into a dark, savage loneliness, making him callously self-reliant, bred in him suspicion and distrust, and to find someone who wasn't afraid of him was like a light shining in the darkness.

The following morning, after Anita had gone to work as usual, he decided to quit. Every day he stayed in this room made it more dangerous for her. If she wouldn't take his money, the least he could do was to get out. He left as it was growing dark, an hour or so before she was due back. He went through the skylight and across the roofs, following the same route as he had come.

He had left without telling her he was going, or without leaving a note for her to find on her return.

During the week in New York, while he had been fixing an alibi, he had thought continually of her. Although they had spent so much time together, he knew nothing about her. He knew only that she had a job as a waitress in a steak joint, but he didn't know where the joint was. He had tried to find out her background. It was beyond his powers to ask anything but direct questions, and she quickly blocked off the questions by curtly saying she didn't wish to talk about herself.

In New York he found he missed her. He stayed at a cheap hotel, and each night as he undressed for bed he brooded on those past thirteen days when she was bustling about her room, not saying anything, but keeping him company by her presence, and pushing back the wall of loneliness that surrounded him. He kept thinking of what she had said: *Do you imagine kindness can be bought like something out of a grocery store*? Kindness! To him it was a word in a foreign language, and yet his mind kept coming back to it. Well, he still owed her something. He was determined now to get out of her debt. He had to see her again. He knew she was desperately poor, and for some reason appeared to have no friends. In her way, she was as lonely as he was. She didn't go to the movies or a dance or do anything girls with her looks were doing every night of their lives. Men seemed to have no place in her life. When he had asked her why she didn't go out and enjoy herself, she had said defiantly, "I do enjoy myself. I don't have to go out to do that. Anyway, I don't want men hanging around me. They're only after one thing, and they're not going to get it from me!"

He had given up. She was too complicated for him to understand. Besides, it wasn't his line to ask questions or to show interest in anyone. He felt hopelessly at sea with her, and irritated with himself for bothering about her. But he had to see her again. Although it was after eleven o'clock when he left Eve Gillis' apartment, it didn't cross his mind that it was too late to call on Anita. She got in from work at ten-thirty, and immediately went to bed. He knew she would probably be asleep by now, but he didn't care. He made up his mind to see her that night, and that was the end of it.

On his way down town, he thought about Kile and his proposition. Ten grand to get a man out of jail! With ten grand in his pocket, he would be on easy street for months. But what was behind all this? If he was worth ten grand to him, this man must be worth considerably more to Kile.

The job appealed to Baird: it was dangerous, difficult and well paid. It would mean a change of scenery. He felt in the mood to tackle some impossible task: it would be an outlet for his pent-up mood of savage, aimless anger that had been slowly welling up inside him for the past two weeks.

He had heard about the Bellmore State Prison Farm. It was one of the toughest prisons in the country. Abe Golheim had been there, and Abe had told him about the place. It was surrounded by a belt of swampland, thirty miles long and ten miles broad. Up to now no prisoner had ever got through the swamp, although a number had tried. They had either been caught by the dogs or had drowned. There had been lurid rumours that several had been eaten alive by alligators.

To get a man out of that swamp would be a hell of a job, Baird thought, as he walked quickly along the sidewalk towards the garage where he kept his car and, if the man resisted, it could be impossible.

But difficulties never worried Baird. He never considered defeat. He would try, and if it didn't come off it would be just too bad. If it did the prize of ten thousand was worth having.

But he would have to make certain the money was there. He didn't trust Kile. He knew instinctively that Kile wasn't the top man. Someone was using Kile as a front. Baird was sure Kile didn't want the job to come off. Even before the final arrangements had been made, Kile was jumpy and scared. Someone bigger than Kile was pushing him into the job either by threats or by the inducement of money.

What was the doll-faced blonde doing mixing herself up in this? Where did she fit in? She was scared, too. When he had said the job wasn't impossible, she had flinched as if he'd hit her. Before he committed himself he would have to find out something about these two, and if he could, find out who the top man was and why he wanted this man in jail kidnapped.

There might be even more than ten grand to pick up if he kept his ears and eyes open. The job seemed full of possibilities.

He reached the garage, got into the battered Ford and drove over to the walk-up apartment house where Anita rented her room.

He left the car a hundred yards or so beyond the entrance to the house, walked back and paused to look up at the top window. It was in darkness, and he grimaced, sure now she was asleep.

There were still a number of people in the street and sitting at open windows, and he felt their eyes on him. Two men sat on the doorstep to the apartment house, smoking, and as he came up the steps they looked curiously at him. One of them was Toni, and Baird gave him a hard, menacing stare.

Toni shifted quickly to one side to give Baird room to pass. Baird saw the scared look that came into Toni's eyes, and he felt like taking Toni by his mop of black hair and banging his head against the wall until his brains spilled out.

But he kept on, walking into the smelly, dimly lit lobby, and began to mount the stairs, aware that Toni and his companion were staring after him.

He walked up the five flights of stairs until he came to Anita's landing. He paused outside the door, listening. Then he went back to the banister rail and looked down to make sure no one was coming up or watching him. He saw no one, and he returned to the door and rapped softly.

"Who is it?"

The sound of her voice sent a little prickle up his spine, surprising him.

"Baird," he said, his mouth close to the door. "I want to talk to you."

He leaned against the doorway and waited. He heard the light click on, the pad of bare feet on the floor, then the door opened.

She stood looking up at him, her dark eyes unafraid and enquiring. She had pulled on her shabby overcoat. Beneath it he caught a glimpse of her plain white nightdress he had seen her in so often.

"What do you want?" she said sharply. "I was asleep."

He experienced a pang of disappointment that she wasn't pleased to see him, but he wasn't going to be put off.

"I guessed you would be," he said. "I've just got in from New York. I thought I'd see how you were getting on." He moved forward, riding her back into the room.

"I don't want you in here," she said, stepping away from him. "Not at this hour."

"Take it easy," he said, moving around her to the sagging armchair. "You're not scared of me, are you?"

"Why should I be? I just don't want you here so late." He sat down, his eyes searching her face. No, she wasn't afraid of him. He could tell that by looking at her.

"Get into bed," he said. "I won't keep you long."

"No." She sat on the edge of the bed and ran her fingers through her hair. She looked tired and pale, and he noticed her lips were whitish without the lipstick camouflage. "I'm dead beat. I wish you'd go. I don't want you here."

He felt a wave of irritation run through him, but he controlled it.

"I shouldn't have gone off like that without saying goodbye," he said uneasily. "I've had you on my mind. I've still got that money. I'd like to lend it to you."

She sat for a long moment looking at him. She saw his embarrassed uneasiness, and she felt sorry for him. Suddenly she smiled. She looked pretty when she smiled, and Baird found himself smiling stiffly back at her. He couldn't remember the last time anyone had smiled at him. He felt as if he had been given a costly and unexpected present.

"Why do you want to lend it to me?" she asked.

"Because you're such a damned mug you won't take it as a gift," he said, sitting forward. "I owe you plenty, and it gives me the bellyache to know you're short of dough when I could help you."

"Thank you," she said. "I appreciate that, but I can't take money from you. I guess I am a mug, but that's the way it is. I don't suppose you'll understand, but I must stand on my own feet. I can't see you borrowing money if you were in a jam. You would want to be independent. Well, I guess I'm like that, too."

He studied her.

"But if a guy owes me something, I'd expect to be paid," he said. "And I owe you plenty."

"Can't you forget that? It just happened you were lucky to come here. I would have done the same for anyone else.

I always side with the one against many. It's the way I'm made."

He didn't like that. He had hoped that she had helped him because of himself, not because of some cock-eyed kink about helping one against many. His expression changed, and his eyes became hostile.

"You can't expect me to keep on begging you to take the dough," he said roughly. "If that's the way you feel about it ..."

"I'm sorry," she said quickly. "I didn't mean to hurt you. I do appreciate ..."

"Ah, the hell with it!" he said in disgust, and got to his feet. What had promised to be a pleasant and unusual evening was turning sour. He stood staring at her, then blurted out, "I don't mean a thing to you, do I?"

He could read the answer in her surprised expression. The idea of caring for him had never entered her head.

"Why ..." she began, and stopped.

"Skip it," he said. "I'm getting soft in the head. The trouble with me is I'm not used to dealing with a girl like you. The women I mix with would take the gold out of my teeth if I give them the chance. You're different. I was beginning to get ideas about you. You're the first woman I've ever met who hasn't been scared of me. Even my old lady was scared of me when I was a kid."

"She wasn't afraid for herself," Anita said, looking straight at him. "She was afraid for you."

Baird frowned. He had never thought of it in that way.

"Maybe you're right," he said uneasily. "She was the worrying kind."

She drew her coat closer about her and moved her bare feet on the threadbare mat.

Watching her, Baird felt a sudden pang of desire shoot through him. He would have given a lot for her to have made a sign of encouragement, but she didn't. She didn't seem to realize he could reach out and grab her, and she wouldn't have the strength to protect herself against him. He felt a sick disgust with himself for even thinking of this.

"I guess I'll go," he said thickly. "Want to change your mind about that dough?"

She looked up and saw at once what was going on in his mind. Even then she showed no fear. She stood up and put her hand on his arm.

"I can't take it. Thanks for the offer. I'm sorry I'm not like your other women friends, if that's what you want."

He smiled crookedly and pulled her to him.

"You're okay as yourself."

Her hands on his chest stopped him from kissing her. She didn't push at him, but the pressure was firm, as if her hands were asking him not to do it.

He released her and stepped away.

"I guess I'm getting soft," he said. "Well, so long. I guess we won't see each other again, but if you're ever in a jam you'll find me at 223 Hundred and Twenty-fifth Street. It's not more than five minutes walk from here. Up on the top floor. Any time you're in trouble and want help, come and see me." He opened the door, turned to look hard at her. "I owe you plenty. Don't forget the address. You never know. You might need me one of these days."

He went downstairs quickly, cutting off her reply. Toni and his companion still sat on the steps. They made way hurriedly as Baird came through the lobby.

He ran down the steps, and walked quickly along the sidewalk to his car.

Jack Burns, who had been lolling against a lamp standard, reading a newspaper, watched him drive away. Then he headed for a nearby drugstore. He got Harmon Purvis on the phone after a delay.

"Burns reporting," he said, pushing back his hat and speaking rapidly. "Baird left Roxburgh House at eleven-five. Rico didn't come out with him. Baird's been calling on a girl who has a room on the top floor of an apartment house on Twenty-fifth Street. He stayed about a quarter of an hour. It's my bet he holed up with this girl when the cops were hunting for him."

"Who is she?" Purvis asked.

"Her name's Anita Jackson," Burns said. "I managed to get one of the tenants of the house to talk about her. He says her morals are no better than they should be: whatever that may mean. She works at a steak joint on Western Street. Want me to do anything about her?"

"Not yet," Purvis said. "Stick to Baird. If he sees her again we might put a tail on her. Don't let Baird out of your sight. I have an idea things will start moving in a day or so."

"Yeah," Burns said, yawning. "Maybe sooner. I'll get over to his place. Tell Ainsworth not to be late. I want some sleep tonight."

"You've got all tomorrow to sleep," Purvis said heartlessly. "There're more important things to think about."

"Don't let me keep you out of your bed," Burns said sarcastically, and hung up.

IV

Adam Gillis went over to the window and looked down into the street. He was utterly bored now with the girl on the bed. It had been a mistake to have brought her up to his room. Her appearance had been deceptive. She was a common little beast, he thought, and not particularly clean. Her awful voice jarred on his nerves, and her perfume was simply hell.

He watched a taxi coming along the street, wondering how best to get rid of her without causing a scene. The only thing in her favour was she hadn't asked for money, but it was obvious by the way she was making herself comfortable she expected to stay the night.

The taxi pulled up outside his apartment house, and a girl got out.

Eve!

Gillis swore under his breath. What did she want, coming here? He turned swiftly away from the window.

"Get your clothes on quick and get out!" he said. "My damned sister's coming. Hurry up! Do you hear me? She'll be here in a minute or so!"

"Who cares?" the girl on the bed said sulkily. "You don't have to answer the door, do you? Let her ring."

Gillis went over to the bed, caught hold of her arm and pulled her to her feet.

"Let go of me, you big stiff!" the girl said angrily. "Who do you think ..." She broke off with a squeal as he slapped her buttocks viciously.

"Do what I tell you," he said, giving her a push that sent her reeling across the room. "Get dressed and get out!"

The venomous look in his eyes frightened her, and she hurriedly snatched up her dress and struggled into it.

"You dirty, rotten creep," she wailed. "Where do you think I can go at this time?"

"I don't give a damn, and keep your mouth shut or I'll take the skin off your hide," Gillis snarled. He grabbed up her stockings, underthings and hat and threw them at her.

"Come on; outside! You can finish dressing in a taxi." He opened the door. "Here, take this, and get out." He pushed a dollar bill into her hand, ran her into the passage. "On your way, and be quick about it."

As she began to curse him, he gave her another slap that shot her forward to the head of the stairs. She bolted down them like a scalded cat.

Gillis shut the door and turned the key.

The room stank of cheap perfume and, cursing, he threw open another window and began to fan the air with a newspaper until the rumpled bed caught his eye and he dropped the paper and ran over to straighten the sheets and pillows.

He was emptying an ashtray full of cigarette butts stained with lipstick when a knock came on the door.

He took a quick look at himself in the mirror. His pyjamas were grubby and most of the buttons on the jacket were missing. There were lipstick smears on his chest and neck. He bolted into the bathroom and hurriedly sponged them off, then slipped into a faded dressing gown before re-entering the bedroom. The knock was repeated. He unlocked the door and opened it.

"Why, Eve!" he said, staring at her. "What on earth are you doing here?"

"I had to see you," she said. "Can I come in?"

"I suppose so," he said reluctantly. "It's a hell of a time to call. I was asleep." He stood aside to let her in. "Sorry about the stink in here. I upset a bottle of perfume. As a matter of fact I'd bought it for you. It smells pretty horrible, doesn't it, and the blasted girl swore it was full of allure."

Eve glanced around the big, shabby room. She had been here only once before. It was a room that set her teeth on edge. It was dirty and dusty. Two naked French dolls stood on the mantelpiece, either side of a row of tarnished silver sporting trophies. Above them, slung perilously on two hooks, was a sculling oar; above the oar were two crossed squash rackets. On either side of this sporting set were boxing gloves that hadn't been dusted since they had been hung in position.

Eve had certain knowledge that her brother had loathed sport of any kind during his very short stay at college. He had been sent down after six months of college life for "infamous behaviour", the details of which she had never learned. Where he had filched the sporting trophies from she couldn't imagine, and didn't like to ask.

Over the bed was a large framed photograph of the men of his year, sitting bolt upright with arms crossed and chins thrust out: young men looking into the future with aggressive determination. She looked at the photograph, and for a moment she couldn't find Adam amongst these determined young men, then she spotted him by his shifty expression, and jeering, untrustworthy smile. He was not so thin as he was now, and she noticed with surprise that his hair was thicker, and it came as a shock to realize his hair now was thinning fast, hinting at a premature baldness.

She moved away from the photograph, feeling ashamed as if she had been caught looking through a keyhole. The years that had passed since he had left college had taken a heavy toll. At least, in the photograph, he looked amused, happy and cared for, but looking at him now, as he stood scowling at her, he looked seedy and disreputable and forsaken.

"Well, what is it?" he asked crossly. "Do sit down, can't you? Must you wander around sticking your nose into everything?"

She sat down, and as she did so she saw something on the floor, half hidden under the bed, and she felt a sense of sick shock as she hurriedly averted her eyes.

"Oh, I know what you're thinking," he said, sitting on the window sill and staring at her. "You're thinking I've had a woman up here. Well, you're quite wrong. I was sound asleep when you knocked."

"It's nothing to do with me who you have here," she said quietly. "But you don't have to lie about it. She dropped a stocking on the stairs. You'd better give it to her. She didn't look as if she could afford to lose it."

Gillis' face registered surprised blankness.

"I haven't the faintest idea what you're drivelling about. I'm not the only lodger in this cesspit. Why, only yesterday I found a pair of panties in the telephone box," and he sniggered, watching her warily.

"She looked very young," Eve said, as if he hadn't spoken. "Almost a child. Adam, do be careful what you're doing."

"Oh, shut up!" he said furiously. "I've had enough of this. I tell you no one's been here. So shut up!"

There was a long silence. Eve sat motionless, her hands folded in her lap, her eyes closed. The sordid room, the knowledge that that vicious little chit of a girl – she couldn't have been more than sixteen – had been here, the phoney sophomore atmosphere and the smell of the cheap perfume made her feel physically ill.

Adam said impatiently, "Well, I don't suppose you came here to admire the scenery. What is it?"

Without opening her eyes she said, "Rico brought Baird to see Preston tonight. They've just gone."

"Baird!" Adam left the window and came over to her. "Did you see him?"

She nodded.

"Is he going to do the job?"

"I think so. He wants to look the territory over first."

"What happened? Tell me everything. I want to know exactly what was said."

He sat on the bed and listened while she gave him a detailed account of the meeting. When she had finished, he lit a cigarette and smiled at her, his thin, handsome face animated.

"That's fine. Of course he'll do it. I knew I wasn't mistaken in my man. He's really got something. What did you think of him, Eve?"

She gave a little shiver.

"He frightened me. He's dangerous, Adam. There's something about him – he – he's like a wild animal: like a tiger."

"He's a killer," Gillis said admiringly. "One of the few genuine killers left. There never were many: Dillinger, Nelson, the Barkers – you can count them on your fingers. Baird's about the last of them, and he's just the right man for the job."

"Adam, this whole business is worrying me," she said, sitting forward. "It's too dangerous. Even if you succeeded in getting Hater out of prison, what makes you think he's going to tell you where the jewels are hidden?"

The animation in his face went away, and the shifty expression returned.

"Of course he'll tell us," he said breezily. "He's going to be grateful we've got him out, isn't he? When I've explained to him the Rajah's willing to do a deal with him, he'll only be too glad to tell us. Without us he can't do a thing."

"But he can!" Eve said. "Do you think I'm an idiot, Adam? You're not planning to help this man to escape:

you're going to kidnap him. You told me that's what you're going to do. You're expecting him to resist. Of course he's going to resist. In two years time he'll be released. If he escapes now, he is a fugitive, and if he's caught, he'll go back to prison for another long term. He's waited fifteen years: two more are nothing to a man like that. How can you, Adam? Why don't you wait until he comes out a free man?"

Gillis mashed out his cigarette in the ashtray on the dusty bedside table. His eyes were hard.

"You can scarcely expect me to wait two years," he said with deceptive mildness. "It was only by the merest fluke I heard the Rajah was planning to gyp the insurance companies if he could. If it hadn't been for that little rat of an ADC who got tight when he and I were in the Bazaar, I never would have got the information. If I wait until Hater comes out, someone else may have the same idea and beat me to it. I've got to go ahead now if I'm going to collect that money, and if it's the last thing I do, I'm damn well going to have it. A half a million! Think of it, Eve! Think what we can do with it."

She wasn't deceived for a moment by his use of "we". She knew she wouldn't see any of it. It was his way of encouraging her to help him. Not that she wanted the money. If he offered it to her she wouldn't touch it. She was keeping in step with him so she shouldn't lose him: that was her reward for meddling in this dangerous business.

"But it won't be half a million," she said, watching him. "You'll have to give Hater a share. He may even want half."

Gillis laughed. He saw the trap, and he sidestepped it with his usual slick adroitness.

"All right: a quarter of a million, then," he said, smiling at her. "Even two hundred and fifty thousand isn't to be sniffed at."

But Eve wasn't to be put off.

"You don't intend to give him anything, do you, Adam?"

"You mean Hater? Why, of course. He isn't likely to part with any information unless he gets well paid. Of course he'll have to have something: not half, but certainly something pretty big."

"And Kile? Isn't he to have anything?"

"Well, it may be necessary to give him something to keep him quiet," Gillis said. "How curious you are."

"But as he is dealing direct with the Rajah, what's to stop him taking the lot and leaving you out of it?" Eve persisted. She had a feeling that Adam's plans had taken care of all contingencies, and she wanted to know just what he was up to.

"What's to stop him?" Gillis repeated. His eyes narrowed. "I would stop him. That's something I was meaning to speak to you about, Eve. It's up to you to find out something about him that we could use if he makes himself awkward."

She shied away from this.

"We're getting into an awful jam, Adam," she said, twisting her hands anxiously in her lap. "I'm scared. Kile expects to have all the money. Then there's Baird. Suppose he finds out why Hater's to be kidnapped? Do you think a man like Baird will let you walk off with all that money when he has the most dangerous part of the job to do?"

He laughed.

"You're continually thinking up difficulties, aren't you?" he said lightly. "The trouble with you is you worry too much. As soon as Baird starts on the job, you don't have to think anything more about it. I'll handle it."

"That doesn't answer my question. What are you going to do about Kile? What will you do if Baird finds out there's a half-million involved?"

Gillis lit a cigarette and flicked the match out of the window.

"I'll wait until the time comes. But it wouldn't do any harm to keep your eyes and ears open so far as brother Kile is concerned. He must have a few secrets he doesn't want to broadcast. Suppose you concentrate on that angle, pet? If we could get something on him, we'd have him where we wanted him if he did turn nasty."

"I'm not going to do it," Eve said evenly. "It's blackmail."

"Why must you always put a label on everything? Suppose it is blackmail: what of it? Or do you want me to leave you to be Kile's toy until you lose your looks and he boots you out?"

She stood up.

"Please listen to me, Adam," she said quietly. "You may be able to handle Kile, but I know you won't be able to handle Baird. Kile doesn't matter. He's old and ill and finished, but Baird's not. He's dangerous and he's no fool. If he finds out ..."

"I know, I know," Gillis said, giving her his charming smile that was a little faded at the edges. "I heard you the first time. It may surprise you to know I'm not worried about Baird. I hope I've enough brains to outwit a man of his calibre. I know he's a killer; but that's all. A good boxer can always beat a good slugger, and that's what Baird is. He doesn't scare me in the slightest." She caught hold of his arm.

"Darling, I beg you not to go on with this," she said imploringly. "It won't work. Oh, yes, I'm sure Baird'll get Hater out of prison. He could do anything, but it's when Hater is free that your troubles are going to start. Please give up the idea before it's too late. You're running into something that's more dangerous than anything you've ever mixed yourself up in before. You must give it up, Adam, before it's too late."

Gillis patted her hand.

"I think I'll go to bed now," he said, yawning elaborately. "I'm dead tired. Go to bed yourself, Eve, and take my advice: mind your own business and leave me to mind mine."

She looked at him helplessly.

"All right, darling," she said. She knew in a moment he would begin his threats again. "I'll go to bed."

"You wouldn't have ten dollars on you, would you?" he said, as he steered her to the door. "It's a debt I promised to settle."

She opened her bag and took out two ten-dollar bills. "Take them," she said, without looking at him. "Only ten," he said, taking one of the bills. "Never let it be said that I sponge on you."

As he opened the door, she turned to face him. "Adam, please think about this. Can't you see how dangerous ...?"

"Don't let's go all over that again," he said, a sudden rasp in his voice. "You'll begin to bore me."

"I'm sorry, but do think about it, darling, before it's too late. Don't blame me if something horrible happens. I can't keep warning you."

"Have that engraved as one of those motto things, pet," he said, "and I'll hang it over my bed. Goodsweet dreams."

He gently pushed her into the passage and shut the door.

V

Jack Burns sat in his car, a cigarette hanging from his lips and a heavy scowl on his fat face. From time to time he shot his cuff and stuck his arm out of the window to see the time by his wristwatch in the light cast by the street standard. It was getting on for a quarter past one, and still no sign of Ainsworth.

He yawned and cursed Ainsworth, using all the bad words he knew. It took a little while to run through his entire vocabulary, and when he had finished, he felt a little less annoyed.

If only this punk Baird would go to sleep, he thought, he'd chance it and go home, but so long as the light burned in the top window, he knew he couldn't take any risks.

He lit another cigarette and groaned. This was a hell of a life, he decided, for a guy who likes his sleep. Purvis, the old goat, would expect him to take over day duty by eleven o'clock. At this rate he wouldn't get more than eight hours sleep, and he needed ten to feel anything like normal.

Every now and then he caught sight of Baird's shadow as he crossed the blind. He was up to something, moving backwards and forwards like that. He didn't give the impression of a man preparing for bed.

Again Burns leaned out of the window to see the time: one twenty-five! He yawned again, threatening to dislocate his jaw.

A patrolman came slowly along the sidewalk, gently whacking the side of his leg with his nightstick. He looked over at Burns, sitting in the car, paused, then came across the street and stopped beside the car.

"Waiting for someone?" he asked, eyeing Burns suspiciously.

"For the end of the world," Burns said sarcastically. "Haven't you heard? You and me and all the rest of the lousy bunch will come to an end in half an hour. If you want proof, my tea leaves told me, and they're never wrong."

The cop rested his foot on the running-board. The situation seemed to him to have possibilities.

"Been drinking?" he asked hopefully.

"Look, I'm busy," Burns said. "Go away and catch a burglar. Do anything, but don't bother me."

"What's this about the end of the world?" the cop asked. "My tea leaves didn't say nothing about it."

"Maybe you use the wrong make of tea. Why don't you run away and make yourself some more? If you don't want to drink the stuff, and if you've made enough of it, you can always drown yourself in it."

The cop considered this, cocking his head on one side and squinting at Burns.

"This could be a pinch, fella," he said amiably. "I haven't made a pinch for a week, and it's time I did. Suppose you and me take a ride down to headquarters."

Burns shook his head.

"I'll play cops and robbers with you some other night," he said. "I've got work to do right now. Be a nice guy and fade away. If you're all that hard up, why don't you go pinch yourself a tart?"

"You'll do," the cop said, his voice suddenly aggressive. "The Sarge hates funny men. He'll put you in cell 6, the one that leaks and has beetles. Start rolling, brother, you and me are going for a ride."

With an air of bored weariness, Burns produced a card and pushed it under the cop's nose.

"Take a look at that, ambitious, if you can read. My old man and Lieutenant Olin are like that." He held up two fat fingers, pressed tightly together. "Interfere with me and you'll lose your badge so fast you won't know it's gone till you come to clean it – if you ever do clean it."

The cop read the card, then spat in the gutter.

"A shamus," he said bitterly. "I might have known it. Okay, forget it. That Purvis creep's always making trouble for us workers."

"He makes trouble for me, too," Burns sighed. "I haven't had a good night's rest since last week, and then that was an accident."

"It beats me how you punks who peep through other people's keyholes can sleep at all," the cop said virtuously. "If I had your job my conscience wouldn't let me sleep."

Burns saw the light in Baird's room had gone out.

"Pipe down," he said tersely. "The pigeon I'm watching's going to roost."

The cop looked up at the darkened window. "That guy Baird? You interested in him?"

"What do you know about him?"

"I've got my orders. Never mind what I know about him."

"Aw, forget it. If there's a thing I hate more than a stye in the eye, it's a mysterious cop."

The front door to Baird's apartment house opened, and Baird came quickly down the steps.

"Jeepers!" Burns muttered. "The punk's going for a walk."

"Looks like he's going on the lam," the cop said.

Baird was carrying a grip. He glanced at the cop and the parked car and went quickly down the street away from them.

Burns scrambled out of the car.

"Listen, brother, this is important. One of my buddies is due along any moment to relieve me. Will you tell him Baird's left with a grip, and I'm going after him?"

"I don't mind," the cop said. "Not if you make it worth my while."

"And they say the police aren't corrupt in this town," Burns said bitterly. He produced a five-dollar bill. "Stick around until he turns up. You can't miss him. He walks pigeon-toed and wears a hand-painted tie."

"I'll tell him," the cop said, pocketing the bill. "Nice to have known you."

Burns snorted and set out after the fast-disappearing figure in the distance.

He had some difficulty in shortening the distance between Baird and himself. Baird swung along at a fast clip, and once or twice Burns had to break into a run or he'd have lost him.

Baird's quick, suspicious ears heard the patter of feet behind him, but he didn't look around. He kept on, not sure yet if he was being tailed. Was it the police? he wondered. He turned down a side street, swearing softly under his breath. He had cut it fine. The train was due out at two, and he had yet to reach the depot and get his ticket. But he had to be sure no one was following him.

When he reached a dark patch of the road, he glanced back. A short, fat man was walking rapidly after him, keeping in the shadows. He didn't look like a cop, and he puzzled Baird.

Baird kept on until he reached an alley that cut through to the railroad depot. He had ten minutes before the train left. Once in the darkness of the alley, he stopped and set down his grip and waited.

But Burns was too experienced to walk into that kind of trap. As soon as he could no longer hear Baird's footfalls, he guessed Baird had spotted him and was waiting for him in the alley.

He walked slowly past the mouth of the alley, so Baird could see him, and kept on down the street until he was out of earshot, then he doubled back on tiptoe until he reached the mouth of the alley again. He stood just out of sight, listening.

Although he had moved silently, Baird had heard him. Baird guessed this fat punk wouldn't venture into the alley so long as he was uncertain Baird was still there.

Time was getting on. Baird couldn't afford to hang about any longer, nor could he afford to let anyone interested in him know he was catching a train.

His hand slid inside his coat and came out again, holding his Colt. Silently he began to edge back along the alley, moving like a ghost.

Burns stood straining his ears, sure now that Baird was still in the alley. He decided not to show himself, but to wait Baird out. He didn't hear Baird creeping along the alley, and he had no idea of his danger until a hand came around the corner of the wall and grabbed hold of his coat.

He let out a yell as he felt himself jerked forward, and he hit out blindly. Then something hard and heavy smashed down on his head, and his world snuffed out into darkness.

Baird dragged Burns into the alley, turned him on his back and went through his pockets. He found one of Burns' cards and he struck a match to read it.

International Detective Agency! A shamus following him! He gave Burns a hard nudge with the toe of his shoe and stood up, his face hard and set.

He hadn't time now to think what it meant. If he didn't hurry he'd miss his train. He left Burns' body in the alley and ran towards the railroad depot.

Forty minutes later Harmon Purvis was startled out of a heavy sleep by the furious ringing of his telephone bell. As he picked up the receiver he glanced at his bedside clock. It showed a quarter past three.

"Who is it?" he demanded.

"This is Ed," Dallas' voice barked over the line. "Baird's given us the slip. Burns is in hospital with a fractured skull. I thought you'd welcome the good news."

"Any idea what happened?" Purvis said, dropping back on his pillow and frowning up at the ceiling.

"The Gillis girl called on her brother tonight. She left around eleven-thirty. I watched Gillis' window until he turned off the light and presumably went to bed. It was after two before I got away. I ran into Ainsworth on his way to relieve Burns. I went with him. We found Burns' car near Baird's place, but no Burns. A cop told us Baird had left his house, carrying hand baggage, about five minutes before we showed up, and Burns had gone after him. We went after them. Obviously from the direction, Baird was heading for the railroad depot. We found Burns in an alley, bleeding like a pig, and the top of his head shoved in. No sign of Baird."

Purvis made clicking noises with his tongue.

"Is Burns bad?"

"Yeah, but the croaker says he'll survive."

"Did you go to the depot?"

"Ainsworth did while I took Burns to hospital. The ticket agent told Ainsworth that Baird had booked through to Shreveport."

Purvis sat bolt upright in bed.

"Shreveport! You sure?"

"Of course I am. What's the excitement?"

"You and Ainsworth grab a taxi and come here pronto," Purvis bawled. "This is important."

"Why? It's after three and I haven't had any sleep ..."

"That's all you damned operators think of," Purvis snarled. "I don't pay you to sleep. The Bellmore Prison Farm is within fifteen miles of Shreveport, and that's where Paul Hater's serving his sentence! That mean anything to you?"

Dallas gave a long, low whistle.

"I'm on my way," he said, and slammed down the receiver.

PART THREE

Baird pushed open the door to the back entrance of the Frou-Frou Club, glanced over his shoulder to make sure no one was watching him, and then stepped into the dimly lit passage. He walked silently to Rico's office. As he reached the door he caught sight of a movement ahead of him and looked up quickly.

Zoe Morton ducked back out of sight behind her dressing-room door, but not quickly enough for Baird to miss seeing her. He stood for a moment staring thoughtfully at the door that stood ajar, then he moved softly along the passage and pushed the door open with his foot.

Zoe was sitting at the dressing table, making up her face. She looked a little flustered, and gave a start when she saw Baird in the doorway.

"What do you want?" she demanded, swinging around on the low stool. "Who said you could walk in here without knocking?"

Baird leaned against the doorway, his eyes on her face.

"Hello, Toots," he said. "I saw you peeping. Anything I can do for you?"

She felt a little sick as she looked into his cold, murderous eyes.

"I – I don't know what you're talking about," she said defiantly. "As if I should want to peep at you. Would you mind fading away? There isn't much air in this hole, and I don't see why I should have to share it with you."

He studied her, then his eyes shifted to the telephone on her dressing table and back to her.

"Watch your step, Toots," he said evenly. "I shan't tell you again."

He gave her another hard, menacing stare that made her feel weak at the knees and went out, closing the door behind him. He walked thoughtfully along the passage to Rico's office and went in.

Rico glanced up from his desk.

"Come in," he said, pushing back his chair. "Lock the door. I've got news for you."

Baird turned the key in the lock, crossed over to the desk and sat down.

"Don't yell at the top of your voice," he said softly. "Someone may be listening in."

Rico looked startled.

"What do you mean? Who's listening in?"

"Forget it," Baird said impatiently. "Just keep your voice down. What's the news?"

His expression puzzled, Rico shrugged his shoulders.

"You don't have to worry about this place," he said. "No one listens in here."

"What's the news?" Baird repeated.

"I've seen Kile. I told him you've looked the ground over and you think you can pull it off. We can go ahead. He's leaving all the arrangements to us. I've five grand to split between us. Pretty good, huh?"

Baird lit a cigarette and stared across the room. "What makes you think you rate anything?" he asked casually. "Who's doing the job – you or me?"

"We're both in it," Rico said, smiling ingratiatingly. "But if that's the way you feel about it, I'm willing to take two and you three."

"Did you find out who the man is?" Baird asked.

"Sure. I've got all the necessary dope." Rico opened a drawer in his desk and took out a big envelope.

"Don't you keep that locked up?" Baird asked sharply.

Rico stared at him.

"It's safe enough. No one ever comes into my office when I'm not here. What's biting you?"

"Nothing," Baird said, flicking ash on to the floor. "Who is he?"

"Paul Hater. Here's his picture." Rico tossed a police photograph across the desk. "He shouldn't be difficult to spot."

Baird looked curiously at the photograph. Rico was right. Hater would be easy to identify. He was small and thin. His dome of a forehead was accentuated by heavy eyebrows and a balding head. He had deep-set, dark, staring eyes and a livid white scar that ran from his right eye to his mouth. He reminded Baird of the fanatical prison chaplain he had met when he had visited his brother for the first and only time.

"He looks as if he's got a screw loose," Baird said, tossing the picture back to Rico. "He won't be difficult to spot. When do we start?"

"Any time we like," Rico said eagerly. "The sooner the better."

Baird nodded.

"And the money?"

Rico tapped the envelope.

"Plenty more where that comes from."

"How do you know?"

Rico laughed.

"What's the matter with you? Kile's a big shot. He's rolling in the stuff. He and I have worked together ..."

"How do you know he's rolling in it?"

"How do I know?" Rico stared. "What are you driving at?"

"Do you imagine Kile's the top man in this set-up?"

"Of course he is."

"If you're so sure," Baird said, "how do you know?"

Rico began to look uneasy.

"What's cooking?" he asked, leaning forward to stare at Baird. "Sounds like you've found out something."

"I've found out plenty," Baird said. "The moment I set eyes on Kile I knew there was something phoney about him. I've been digging in his backyard, and does it stink! He owes money everywhere. He hasn't paid for that big house on Roosevelt Boulevard. He's hanging on by the skin of his teeth, and isn't expected to last six months."

Rico stiffened.

"You sure?"

Baird made an impatient movement.

"If you hadn't been hypnotized by his front you could have found out about him as easily as I did."

Rico began to sweat.

"How about this five grand?" he asked, tapping the envelope. "He can't be all that broke."

"Don't I keep telling you? He isn't the top man."

Rico thought for a moment, then shrugged.

"Does it matter? At least we've got the dough."

"I like to know who I'm dealing with. Ever asked yourself why Kile wants Hater out of jail?"

"I asked Kile. He wouldn't say. I don't see why we should worry." Rico spread out his hands. "We're getting paid for the job. The money's good enough, isn't it?"

"You're a bigger sucker than you look," Baird said. "Don't you know who Hater is?"

Rico shifted uneasily in his chair.

"I don't know what you're getting at," he said. "Hater used to be one of the big operators about twenty years ago. He specialized in jewellery. I seem to remember he pulled off a big deal and a fence shopped him."

"About fifteen years back he pulled off a four-million-dollar job and cached the stuff. It was never found," Baird said softly.

"Four million?" Rico gulped. "It was never found?"

"That's right. Doesn't the nickel drop now?"

"You mean Kile's after the stuff?"

"Kile and someone else. It looks like it, doesn't it? Why should they want to kidnap Hater? He's only got two more years to serve. If he escapes now, he'll be on the run for the rest of his life until he's caught."

"Four million dollars!" Rico got up and began to pace up and down. "Jeepers! That's dough."

"That's about the first sensible thing you've said tonight," Baird said sourly. "And they're paying me ten grand. That's a laugh, isn't it?"

Rico wiped the sweat from his forehead. He went over to the cellaret and made two highballs.

"I'd better talk to Kile," he said as he brought the drinks to the desk. "He'll have to jack up the ante."

"You'll keep your trap shut," Baird said. "I'm handling this. If we play our cards right, we should collect the whole bundle."

Rico lost colour and gripped the edge of his desk until his knuckles turned white.

"Are you crazy?" he asked. "What would we do with stuff like that? We couldn't handle it. Four million dollars! There's not a fence in the country who could handle it."

Baird took off his hat and ran his fingers through his thick blond hair.

"I don't know why the hell I bother with you," he said, exasperated. "Haven't you any brains? Do you think I'm mug enough to imagine you could handle the stuff? No, the obvious thing to do is to wait until Kile gets rid of it. He must know someone he can unload it on or he wouldn't be paying us to snatch Hater. The time we move in is when Kile collects the dough. Then we take it away from him. If he knows what he's doing, the take should be worth half a million at least, probably more, and that's better than a lousy ten grand. Now do you see what I'm getting at?"

Rico licked his dry lips.

"It sounds all right," he said cautiously, "but how do we know when he gets paid off?"

"That's something you can find out. He's got to be watched night and day after we've turned Hater over to him. And another thing, we've got to find out who the top man is, too. And then there's that shamus who followed me: we've got to find out who employed him, and why."

Rico started out of his chair.

"What shamus? I haven't heard anything about a shamus."

Baird eyed him jeeringly.

"Don't get so steamed up. The night I went to Red River Basin I spotted a fat guy tailing me. I caught him napping and softened his skull for him. He was an operator working for the International Detective Agency. Someone who doesn't mind spending dough is having me watched. Maybe it doesn't have anything to do with the Hater snatch, but somehow I think it does. We've got to find out why I was being tailed, and pronto."

Rico took a long drink. His nerves were fluttering.

"Maybe it's Kile," he said hopefully.

"I don't know, but I mean to find out. How long's this redhead been working for you?"

"You mean Zoe?" Rico's face was startled. "What's she got to do with it?"

"I don't know, but every time I've shown up here she's been watching me. Maybe she's a plant."

"Zoe, a plant? Don't make me laugh," Rico said. "I've known her three or four years. She came to work at the club when it first opened. I knew her when she was in show business before that. She's okay. Maybe she's interested in you. She has a yen for a big guy like you; she told me so."

Baird jerked his thumb at the photograph on the desk.

"Put that in your safe and lock it up," he said. "I think she's mixed up in this. It'll be easy enough to prove. Now, listen, here's what you have to do ..."

When Baird closed the door, Zoe drew in a deep breath of relief. She sat for a long minute, staring at herself in the mirror. She saw she had gone pale under her rouge, and she laughed a little unsteadily.

"That guy sure scared the lace pants right off you," she said, addressing her reflection in the mirror. "Phew! He's enough to scare anyone. Zoe, my child, you've got to be a lot more careful in the future. Take my advice and call Ed. He'll know how to handle this."

She got up and went to the door, opened it a crack and looked down the deserted passage. Satisfied there was no one to hear her, she shut the door again and rang Dallas' apartment. There was no answer. She replaced the receiver, feeling a little lost and sat for a moment thinking. It was only a few minutes after ten. Maybe Ed would blow in. He came in most nights now. Maybe he was on his way down at this very minute.

She began to finish her make-up, and while she painted her lips with a fine-haired brush, she wondered what Baird was doing in Rico's office. She had promised Ed to find out all she could of Rico's and Baird's movements, and she didn't want to let Ed down. By now she was half in love with him, and besides, he was paying her well.

She went to the door again and opened it. She hadn't the nerve to go down the passage and listen outside Rico's door. Baird had given her a bad scare.

Watch your step, he had said. I shan't tell you again.

A little shiver ran down her spine as she remembered the way he had looked at her. But with Ed around, she told herself, trying to bolster up her courage, there wasn't anything to be scared about. Baird wouldn't dare touch her. All the same she wasn't going to take unnecessary risks until she had consulted Ed. He'd know how far she could go.

Leaving the door ajar, she went back to complete her make-up. Then she took off her wrap and slipped into her green evening dress. In twenty minutes she would have to go into the restaurant. It was her late night, and she wouldn't be through until three o'clock.

She heard the door open at the far end of the passage and she jumped to her feet, running to her door to listen.

She heard Baird say, "What are you worrying about? We'll be back in an hour at the latest. You're not chained to this dump, are you?"

"I shouldn't be going out," Rico grumbled, "but I'll take a chance. Maybe nothing will blow up while I'm away."

"Aw, forget it. Did you lock up that envelope – the one Kile gave you?" Baird asked.

"It's in my desk. It's okay. No one ever goes into my office when I'm out. Come on, for the love of Pete, if we're going," Rico said impatiently, and she heard them walk down the passage to the street door.

Cautiously Zoe peered into the passage. She was in time to see Rico disappearing into the alley at the back of the club.

She stood hesitating. Something from Kile! That's what Ed wanted.

She ran over to the telephone, and again dialled Dallas' number, but there was still no answer.

Where was he? she wondered feverishly. They said they would be back in an hour. If Ed was to get a look at that envelope she would have to take action herself.

She went back to the door and looked at Rico's door. It seemed now a long way down the passage. Should she take a chance and get the envelope? If she went at once there couldn't be any risk.

She started down the passage, her heart beating violently, and her knees shaky. She reached the office door, paused outside while she screwed up her courage to go in. Then she rapped softly on the door, turned the handle and pushed the door open. The office was in darkness.

"Is anyone there?" she asked in a quavering voice. The silence that came out of the darkness reassured her, and she slipped into the room, shut the door and groped for the electric light switch.

The lights over Rico's desk went on. She moved quickly to the desk and jerked open the top drawer. The first thing she saw was a big envelope with Rico's name scrawled on it.

As she reached forward to pick it up, the shadow of a man fell across the desk.

The shock paralysed her for a moment, then she spun around.

Baird was standing just behind her. At the door, Rico stood, white-faced, staring at her in horror.

"Hello, Toots," Baird said softly. "Still peeping?" The scream that rose in her throat was cut short as his fist smashed against the side of her jaw. She felt herself falling into dark, suffocating oblivion.

II

Adam Gillis stood under the bright lights of the Elite cinema and looked impatiently at the stream of passing traffic.

About fifty yards away, Dallas sat in his car, parked in the shadows, watching him.

From time to time Gillis glanced at his strap watch, and Dallas guessed he was waiting for someone. He wasn't surprised when he saw a small coupé pull out of the stream of traffic and stop within a few feet of Gillis.

Gillis opened the door and got in.

"About time," he said crossly. "Why can't you be more punctual? Do you think I haven't other things to do except wait at street corners for you?"

Eve edged the car once more into the slow-moving traffic.

"I'm sorry, darling, but he didn't leave until five minutes ago. Besides, I'm not more than five minutes late."

Dallas started his engine and slid into the traffic after them. He had caught sight of Eve at the driving wheel, and wondered where these two were going.

"Has Rico been along?" Gillis asked, lighting a cigarette.

"Yes. Baird got back last night. He says it'll be difficult, but not impossible. Rico said Baird's going to get Hater out this week."

Gillis breathed heavily. His eyes were alight with excitement.

"Did Rico say how he was going to do it?"

Eve shook her head.

"Preston didn't want to know. He gave Rico the five thousand and the photograph. He's arranged to hand over the rest of the money at the shooting lodge as you said. That's where Baird will take Hater."

"Fine," Gillis said. "Well, we're coming along. If anyone can do the job, Baird can."

"Preston's getting nervy, Adam. He worries me."

Gillis shrugged indifferently.

"Keep him going. It won't be long now. As soon as he's collected the money from the Rajah, I'll move in and take over."

"But, darling, how can you be so sure you'll succeed?" Eve said anxiously. "You just can't take the money away from Preston like that. He'll never stand for it."

"Oh, yes, he will," Gillis said airily. "A couple of nights ago, when he was with you, I broke into his stately home. I opened his safe. What do you think I found in it?"

"You – you opened his safe?" Eve exclaimed, horrified. "Adam! How could you?"

"Oh, shut up!" he said impatiently. "If you'd been more helpful I needn't have taken the risk. I told you we had to get something on Kile. Well, I've got it. I found Jean Bruce's bracelet in the safe. That'd get him ten years in jail."

Eve gripped the steering wheel tightly.

"How do you know it's Jean Bruce's bracelet?"

"My dear pet," Gillis said, and laughed. "Jean used to amuse herself with me when she felt she wanted to be a naughty girl, and I can tell you that was quite often. I've seen the bracelet a dozen times."

Eve felt sick.

"Oh! I didn't know you knew her."

"There are lots of girls you don't know I know," Gillis returned. "As a matter of fact, I'm damned sorry Jean's dead. When she was in the mood, she could be vastly diverting."

"But the bracelet was stolen," Eve said, turning to stare at Gillis.

"Watch the road, can't you?" he said sharply. "Of course it was stolen. The police are looking for it now. If Kile doesn't play ball, I'm going to be one of those anonymous callers you read about in the papers and tip the police off he's got the bracelet in his safe."

"You can't do that!"

"Not if it isn't necessary."

"But how did he get it?"

"I should worry about that. He can explain that to the police if he wants to, but somehow I don't think he will."

Eve drove in silence for a while, her mind frozen with fear and worry. It was still not too late to draw back. She felt she had to warn Adam again.

"Preston's worrying about Baird," she said. "He's beginning to think as I do. Suppose Baird finds out who Hater is, or suppose Hater tells him about the collection?"

"Baird is almost certain to find out who Hater is," Gillis said carelessly. "But he can't do anything about it until the money's paid over. I should think it's more than possible he knows already and is planning to double-cross Kile. I've taken all that into account. It's simply a matter of working faster than Baird, and I've no doubt I can do it." He glanced at his strap watch. "Make for the Frou-Frou Club, will you? I've got to meet a man there in ten minutes."

"Oh, Adam, I do wish you would give this up," Eve said feverishly. "It's too dangerous. You don't know what you're walking into. I'll go back to the Follies. I can earn enough for both of us."

"Will you shut up!" Gillis snarled furiously. "Don't be so damned gutless! This is the chance of a lifetime, and I'm not going to miss it!"

She drove in silence to the club and stopped the car before the lighted entrance. Dallas, fifty yards behind them, increased speed to pass them. He drove into the parking lot at the side of the club.

As he walked to the entrance, he saw Eve's coupé driving away. He caught a glimpse of her white, set face, and guessed the talk she had had with her brother hadn't been a pleasant one.

He entered the club. Gillis was just coming out of the cloakroom. He smiled at Dallas and came over to shake hands.

"Haven't seen you in weeks," Gillis said breezily. "How are you?"

"Alive, but no more," Dallas returned. "I've been out of town. I thought it was time I looked up Zoe again."

"How did you find her?"

"All you said she would be."

Gillis nodded.

"I'm glad. Let me see, don't I owe you some money? What was it – five dollars?"

"Ten," said Dallas, "but there's no hurry."

"Oh, but there is. One must pay one's debts," Gillis said,

and took out a small roll of bills from his pocket. He handed Dallas two fives. "Sorry to have been so long about it."

"That's okay," Dallas said, surprised to be paid, and thinking Gillis must have put a pretty hard bite on his sister. "What's ten bucks between friends? Come and have a drink."

Gillis shook his head.

"Not tonight. I'm expecting a blonde: one of those wild, woolly and wanton females I specialize in. She should be waiting at the bar if she isn't going to be late. See you some other time."

Dallas watched the tall, thin figure walk into the bar. Then he went into the cloakroom, parked his hat and returned to the lobby. He decided he would see Zoe right away, and then keep an eye on Gillis. Zoe would be on duty in ten minutes. He would have to hurry to catch her in her dressing-room.

He went down the stairs that led to the rear of the building, along the passage to Zoe's room. The door stood ajar. He knocked and pushed it open. The lights were on, and Zoe's silk wrap lay across the divan. There was a smouldering cigarette end in the ashtray. But there was no sign of Zoe.

Absently, Dallas stubbed out the cigarette, and then went back along the passage to the restaurant. Luigi, the Captain of waiters, came to meet him.

"Good evening, Mr Dallas," he said. "Your usual table?"

"Not at the moment," Dallas said, looking beyond him into the crowded restaurant. "Miss Norton around?"

"She's not due in the restaurant until eleven-thirty," Luigi said, and consulted his watch. "About five minutes. Shall I tell her you would like her to join you?"

"Yeah, do that. I'll be in the bar."

Dallas went across to the lobby. Schmidt touched his cap when he saw him. He approved of Dallas.

"Seen Miss Norton?" Dallas asked, pausing.

"Yes, sir. She's in the club. I expect you'll find her in her dressing-room."

"She's not there. If you spot her, tell her I'm in the bar."

He saw Gillis sitting in a corner of the bar with a blonde girl who didn't look much older than seventeen. She had a pretty, vicious little face, and she was leaning forward across the table so Gillis could see down the front of her low-cut gown. Gillis looked casually amused, and glanced up. He saw Dallas come it and gave him a broad wink.

Dallas called for a double Scotch and sat on a stool up at the bar and talked to the barman. He watched Gillis in the mirror behind the bar. After a while, Gillis and the girl went into the restaurant. Dallas decided he'd have another look for Zoe.

Luigi was just coming back to the entrance after seeing Gillis and his companion to their table. He shook his head at Dallas.

"Miss Norton hasn't shown up yet," he said, and there was an annoyed look in his eyes. "I can't understand it. She hasn't been late since she's been here."

The waiter came up at this moment and whispered in his ear.

"She isn't in the club," Luigi told Dallas when the waiter had gone away. "I'm very sorry, Mr Dallas, I haven't an idea where she is."

"That's okay," Dallas said shortly, and went back to the lobby.

"Miss Norton has left the club," he told Schmidt. "Did

you see her go?"

"She hasn't been this way, sir," Schmidt said, looking surprised. "If she's left the club she'll have gone by the back exit."

"Thanks," Dallas said, and went quickly down the stairs to Zoe's room again. He was worried now. What had happened to her? he wondered, as he again entered her room. He stood looking around, then he went to her wardrobe, opened it and found her hat and coat on a peg. He stood for a moment staring at them, his uneasiness turning to alarm.

If she had gone out, why on earth hadn't she taken her coat? It was raining a little outside, and she couldn't have gone just in her evening dress.

He went over to the telephone and dialled her home number. There was no answer, and he dropped the receiver back on its cradle.

Had she slipped up somewhere? He had warned her not to attract suspicion. He knew how dangerous Baird might be, and he cursed himself for involving her in this business.

He picked up the receiver again and called Purvis.

"Zoe's missing," he said, when Purvis came on the line. "It may be a false alarm, but I don't think so. Can you send Ainsworth over to take care of Gillis? I want to look for her."

"Think anything's happened to her?" Purvis asked sharply.

"Your guess is as good as mine. Has MacAdam reported about Baird's movements tonight?"

"Baird's in the club now."

"I haven't seen him. You sure?"

"Mac phoned through about twenty minutes ago and

said he tailed Baird to the club. He's been watching the front entrance, and hasn't seen Baird come out."

"There's a rear exit. Doesn't the fool know?" Dallas said angrily. "Well, he can look after Gillis. I'll tell him. Baird's not in the club, unless he's in Rico's office. I'd better go along and check that."

"If you want Ainsworth, I'll keep him standing by," Purvis said.

"Yeah, do that. I'll call you back."

Dallas hung up and walked down the passage to Rico's office. He rapped sharply. There was no answer, and turning the handle he pushed open the door.

The room was in darkness, and with a grunt of disappointment Dallas was about to back out when he paused and sniffed the air. His sharp nose detected a faint smell of musk. He sniffed again. It was musk all right, and he knew Zoe's latest fad was to use a musk perfume. He groped for the light switch and turned on the light.

The office was empty. He stood looking around, but saw nothing to excite his interest, but he wasn't satisfied. He went over to the desk, and bending, he sniffed at the blotter on the desk. The smell of musk was stronger there, as if Zoe had touched the blotter.

Something caught his attention and he glanced down. Half hidden under the desk was a small evening bag. He knew it at once. It was the one he had given Zoe a week or so ago. He had a tight feeling in his throat as he bent and picked it up.

III

Rico sat beside Baird and stared through the windshield of the Buick as Baird drove slowly along the waterfront. The headlights of the car picked out the oily puddles, the litter and squashed fruit that covered the narrow causeway, bordered on one side by tall, dark warehouses and on the other by the river.

Rain pattered down on the roof of the car and splashed on the still water of the river. They had been driving fast for the past twenty minutes, and now they had reached the waterfront, Baird had slowed down as if uncertain where he was going.

Zoe lay on the back seat. Her wrists and ankles were tied with cord, and an adhesive bandage covered her mouth. From time to time Rico glanced over his shoulder at her. Her eyes were closed and she didn't move. Rico was scared Baird had broken her neck as he had broken Jean Bruce's neck. It came as a sick sense of relief when he heard her moan softly through the gag.

The sight of the river made him break out into a cold sweat. The one thing he had sworn to avoid was murder, and now, he felt certain, he was going to be forced to take part in the girl's death.

"You won't do anything to her?" he said, forcing words through his stiff lips. "I – I won't stand for murder ..."

Baird glanced at him, and then shifted his attention back to the narrow causeway.

"Do you want her to sick the cops on you?" he asked softly. "This is a kidnapping rap: could get you the gas box."

Rico gulped. He hadn't thought of that. The tiny spark of courage that had forced the words out of him abruptly snuffed out. He shut his eyes, while his heart banged against his ribs, and his mouth turned sour and dry.

The car jolted slowly on for some time, but Rico didn't open his eyes. It wasn't until he felt the car stop and heard

Baird open the door that he looked fearfully through the windshield to see where he was.

Baird had turned off the headlights. Rico couldn't see much in the feeble lights of the parkers. He seemed to be in a cul-de-sac. He could smell the river, but couldn't see it. Surrounding him were high walls of rotting timber, black with tar.

"Come on out," Baird said impatiently.

Rico got out of the car. His legs could scarcely support him. The rain felt cold against his feverish face. He looked up. High above him he could make out the outline of the roofs of the buildings against the rain-swollen sky. Two or three derricks hung lifelessly from the upper storeys. The warehouse had an air of neglect and disuse. But it was the silence that unnerved Rico. Only the soft patter of the rain and his own heavy, uneven breathing came to his listening ears. He had a suffocating feeling of being buried alive, and when Baird jerked open the rear door of the car, he started violently.

"Take this," Baird said, turning and pushing a flashlight into Rico's hand. "What's the matter with you? Can't you hold it steady?"

He leaned into the car, dragged Zoe out, and hoisted her over his shoulder. She struggled feebly, but he took no notice, handling her with the impersonal indifference of a slaughterman preparing cattle for the hammer.

"Give it to me," he went on to Rico, and snatched the light from him. "Come on."

"Where're we going?" Rico muttered, staring up at the building.

"A place I know," Baird said. "Come on and stop yapping."

Rico followed him through an archway into a long, dark passage. The uneven floor was strewn with refuse: an evil smell came out of the passage and sickened Rico. As they moved slowly forward, he could hear the rustle of rats ahead of them. Huge spiders scuttled into the shadows as Baird flashed his light up to the ceiling.

At the end of the passage they came to a flight of stone steps that eventually brought them into a vast barn of a room full of packing cases, barrels, litter and the smell of damp and decay.

Baird lowered Zoe to the floor, and as he straightened up he swung the beam of his flashlight around.

"Safe enough," he said under his breath. "No one is likely to hear her."

Rico didn't say anything. He leaned against one of the rotting packing cases and stared at Baird in horror.

No one is likely to hear her.

His mind shied away from the implication. Pain and violence had always demoralized him.

"What's the matter with you?" Baird asked roughly, shining the light full on Rico's face. "Losing your guts?"

"What are you going to do with her?" Rico whispered, holding up his hand to shield his sweating face.

"What do you think?" Baird said. "She can tell us what we want to know. Someone's got at her to spy on you, and we want to know who."

He bent over Zoe, loosened the tape round her mouth and jerked it off.

"Hello, Toots," he said, kneeling by her, "I warned you how it'd be. Now you better start talking. Who's behind your racket?"

Zoe stared at him, terror in her eyes.

"Let me go!" she gasped. "Rico! Make him let me go! You'll be sorry if you don't! I'll make trouble ..."

Baird slapped her face, and her words choked off in a scream.

"Shut up!" he said softly. "Who's behind your racket?"

"No one, and it isn't a racket," Zoe sobbed. "Let me go!"

Baird's hand reached out and his fingers caught hold of Zoe's chin. He raised her face and flashed the light in her eyes.

"Better start talking, Toots," he said. "I'm in a rush. You don't want me to persuade you to talk, do you?"

"I tell you I don't know what you mean," Zoe gasped, trying to break Baird's grip.

"Okay," Baird said, letting go of her. "If you want it the hard way, you can have it the hard way."

Rico felt suddenly sick.

"I feel ill," he said. "I – I can't watch, Baird. Let me wait in the car."

Baird stood up.

"Go and wait in the car, you gutless monkey, but don't run away."

"I'll wait," Rico said feverishly, and began to back away. Baird caught hold of his coat front and shook him. "Don't run. If you want your share, you're damn well going to earn it!"

He gave Rico a shove that sent him reeling into the shadows.

"Don't leave me!" Zoe screamed, struggling to sit up. "Rico! Don't leave me with him! Rico! Come back!"

Rico blundered down the stairs, sweat pouring down his face. Zoe's screams suddenly stopped and, shuddering, Rico began to grope his way along the pitch-black passage. The darkness came down on him as if a blanket had been thrown oven his head. He could see nothing, and he stopped short, his heart pounding, while he tried to see where he was going.

He remembered the huge spiders, the stinking refuse on the floor and the rats, and he knew he couldn't go on without a light. He turned and groped his way back until he reached the steps. He sat down, holding his head between his hands.

It seemed to him he sat in the evil-smelling darkness for a long time. Somewhere in the passage he could hear the busy gnawing of rat's teeth on wood, the occasional drip of water, and the persistent patter of the rain against the walls of the building. But he didn't pay any attention to these noises. His ears were straining for the sound of any activity in the vast room above him. At first he heard nothing, then he imagined he heard the sound of breathing until he realized it was the curious echo of the thumping of his own heart as he sat there, his blood hammering through his veins.

The minutes dragged by. What could Baird be doing? he wondered stupidly. Perhaps after all she was talking, telling Baird what he wanted to know, and it would mean ...

A long, blood-chilling scream rang suddenly through the building. It came down to Rico like the rush of wind, past him, and on down the passage, making the rats scramble up the walls in a panic of agitation.

Rico put his hands over his ears as the scream was repeated, but he couldn't block it out. It seemed to run round and round inside his head like the rats running up and down the walls.

The screaming went on for a long time.

"Please don't!" he heard Zoe cry. "No... oh, no! I don't know anything ..."

Then she went back to the high-pitched screams that tore Rico's nerves to shreds, and finally the screaming gave way to a soft moaning that was as horrible to listen to as the screaming.

The moaning kept on, until Rico thought he'd go crazy. He tried to stand up, but his shaking legs wouldn't support him. He sat there, his hands over his ears, his eyes shut and his heart pounding. He had sweated right through his clothes, and he felt exhausted, as if he had been running without rest for miles.

He became aware suddenly that the moaning had stopped. For some moments he only heard the rustling of rats and the sound of the rain against the walls. He sat in the darkness, not moving, his nerves screwed up to meet another outburst of screaming.

Then the choked bang of a gun shattered the silence. The violence of the sound threw Rico on his knees. The echo of the shot rolled through the empty building, sending the rats scurrying madly to their holes.

Rico remained on his knees, too sick to move or think. He was still there among the slime and muck on the floor when Baird came down the steps.

"What the hell do you think you're doing?" Baird asked, and dragged Rico to his feet. "Lost the little guts you had?"

Rico made an effort to pull himself together.

"She's dead?" he asked without hope.

"What do you think?" Baird said. "I dropped her into the river. With any luck they won't find her for months. Come on, let's get out of here." He shoved Rico along the passage, under the archway to where the car was waiting.

"I've got some news for you," Baird said as he paused to light a cigarette. "That fella Dallas works for the International Detective Agency. He's been hired by the insurance companies, who're trying to find the stuff Hater cached. Dallas is on to you and Kile and me. We've been watched day and night for weeks. And listen, the top man's Gillis, the guy who comes into your club. That redhead you were so sure about has been reporting every move you've made."

Rico stood staring stupidly at Baird. He scarcely heard. The sound of the shot was still ringing in his head.

"Kile's going to unload the stuff when he gets it on the Rajah himself, who's planning to gyp the insurance companies. A sweet set-up, isn't it?" Baird went on.

Groaning, Rico turned away and suddenly vomited.

With a grunt of disgust Baird got into the car and started the engine.

"Come on, let's get out of here," he said.

IV

Dallas found MacAdam in a bar opposite the Frou-Frou Club, where he had a good view of the main entrance of the club.

MacAdam, a dark, beefy man, who looked too big for his clothes, was nursing a pint of beer, and staring through the window of the bar, a faraway expression in his eyes.

Dallas gave him a jab in the ribs that made him spill some of his beer. He turned wrathfully.

"Oh, you," he said in disgust. "I might have known it. I saw Gillis go in about a quarter of an hour ago. I guessed you'd be around like bad news."

"Where's Baird?" Dallas demanded.

MacAdam eyed him sharply. He didn't like the expression on Dallas' face.

"What's cooking? You look like you swallowed a bee."

"You'll think you've swallowed a goddamn hornet in a moment," Dallas snarled. "Where's Baird?"

"In the club, of course. Why else do you think I'm here?"

"He isn't in the club. Don't you know there's a rear exit?"

MacAdam sighed.

"So what am I supposed to do?" he asked, waving his beer in Dallas' face. "Cut myself in half? I can't watch the rear exit as well as the front, can I?"

"If you'd watched the club farther down the road," Dallas said angrily, "you could have seen him if he had come out either exits."

"Yeah, I guess that's right," MacAdam said, his face falling. "I had a thirst on me like an oil fire. I just had to put it out."

"Well, he's gone, and it's my bet your job's gone, too. Rico isn't in the club, and Zoe's missing. If anything happens to her, you're for the high jump. I'll damn well see to that! Get out of here and watch for Gillis when he comes out. I'm turning him over to you while I look for Baird."

MacAdam hurriedly emptied his glass.

"What do you think's happened to Zoe?" he asked, looking worried.

"Anything can have happened to her. Get going before Gillis slips through your fingers."

They went out on to the street together.

"If I don't pick Baird up, you'd better quit," Dallas said. He was cold with fury. "We're responsible for that girl. She was one of us."

"Yeah, yeah; take it easy," MacAdam said. "I slipped up, but how the hell was I to know? How do you hope to find Baird? He's got a start on you, hasn't he?"

"Rico owns a Roadmaster Buick. It's a showy job, and it isn't in the parking lot. It's my bet they've taken Zoe somewhere in it. I'm going to try and trace it."

"Rather you than me," MacAdam said. "Sounds like you've got plenty of exercise coming to you."

"Watch Gillis and save your sympathy," Dallas snapped, and walked off to where he had parked his car.

The parking attendant came over as Dallas turned on his headlights. Dallas gave him half a buck.

"Mr Rico took his car out about twenty minutes ago. I'm trying to find him. Know which way he went?"

"He turned left and headed towards his apartment," the attendant said. "I reckon he's gone home, although he's never been as early as this before."

Dallas nodded. He thought that was unlikely.

"Mr Baird was with him, wasn't he?"

"That's right."

"Anyone else?"

The man shook his head.

"Just the two of them. Mr Baird was driving."

Dallas started his car.

"I'll try his apartment," he said, and drove out of the park. Swinging his car to the left he drove as fast as the traffic would allow him to the intersection. Straight ahead would bring him to Rico's apartment block, but he couldn't imagine Rico would take Zoe there: he was too cautious for that.

Dallas swung the car to the kerb, a few yards from the traffic lights. He got out and went across to a man selling newspapers, hunching his shoulders against the drizzling rain.

"Hey, Joe," he said. "Have you seen a big Buick with yellow fenders pass this way?"

"You mean Rico's car?" the man asked, and shook his head. "I didn't notice it. The cop on the corner might have seen him. He's been airing his corns for the past hour right there."

"Thanks," Dallas said, and went over to the patrolman, who looked as if his feet had taken root on the kerb. He eyed Dallas without interest as he came up. Dallas poked one of his cards at him. "Seen Rico's Buick pass this way within the past twenty minutes?"

The cop read the card, nodded and handed it back. Purvis subscribed heavily to the police fund each year, and most of the cops played ball with the Agency.

"Yeah," he said. "I seen the little rat."

"Which way did he go?"

"Turned right at the lights, and headed towards the river."

Dallas felt a little chill run up his spine. He might have guessed that's the way they'd go.

"Thanks," he said, turned and ran back to his car. He drove rapidly along West Street, turned left at the next intersection, increased his speed along the broad, deserted dock road. A couple of miles of fast driving brought him to the river. Again he pulled to the kerb and got out. He spent ten minutes trying to find someone who had seen Rico's car before he succeeded.

A red-headed street walker volunteered the information.

"Sure, it was heading for the old causeway," she told Dallas, while she ogled him from under her hat brim. "It's

Rico, isn't it? I thought I recognized him. Why worry about him, sugar? Let's you and me have fun."

"Some other night," Dallas said, scarcely hearing what she said. "I've got to find this guy."

"No accounting for taste," the girl said, shrugging her thin shoulders. The rain dripped off her umbrella on to her sandalled feet. "Me – I wouldn't look for Rico if he was the last man on earth."

Dallas got into his car and headed along the narrow causeway. He was sure now that Baird and Rico had brought Zoe here to murder her. Why else should they come down to the river? He felt responsible for Zoe, and he drove recklessly, refusing to accept what his common sense was telling him: if they were going to murder her, they would have done it by now.

Very soon he got completely lost in the narrow alleys that ran between the derelict warehouses. It became impossible to drive fast and, exasperated, he stopped the car and got out. Rain poured down on him as he swung the beam of his flashlight up at the high buildings. He cursed softly, wondering which way to go, when suddenly he heard the sharp bang of a heavy calibre gun.

The shot sounded close. As far as he could judge it came from a building a little way up the alley.

As he broke into a run, he knew he was too late to save Zoe, and he groped for his .38 police special. He reached the end of the alley, paused to listen again, but heard nothing. It had been somewhere near here, he thought, looking up at the row of high buildings. Their doors were boarded up, and he guessed there must be an entrance somewhere at the back. He ran down the next alley he came to and reached an intersection that he calculated would bring him to the rear of the buildings he had just passed.

Then he heard a car start up. He increased his speed and raced down the alley to another intersection. As he rounded the corner he was in time to see a big car moving swiftly away from him. Its parking lights lit up its bright yellow fenders.

It was moving too fast for him to hope to overtake it. He stopped, raised the .38 and fired. The smash of glass told him he had scored a hit. The car increased speed, and before he could fire again, it had whipped around a bend and had disappeared.

He stood there for a moment, trying to think what to do next. It would be hopeless to try to find Zoe's body. They were certain to have dumped her into the river, but if he acted fast it might be possible to get the body before the currents took it away.

He raced back to his car, scrambled in, and drove as fast as he dared back along the causeway. There was no sign of the Buick. The delay in getting back to his car, finding his way to the causeway, had given Rico too big a lead to hope to overtake him.

Dallas spotted an all-night café at the corner of West and Union. He crammed on his brakes, swung the car to the kerb and ran across the sidewalk into the café.

The place was full of steamy moisture, the smell of frying onions and hot, strong Java. A dozen dockers sat around a big table playing dominoes and drinking beer. The red-headed street walker who had identified Rico's car was sitting on a high stool at the bar, showing off her legs in the hope of drumming up some trade. None of the dockers seemed interested. She smiled archly at Dallas when he came in, but he went past her like a miniature hurricane and dived into a phone booth at the end of the room.

He caught Olin as he was leaving for the night.

"I can hand you Baird on a plate," he said urgently. "Listen: it's a safe bet Baird's just knocked off one of Rico's taxi-dancers. Rico's in it, too. They've slung her in the river. I spotted their car leaving and took a shot at them. I think I smashed a window. If you get moving fast there's a chance of recovering the body before the tide gets it."

Olin knew Dallas didn't make mistakes. He had worked with him a lot in the past, and to Dallas' delight he didn't waste time asking questions.

"If you're pulling me out on a false alarm I'll slap a charge on you," Olin said. "Is this the McCoy?"

"This isn't a false alarm, George," Dallas said, and the grimness in his voice convinced Olin. "Get some boys and come down to West and Union fast."

"Stick where you are," Olin said. "I'll be right with you."

Dallas hung up and went to the bar. He ordered a double Scotch.

"Did you find him?" the redhead asked, hitching up her skirt so he could see the top of her stocking.

The bartender leaned over the bar.

"Hey, you! Take it outside and peddle it in the rain," he said, "or you'll get bounced out on your fanny."

Dallas said, "Pipe down. She's a friend of mine. Give her a Scotch."

The redhead sneered at the bartender and gave a little wriggle inside her clothes for Dallas' benefit.

"Let's get out of this hole," she said. "I've got a swell apartment you'll love."

"Drink your Scotch and shut up," Dallas said. He finished his drink, patted her on the shoulder and went out into the rain.

Four minutes later he heard the first of the sirens. In another minute West Street was alive with noise and black and white police cars.

Olin leaned out of the front car and waved to Dallas.

"Well, you've certainly started something," Olin said, as Dallas scrambled into the car. "I hope for your sake you can finish it. Let's have it quick as we go."

"Make for Pinder's End," Dallas told the driver, and while the car shot down West Street, he gave Olin his prepared story.

"The girl's name is Zoe Norton," he said rapidly. "She and I sleep together when we've nothing better to do. Nothing serious, but I like her and she likes me."

"Okay, okay," Olin said impatiently, "never mind about your love life. Where's Baird fit in this?"

"I don't know," Dallas lied. "I went to the club to see Zoe tonight. Like I told you, she works for Rico. She was missing. She'd been in the club; her hat and coat were in her dressing-room, but she had disappeared. I found her bag in Rico's office. He had vanished, too. I found out he and Baird had taken Baird's car and had gone off together. I traced them to Pinder's End on the waterfront. Then I lost them. I was nosing around when I heard a shot. I was in time to see Rico's Buick driving away like a bat out of hell. I took a shot at it, and smashed one of the windows. It's my bet Zoe found out something about those two and they've silenced her."

"Found out what?" Olin barked.

"No idea, but it could be something to do with the Bruce killing."

Olin snorted.

"You don't even know if they had her in the car."

"Where else is she, then?"

"Anywhere. You're sure about the shot?"

"Yeah, I'm sure about that."

"Maybe Baird has rubbed Rico out," Olin said hopefully. "I'll get myself good and drunk if he has."

"It's Zoe all right," Dallas said. "I'm sure of it."

"Why the hell should they want to knock off a taxi-dancer?" Olin asked. "Talk sense." He gave Dallas a sharp look. "Or are you keeping anything back?"

"You know as well as I do the whole of my life's spread out for you to pick over," Dallas said. "Don't be so damned suspicious."

The car skidded to a standstill.

"This is it," the driver said.

Dallas and Olin got out. The three other police cars emptied. The prowl boys stood around in the rain expectantly, looking at Olin for orders.

"Where did you hear the shot?" Olin asked.

"Right here. It seemed to come from those buildings." Dallas waved at the high, dark warehouses.

"Okay, boys," Olin said. "Get busy. Look these joints over. If you find anything, sound your whistles."

The prowl boys broke up into parties of twos and began a systematic search of the warehouses.

"I'm going to the waterfront," Dallas said. "Coming?"

"Leave it to the River Police," Olin said shortly. "I tipped them off before I left."

"That's where she's going to be found," Dallas said, "and that's where I'm going."

Olin shrugged, but followed Dallas to the end of the alley into what appeared to be a cul-de-sac.

"You won't get to the river this way," Olin grunted.

Dallas swung his flashlight beam on the ground.

"There's been a car here. Look, tyre and oil marks. Where's that lead to?" He flashed his light on a low, dark archway. "Come on, let's take a look."

Olin followed him through the archway into an evil-smelling passage. In the mud and slush that covered the floor they could see footprints.

"Someone's been here, and recently," Dallas said.

He began to mount the stone steps at the end of the passage, stopped and sniffed.

"Gunpowder!" he exclaimed. "Can you smell it?"

"Do you imagine I haven't got a nose?" Olin growled, jerking out his gun. "Get out of the way. I'll handle this."

He ran up the rest of the steps into a vast, barn-like room with Dallas on his heels. The smell of gunpowder hung in the thick atmosphere. Among the other smells Dallas imagined he could smell musk.

"Look at that!" Olin barked, dropping the flashlight beam to the floor. A dark-brown stain made an irregular pattern on the dirty boards: close by was a small pile of half-burned matches.

"That's blood."

Dallas spotted a door in the wall. He went over to it, pushed it open. He found himself looking down at the dark waters of the river, some thirty feet below.

"He killed her and threw her out this way," he said, through clenched teeth.

Olin joined him.

"Looks like it," he said. "There's the river boys. We'd better get them working here." He flashed his light on and off. In the distance a light answered. "They'll be up in a couple of minutes. Wait here and guide them in. I'll get my lot together."

Dallas sat on the floor, flashing his light on and off. At the back of the building he could hear Olin's whistle. The lights of the police launch came closer. By the time Olin had returned, the police launch was bobbing up and down just below where Dallas was sitting.

"There's a body down there somewhere," Olin shouted. "It was thrown in from here. Get busy and find it. It couldn't have drifted far."

A powerful searchlight was turned on that lit up a big expanse of water. It made Dallas feel sick to think that Zoe was somewhere in that dark, oily grave. He sat there, smoking, for a long time, while the River Police threw out their drags and systematically combed the river.

It was over an hour before they found Zoe. By that time both Olin and Dallas had joined them on the launch.

"Here she is," one of the River Police said, as the drags came in. Gently he and another cop rolled Zoe's half-naked body off the hooks.

"This the one you want?" the sergeant asked, looking up at Olin.

"Is it?" Olin asked Dallas.

"I guess so," Dallas said huskily.

Zoe had been shot through the head. The big .45 slug had torn a chunk of her skull away. She didn't look like the Zoe he had played around with. He stood staring down at her, a cold, sick feeling creeping over him.

"Looks like someone's been burning her," Olin said, in a hushed voice. "Look at the state she's in."

The sergeant tossed a blanket over Zoe's broken and tortured body. His usually red, cheerful face looked a little green.

"Well, what are we waiting for?" Dallas said, his voice rasping. "Let's go get those two bastards."

V

Baird saw a flash of flame in the driving mirror; at the same instant there came a crash of breaking glass. Glass splinters flew inside the car like shrapnel.

Rico cried out as he ducked down on the floor of the car. Automatically Baird's foot trod down hard on the gas pedal. The big Buick surged forward, and he whipped it around the bend in the causeway.

He sent the big car hurtling along the narrow road. He could feel blood running down the side of his neck from a cut from a glass splinter, and he swore softly.

"What is it?" Rico quavered from the floor of the car. "Who shot at us?

"How the hell do I know?" Baird snarled.

But he was quick to realize what this meant. Someone had been close by when he had shot that damned spying redhead. A car like Rico's could easily be identified. If whoever it was called the cops, and they found the body before the current took it away, Rico would be on the spot. Baird hadn't any illusions about Rico keeping his trap shut. Any tough cop could make Rico sing like a canary, and Rico would try to pin the whole weight of the killing on Baird.

He kicked Rico hard in the ribs.

"Get up!" he said furiously. "See what the damage is!"

Rico pulled himself off the floor and looked back at the gaping hole in the rear window. With relief he saw there was no car following them, and he sank down on the bench seat beside Baird, groaning.

"Aw, shut up!" Baird snarled. "It must have been one of those shamuses who's been following me. Start using your head, Rico. We've got to take action fast if we're going to beat this rap. He's seen the car. We can't get that window fixed before the cops descend on us. If they don't find the body we can cook up some yarn, but if they do, we're sunk!"

Rico turned cold.

"You got me into this!" he wailed. "I told you I wouldn't stand for murder! Damn you! Let me get out of here! I'm not going to be caught with you!"

Baird swung his arm. The back of his hand caught Rico across his nose and mouth, stunning him.

"Shut up, you squealer!" Baird exclaimed. "We're both in this! You try and walk out on me, and I'll put a slug into you!"

Rico wilted. He lay back, his hands over his face. "Maybe we can tell them the car was stolen from the park," Baird said. "If you and me can fix an alibi ..."

"That shamus saw us," Rico said, fear steadying his nerves and letting his rat-shrewd brain function. "You've fixed me this time, damn you! There's no way out of it! Olin's been waiting for something like this to break."

"Take it easy," Baird said coldly. "Maybe they won't find her. We'll get back to the club and find out what's been going on. Until we know who's been talking we can't do a thing."

"Listen!" Rico said, stiffening. "Police sirens!"

Baird stamped on the brake, swung the car across the street with a screech of tortured tyres and drove up a narrow side street. He stopped the car, jumped out and stood on the sidewalk, his hand on his gun.

Fearfully, Rico peered through the broken rear window and looked towards the main street. The clamour of sirens grew louder. They watched three black and white police cars flash past, heading for Union Street.

"That punk tipped them off fast enough," Baird growled as he got back into the Buick. "But they still mayn't find her."

He drove recklessly along the back streets and reached the club in under five minutes. He drove into the parking lot.

"Get hold of yourself," he said, as he wiped the blood off his neck. "Come on out. We may be rushed for time."

As they got out of the car, the parking attendant came over. He stared at the blood on Baird's collar, then his gaze shifted to Rico's damaged nose, and his eyes popped.

"Some drunk threw a bottle at the car," Baird said. "Smashed the rear window."

"Gee!" the attendant exclaimed. "What did he want to do that for?"

"Anyone been asking for me, Tim?" Rico said, holding his handkerchief across his face.

"Mr Dallas wanted you. I told him you'd gone home. He said he'd try your apartment."

"Got another car, Rico?" Baird asked sharply. "We may have to go out again."

Rico gulped.

"There's the Packard."

"Get it around the rear entrance," Baird said to the parking attendant. "We may be leaving in a hurry."

"Yes, sir."

Baird caught hold of Rico's arm and hustled him to the rear entrance.

"Can we trust that guy?"

"Yes," Rico said. " 'Tim's all right. He'll do anything for me."

"That's swell," Baird said sarcastically. "Dallas fired that shot! He must have come here to see the redhead, found her missing and traced us to the waterfront. I must have been crazy to have used that damned car of yours. A blind man could identify it."

Rico pushed open the door of his office and went in. He turned on the light and went over to the cellaret. With a shaking hand he poured two whiskies, gave Baird one and gulped down the other. He poured more whisky into his glass and then dropped into a chair.

"You got me into this," he said. "You've got to get me out of it."

"It'll be easy if they don't find her. But if they do ..." Baird shrugged. "Can't you find out what's happening?"

Rico gulped down his second whisky, picked up the telephone and dialled a number. After a slight pause, he said, "That you, Sam? This is Rico. Listen, I want you to get down to Pinder's End fast. The cops are there. Find out what they're doing and call back. It's worth fifty if you give me some fast action."

He hung up and looked at Baird.

"Sam'll find out. He'll call me back."

"Where's that five grand?" Baird demanded. "Get it, and get hold of every buck in the place. Get moving: we may have to dust, and dust fast!"

Rico licked his dry lips.

"What do you mean? I can't just walk out of here. It's my living. What are you talking about?"

"Get the dough!" Baird snarled. "You can stay here if you want to, but if they fish her out of the river, I'm going to be well out of reach."

Rico closed his eyes. He had visions of Olin cornering him. He saw the room at headquarters with its one blinding light, and the big coppers crowding around him with their blackjacks. He started out of his chair, sweat running down his face.

"Where can I go?" he yammered, catching hold of Baird's coat front. "What about the club? What the hell am I going to do?"

Baird threw him off.

"You can come with me to Red River Basin. That's where I'm going," he said. "Have you forgotten? There's half a million or more to be picked up there, and it's where Olin can't get at us. What do you care about this lousy club if you can get your hands on money like that?"

Rico gulped and gaped at Baird.

"It'll turn out to be another of your bright ideas," he whined. "How do I know I shan't be in a worse jam?"

"You couldn't be in a worse jam," Baird said brutally. "Get moving. Collect all the dough you can lay hands on, and make it fast."

Rico staggered out of the room, and Baird heard him calling to Luigi. Shrugging his shoulders, Baird sat down and helped himself to another whisky. The only regret he felt for leaving town was that he wouldn't get the chance of seeing Anita again. He had found out where she worked, and most nights he parked his car near the restaurant to watch her come out when the restaurant closed. Sometimes he followed her home and spent a half an hour watching the light in her window, seeing her pass and repass as she moved about the room, preparing for bed. He made no attempt to speak to her, and he was careful that she shouldn't see him. He told himself again and again he was getting soft in the head and he was wasting his time, but the fascination of seeing her from a distance was irresistible to him.

Rico returned ten minutes later. He carried a suitcase which he placed on the table.

"Luigi will look after things for me," he said. "I've got a couple of grand in here, and there's the five grand from Kile. But unless I have to, I don't want to go ..."

The telephone bell rang sharply, cutting off his words. He answered it while Baird lounged in his chair and watched him.

"Yeah, Sam, This is Rico. What's going on down there?" He listened, and Baird saw his face go green. "They have? Okay. Thanks, Sam. Come up to the club and see Luigi. He'll pay you off." He hung up and looked at Baird, who was already on his feet, reaching for the suitcase. "They've found her! Sam saw them hook her out about three minutes ago."

"Come on, then," Baird said. "Let's get out of here fast. First stop Red River Basin."

Rico tore at his hair.

"Leaving all this! I'll be ruined ..."

Baird was already walking rapidly down the passage to the car park. Rico snatched up his hat and coat and rushed after him.

The dark blue Packard was waiting at the rear exit.

"There's another set of licence plates in the boot," the parking attendant said, coming up. "The tank's full, and there's a Thompson under the rear floorboards. Anything else I can do?"

"Can you ditch the Buick?"

The parking attendant grinned.

"I've already done that. I left it in a vacant lot about a mile away."

"Nice work," Baird said approvingly. "If they ask questions, tell them you haven't seen us."

"Sure."

Rico scrambled into the Packard.

"Good luck, Mr Rico. I'll stall them," the parking attendant said.

"Thanks, Tim. Maybe I'll be back," Rico said mournfully.

Baird let in the clutch, swung out of the parking lot, and headed up town.

MacAdam, who had been sitting in his car waiting patiently for Gillis to show, spotted Rico in the Packard. He thought he recognized Baird at the wheel. He didn't hesitate. Instinct told him it was more important to go after Baird and Rico than to wait for Gillis.

He trod on the starter and shot his car away from the kerb.

VI

"Peggy, darling," Gillis said, turning on his boyish charm and leaning across the table to catch her hand, "aren't you getting a little bored with all this? Wouldn't you like to come back to my place? We could have much more fun alone together."

His blonde companion screwed up her eyes to focus the tanned, smiling face that appeared to bob up and down like a toy balloon on a rough sea.

"I'm having fun right here," she announced, in a voice that carried across the restaurant. "I don't want to go to your dreary old place. I've been there, and I know what you call fun. I'm staying right here. Let's have some champagne."

Gillis' smile became fixed. He glanced a little anxiously at the tables close to his. Some of the diners were looking at Peggy, amused smiles on their faces.

"I think you've drunk enough already, darling," he said, keeping his voice low. "Come on, Peggy, let's get out of here."

"I don't want to," she said, with drunken obstinacy. "I want some champagne. I'm not asking you to pay for it. I'll pay for it myself. I've lots and lots of money. Hey, waiter!" she went on, raising her voice. "Where's the lousy waiter? Waiter!"

Gillis went white with suppressed fury. If there was one thing he hated, it was to be the centre of a scene. People were now staring at him, and some of them were whispering to each other.

"Keep your voice down, you little fool!" he said furiously. "You're making a scene!"

"I don't care!" the girl cried. "Why shouldn't I make a scene if I want to? I'm paying for this meal, and if I want to, I'm entitled to make a scene!"

A waiter came up quickly.

"Is there anything madam wants?" he asked, bowing.

"Get some champagne," the girl ordered. "My boyfriend's thirsty. He only drinks champagne if I pay for it. Don't you, Adam darling?"

Gillis pushed back his chair. He was sweating now.

"Sure," he said soothingly. "But excuse me a moment. I'll be right back. I've just remembered I've got to make a phone call."

"Oh, no, you don't!" the girl exclaimed at the top of her voice. "I'm not all that drunk. You're not going to walk out on me just when I'm buying you champagne. Just because I won't go back to your fusty old bedroom and let you maul me around, you're not going to leave me flat!"

The people within earshot had stopped pretending to listen, and were frankly gaping at Gillis.

"Shut your mouth!" he snarled at her, getting to his feet. "You're not fit to go to public places."

Peggy giggled.

"I've got a hundred dollars in my bag for you, Adam, darling. If you go I shan't give it to you."

Gillis was already walking stiff-legged down the long aisle to the exit. Sweat beaded his face as he saw people staring at him.

Peggy picked up a spoon and began to hammer with it on the table, chanting drunkenly, "Gigolo! Gigolo! Dirty little gigolo!"

Gillis went hurriedly into the men's toilet. He was so furious he could have gone back and murdered the bitch. He ran cold water into the basin and plunged his face in it.

That was the finish of him in the club. He couldn't come here again, he told himself, as he groped for a towel. Damn her! He might have known the vulgar little fool couldn't have held her liquor. He was crazy to have thought he could have persuaded her to go back to his room, after what had happened the first time. Then she had smashed a window, scratched his face and nearly wrecked the room. It was a wonder the police hadn't turned up. He had thought if he could get her tight she might be more amenable. Instead, he had let himself in for this scene. To look at her you'd have thought she was an absolute pushover. He stood staring at his reflection in the mirror, while he called her every name he could think of.

Well, he wasn't going to leave by the front entrance. She might be there to start another scene. He'd go by the back exit.

Pushing open the door on his left, he stepped into the passage that led to Rico's office, the changing-rooms and the back exit. He hadn't taken more than a dozen steps when he came to an abrupt standstill.

Someone was talking in Rico's office. He recognized Baird's soft tones. He moved forward silently, opened the door next to Rico's office and slipped into a small, dark room used by waiters for changing into their outdoor clothes. The room smelt of damp wool and unwashed bodies, but Gillis was far too intent to notice. He put his ear against the wall and listened. He heard Baird say, "You can come to Red River Basin. That's where I'm going. Have you forgotten? There's half a million or more to be picked up there, and it's where Olin can't get at us. What do you care about this lousy club if you can get your hands on money like that?"

Gillis held his breath so he could hear better. There was a set, hard smile on his mouth now. Already he had forgotten about Peggy and the way she had insulted him. If the little fool hadn't made the scene he wouldn't be listening to this conversation now.

"It'll turn out to be another of your bright ideas," he heard Rico say, his voice unsteady. "How do I know I shan't get into a worse jam?"

"You couldn't be in a worse jam," Baird returned. "Get moving. Collect all the dough you can lay hands on, and make it fast."

Gillis heard Rico leave the room and go down the passage in a stumbling run. What had happened? he wondered, puzzled. Why had they suddenly decided to leave for Red River Basin in such a hurry? He hadn't been wrong about Baird. Baird was going to gyp Kile if he could. He knew neither Rico nor Baird could hope to handle the jewellery. They would wait until Kile got the money. That's when they'd act. Well, he was ready for them.

But why rush off like this? What did Baird mean when he said Rico couldn't be in a worse jam?

He opened the door and moved cautiously into the passage. He edged his way along the passage to the rear exit and peered into the alley. Immediately facing him was a dark blue Packard. A man in a white coat and peak cap was standing near by. Gillis dodged back and shut the door. He heard Rico coming along the passage. He darted into Zoe's dressing-room and pushed the door to.

The telephone bell rang in Rico's office, and Gillis cursed himself for leaving the waiters' changing-room. Where he was he couldn't hear what was being said. There was a slight delay, then Rico's door opened, and he heard Rico say frantically, "Leaving all this! I'll be ruined ..."

Baird came out of the office, carrying a suitcase. He went to the rear exit, and leaving the door wide open, climbed into the Packard.

A moment later Rico came blundering after him, struggling into his overcoat.

As the Packard started up, Gillis moved swiftly to the open door and stepped into the alley. He was in time to see the Packard shoot into the main street.

"Anything you want, sir?" the parking attendant asked suspiciously.

Gillis ignored him. He ran to the end of the alley and looked after the swiftly moving Packard. From across the road he heard a car start up, and he looked in its direction. He saw a dusty Lincoln pull out dangerously into the thinning traffic. It went after the Packard, cutting in front of other drivers, causing them to swerve and sound their horns. Gillis caught sight of a big fleshy man at the wheel, and he stared after him thoughtfully.

The man in the Lincoln worried him. Was he a policeman? Gillis thought that was unlikely. Policemen usually hunted in pairs. Then who was he? What was he doing, tailing Baird?

He crossed the street and went into the bar. The barman knew him and nodded to him.

"A Scotch, Jack," Gillis said, leaning against the bar. When the barman put the drink in front of him, Gillis went on, "Seen a big fat guy in here? He was wearing a dark green leisure jacket and a brown hat."

The barman nodded.

"Yeah, I've seen him. It's my bet he's a shamus. He's been watching the club for the last hour. Another guy joined him a while back, and they went out together. The fat fella sat in his car and went on watching the club, the other one went into the club."

Gillis finished his whisky and slid a five-dollar bill across the counter.

"Hang on to the change," he said. "What was the other guy like?"

"Tall, lanky, with a crew haircut."

Dallas!

"Thanks, Jack," Gillis said, and pushed himself away from the bar. For the first time since he started on this business he felt uneasy. If Dallas was watching him – how much had he found out?

He stood hesitating for a moment, then walked quickly to a pay booth and shut himself in.

VII

Rico sat huddled up, staring miserably at the two pools of light from the headlamps that raced ahead of the Packard. He was sure now he had seen the last of the Frou-Frou Club and the future yawned before him as a dark, menacing chasm. If Baird didn't pull this job off, he would have to start all over again. Baird had nothing to lose, but it was different for him: he had established himself; he was a man of substance. He was leaving behind him a flourishing business, a newly furnished apartment, a wardrobe full of clothes, and a Buick. He must have been out of his mind to have got himself in a jam like this.

Baird said, "In another fifteen miles we'll be across the State line. We can get an air taxi from Lincoln Falls to Shreveport. If we get the breaks we should be in Red River Basin by tomorrow night."

Rico didn't say anything. He thrust his hands in his coat pockets and huddled further down in his seat. Rain beat against the windshield and drummed on the roof of the car. There was very little traffic on the highway, and Baird kept up a fast speed.

"Getting this guy Hater out of the swamp isn't going to be a picnic," Baird went on, "but it can be done. I've fixed a boat. As soon as we get over the State line you'd better get Kile on the phone and let him know what we're doing."

"If this doesn't come off ..." Rico groaned.

"It's got to come off!"

"Even if Kile pays us when we hand over Hater, how are we to get hold of the pay-off when Kile collects it? He'll probably get it at his house. What can we do if he does? We can't show our faces in town. How shall we know when he does collect the dough?"

"What makes you think we can't go back there?" Baird asked indifferently. "Olin wouldn't scare me away from any town."

Rico began to sweat.

"We'll walk into a trap if we go back," he said, sitting upright and staring hard at Baird.

"If you want the dough you'll have to go back. There's no other way of getting it. That's a risk we'll have to run. When Kile takes delivery of Hater we can't afford to let him out of our sight for a second!"

Rico groaned.

"I wish I'd never touched this," he said in despair. "It's ruined me."

"You can quit any time you like," Baird said. "If you don't want your share, say so: all the more for me."

Rico lapsed in moody silence. He sat still staring at the broad black ribbon of the road as it fled under the wheels of the Packard.

Every now and then Baird glanced into his rear mirror. The two distant headlights he could see puzzled him. There was a car behind him that had kept a hundred yards or so in his rear ever since he had struck the highway. He didn't think anyone was tailing him, but he couldn't afford to take chances. It couldn't be the cops. They wouldn't hang behind like this. They'd overtake and force him to stop. Who else could it be? One of the International operators? That was possible, and his thin lips set in a hard line.

"There's a car behind us I don't like the look of," he said, giving Rico a nudge with his elbow. "Keep an eye on it. I'm going to try and shake it."

Rico caught his breath in alarm and screwed around, staring at the two blobs of light that hung steadily in the rear.

Baird gradually increased pressure on the gas pedal. Slowly the car began to build up speed. From sixty miles an hour the speedometer needle crept up to seventy.

"He's still there," Rico said.

Baird was afraid to drive too fast in the pouring rain. The surface of the road was treacherous, and he had no intentions of having a smash-up at this stage of the game.

"Okay," he said. "We'll stop and see what he does."

Gradually he slowed down the Packard.

"He's slowing down too," Rico said in alarm.

Baird swung on the grass verge and brought the Packard to a standstill.

They both watched the headlights of the approaching car. The driver appeared to hesitate, then increased speed and went past them. Baird caught a glimpse of a big man at the driving wheel of a Lincoln.

Baird lit a cigarette.

"We'll let him get well ahead," he said. "Maybe he wasn't following us, but I'm not taking any chances."

"We're not over the State line yet," Rico said uneasily. "We'd better get on."

Baird grunted. There was some sense in that. He started the car engine and drove along the highway at a steady forty miles an hour.

There was no sign now of the other car's tail lights. A mile or so up the road, Baird spotted a side turning.

"Maybe he's turned off," he said. "I'll get moving again."

He increased his speed and continued along the broad Highway.

"Keep a lookout behind," he told Rico. "Just in case he's foxing."

Rico couldn't see any light, and he remained, screwed around, watching the darkness through the rear mirror. After several miles, he said sharply, "A car behind."

"Same one?"

"I don't know. It's about a quarter of a mile back."

Swearing softly, Baird trod on the gas pedal. The Packard surged forward. He held it steady at seventy miles an hour, but they didn't lose the following car. Another couple of miles took them across the State line. Ahead of them lay the little town of Brentwood; beyond Brentwood, another thirty miles along the highway, was Lincoln Falls.

Brentwood was in darkness as Baird drove along the main street. It was now a little after two o'clock. At the far end of the street he saw the lights of a solitary all-night café.

"Maybe they have a phone here," he said, slowing down. "Get Kile and tell him we should have Hater out in three days. Tell him to bring the dough to that place of his."

He pulled up a few yards from the café, parking the car in the shadows.

As Rico got out of the car, they both looked back along the main street. There was no sign of the following car.

"Maybe he's turned off his headlights and is coming the rest of the way on foot," Baird said, and his hand slid inside his coat and closed around the butt of the Colt. "You fix Kile. Tell him to make sure he isn't being tailed. Tell him about Dallas. He's got to be certain no one's tailing him when he comes to collect Hater. I'll fix this guy. You get going."

Baird watched Rico enter the café, then he moved silently away from the Packard and took up a position in a dark doorway, where he had a clear view of the street. He waited some minutes before his sharp ears told him someone was coming. He looked towards the sound, but couldn't see any movement. Out of the darkness came a soft scrape of shoe leather on rough ground, then he caught sight of a dark shape by the Packard.

This shamus knew his job, he thought grudgingly. He had sneaked up to within thirty yards of Baird without Baird spotting him.

Baird didn't move. The dark, shadowy figure crept up to the Packard, satisfied himself there was no one in it, and moved silently into the light coming from the café. Baird saw the big, fleshy man who had been following him in the Lincoln.

MacAdam was jumpy. He remembered what had happened to Burns, but he had to find out what these two were up to. He knew the risk he was taking. This might be a trap, but with any luck he might have fooled them into thinking they had lost him. He moved forward to peer through the café window. Apart from an elderly man lounging behind the counter, the café appeared to be empty, then MacAdam spotted Rico in a pay booth. There was no sign of Baird, and realizing Baird could very easily be out there somewhere in the darkness, he looked quickly over his shoulder.

Baird was right behind him: the big Colt steady in his hand.

"Get your hands up," Baird said softly. "One false move'll be your last."

MacAdam raised his hands.

"What's the trouble?" he asked. "I was just going in there ..."

"Shut up!" Baird said. "You don't fool me. You've been tailing me since we left town."

"You're crazy!" MacAdam said. "Now look ..."

"Get over to my car and snap it up!" Baird said, moving forward.

MacAdam backed towards the Packard.

Rico came hurrying out of the café. He stopped short when he saw MacAdam and his knees wilted.

"Come on! Come on!" Baird said sharply. "Frisk him. He'll be carrying a gun."

Rico ran his hands over MacAdam as if he were handling a snake. He took from the shoulder holster a .38 police special.

"Get his wallet," Baird went on.

Rico found the wallet, opened it and found MacAdam's buzzer and licence.

"A shamus," he said bitterly.

"Yeah," Baird said. "Okay, brother, do what you're told and you won't get hurt. This is where we part company. Where's your car?"

"At the end of the street," MacAdam said.

"Let's take a look at it," Baird said. "Get going!"

MacAdam walked stiffly down the dark street with Baird at his heels. Rico remained with the Packard. When they reached the Lincoln Baird said, "Open the hood and give me the rotor arm. This is as far as you go."

MacAdam leaned forward and reached for the hood catch.

Baird set himself. He brought the gun butt down on MacAdam's skull, driving him to his knees. He hit him again, then kicked his unconscious body out of his way, lifted the hood and removed the rotor arm.

He left the hood open and MacAdam lying half under the car, and ran back to the Packard.

"That's fixed him," he said, as he slid under the driving wheel. "It'll take him a week to get over that smack. Get Kile?"

Rico nodded miserably. All this violence horrified him, but he was too scared of Baird to protest.

"He said he'll be at the lodge the day after tomorrow with the dough."

"He'll get a slug in the gut if he tries anything funny," Baird said, starting the car. "Did you tell him to watch out for a tail?"

"Yes. He didn't seem to like it."

"He's not supposed to," Baird grunted, and sent the car racing along the highway. After a while he went on, "This isn't going to be a picnic. By the time we've got Hater we'll have carried every nickel of that half million. This may be a fast buck, but don't kid yourself we're not going to earn it."

Rico, who had no idea what was ahead of him, huddled down in his seat and said nothing.

VIII

There was a drag to Dallas' step as he walked up the rose-lined path to Purvis' front door. Before he could ring the bell, the door jerked open and Purvis waved him in.

"I was hoping you'd come," Purvis said, as he led the way into his study. "Did you find the girl?"

Dallas flopped down in an easy chair.

"If you haven't got a drink in this hole, for the love of Mike give me some coffee," he said. "I'm about dead on my feet."

Purvis gave him a sharp look and went over to an electric percolator. He poured two cups of coffee and brought them across the room. He gave Dallas a cup, hesitated, then went to a cupboard and produced a bottle of brandy.

"This any good to you?" he asked, a little reluctantly.

"Sure," Dallas said, and poured a liberal shot into his coffee. He put the bottle down by his chair, out of Purvis' reach. He drank some coffee, sighed and poured more brandy into the cup.

"Did you find the girl?" Purvis repeated, as he sat down.

"Baird and Rico kidnapped her," Dallas said in a flat, cold voice. "They took her to a warehouse out at Pinder's End and burned her with matches. Then they shot her through the head and chucked her into the river. I got Olin on the job, and the River Police fished her out about forty minutes ago."

Purvis breathed heavily. His thin, pale face tightened.

"That's bad," he said. "Sure it was Baird?"

"Yeah. The cops couldn't find the slug, and he hadn't left a clue behind him, but I saw him and Rico on the spot a minute or so after the shooting."

"His word against yours."

"No. I took a shot at the car; smashed the rear window. Olin's found the car about a mile from the club. If Olin gets either of them, he'll make them talk."

"Does he think he can pin it on them?"

"It's a cinch if he knew what the motive was," Dallas said, looking straight at Purvis.

"And what's that?"

"Zoe slipped up somewhere. Maybe they caught her listening outside the door. I'm not kidding myself they don't know the set-up now. You should have seen the way the bastards burned her."

Purvis stroked his nose.

"We paid her well," he said uneasily, "but she didn't deserve that."

"That's pretty white of you," Dallas said heatedly. "This wouldn't have happened to her if we had told Olin what we are doing. He'd have had Baird in jail by now."

"That's a lot of hooey," Purvis said. "Olin's got nothing on Baird. I know you're feeling sore about the girl, but you can't talk like that. If you felt like that about her, you shouldn't have put her out on a limb."

"So it's my fault?" Dallas said, his face white and strained.

"It's certainly not mine. I didn't suggest paying her three hundred dollars."

Dallas didn't say anything. He ran his fingers through his hair and grimaced. He was feeling bad about Zoe.

"What's Ainsworth doing?" Purvis asked, after a short pause.

Dallas drank more coffee, and as he fumbled for a cigarette, he said, "He's watching Kile. At the moment we've lost Baird, Rico and Gillis. When I got to the club with Olin, Baird and Rico had skipped. There was no sign of Gillis. I tried to find MacAdam, but his car had gone. I'm hoping he went after Gillis. Olin took the club to pieces, but we didn't find anything. That guy, Luigi, Rico's Captain of waiters, talked after Olin got tough with him. He told Olin both Rico and Baird had returned to the club about forty minutes before we got there. Rico said he had to leave town in a hurry. He collected all the cash he could lay his hands on, and went off with Baird in a dark blue Packard. No one knows where he was going. Olin's thrown out a dragnet, but so far the car hasn't been seen. While this was going on, I searched around for MacAdam. As soon as Ainsworth reported to me, I sent him down to watch Kile. If Kile slips through our fingers, we've lost the lot of them."

"I imagine Baird and Rico have gone to Shreveport," Purvis said thoughtfully. "I think the balloon's about to go up."

"Yeah," Dallas said. "Think we should tell Olin what's cooking? He could set a trap for Baird."

"Red River's not in his territory. By the time he got any action, Baird would be miles away. Besides, we're losing sight of our objective: we want Baird to take us to the jewels. If Olin barges in now, we're back where we started."

"I don't like it," Dallas said. "The casualties are mounting up. First Burns, now Zoe: maybe it'll be me next."

Purvis didn't look particularly worried.

"I've been working fifteen years on this case," he said. "I'm in sight of pulling it off. I'm not going to bring Olin in to mess it up now."

Dallas shrugged. He felt too tired to argue. He stared down at his feet, brooding.

Rain continued to patter against the window. A car came grinding up the hill towards Purvis' house. Both Purvis and Dallas listened to the sound of the labouring engine. They looked at each other questioningly. The car came nearer, then passed the house and went on up the hill. Both men relaxed again. Then the telephone bell started to ring. Dallas jumped a little and spilt some of his coffee.

Purvis picked up the receiver. He said, "Yes, speaking." He sat still, his face expressionless, his long, bony fingers tapping a tune on the arm of his chair. After a while he said, "Okay, and thanks. I'll be down in the morning. Brentwood hospital? Yeah, I know how to get there. It's before you get to Lincoln Falls. Yeah, sure." He hung up.

"Who's dead now?" Dallas asked, his hands turning into fists.

"MacAdam's been found with a fractured skull," Purvis said slowly. He didn't look at Dallas. "He was picked up in Brentwood's main street."

Dallas stubbed out his cigarette.

"How is he?"

"He'll be all right," Purvis said. "Be some time before he gets around again, but he's not in danger."

"That's swell," Dallas said sarcastically. "Just a fractured skull. Nothing worse than a slight headache. Baird again, eh?"

"I guess so. A man answering to Rico's description used the telephone in a café in Brentwood around two o'clock. A little while later MacAdam was found about a couple of hundred yards from the café. At least we now know they're heading for Red River. There's an airfield at Lincoln Falls. They could get a plane to Shreveport from there."

Dallas got slowly to his feet.

"I'd better get over to Kile's place. If we let him slip through our fingers, we're sunk."

"Rico could have been phoning Kile," Purvis said thoughtfully. "Looks as if they're on their way to get Hater out."

"I can't imagine they're going to Red River to look at the alligators," Dallas said sarcastically. "I'm glad I haven't a wife and children. This job's getting dangerous."

Purvis saw him to the door, and then returned to his study. He listened to Dallas' car start up. He remained standing, his face expressionless, his eyes thoughtful long after the sound of Dallas' car had died away.

PART FOUR

The slow-moving, mud-coloured Red River wound through a dense undergrowth of sawgrass, duckweed and sagittaria. The great naked roots of the mangrove trees, anchored in the mud flats, gave the impression of a forest on stilts. An oppressive, tropical heat hung over the river. The only sound Rico could hear was the thump, thump of a diesel engine a long way away, pounding out a monotonous rhythm.

Rico wiped the sweat out of his eyes. He was sitting in the prow of a flat-bottomed boat that seemed to him to be horribly fragile, and likely to tip over if he moved.

Baird sat in the stern and paddled the boat through the slow-moving water, keeping close to the bank. The Thompson gun, loaded and cocked, lay at his feet. His pale eyes scanned both sides of the bank as they moved slowly upstream.

"Hear that noise?" he said suddenly. "That's the dredge. It's farther away than it sounds. That's where Hater is."

Rico hunched his shoulders. Mosquitoes droned above his head. He was afraid to flap his hands at them in case he upset the boat.

"What a hole!" he said, looking at the tall sawgrass on either side of the bank. "How can we hope to make a path through that stuff? How the hell are we going to get him away?"

"We haven't got him yet," Baird said. "Keep your voice down. Sounds carry a long way across water."

Rico grunted and lapsed into silence. As the boat moved slowly up the river, taking him farther into the dense undergrowth and away from civilization, he regretted still more getting himself mixed up in this crazy, dangerous business.

He noticed a big log of wood, like a tree trunk, floating motionless in the water. Baird suddenly swung the boat's nose away from it, and slightly increased his speed.

"Don't wake that guy up," he said. "That's an alligator."

Rico felt suddenly sick. He gripped the sides of the boat as he stared at the black object that was now in their rear.

"An alligator?" he repeated hoarsely. "You sure?"

"Yeah. This river's lousy with them," Baird said indifferently. 'They'll leave you alone if you leave them alone. It's crocodiles you have to watch. They'll charge you on sight."

Rico gulped.

"Any around here?"

"Not likely," Baird said. "Farther south you might find some, but not here, I guess."

A big bird rose out of the sawgrass with a tremendous flapping of wings, and climbed above Rico's head, making him start violently. The boat rocked, and Baird cursed him.

"Sit still, can't you?" he snarled. "Do you want to have us over?"

A hundred yards farther on Baird swung the nose of the boat towards the shore.

"That is it," he said. "Mind how you get out. The ground's like glue along the bank."

The nose of the boat rammed the bank and sank into it.

"Get hold of the boat and steady it," Baird said.

Rico got out awkwardly. His foot sank up to his ankle in the soft ground. Miserably he held the boat steady while Baird threw their suitcases on to the bank, and then worked his way aft and joined him.

"Most of the ground near the shore's like this," Baird said, hauling the boat into the sawgrass and picking up the Thompson and his suitcase. "Mind you don't lose a shoe. This stuff pulls like hell."

He began to walk through the high grass, forcing a passage, pulling one foot after the other out of the swampy ground.

Rico followed as best he could. He felt he was walking through a sea of molasses, and after he had gone a few yards he had sweated right through his clothes.

Baird seemed indifferent to the conditions. He kept on until he reached higher ground, then paused until Rico came panting up.

"It's okay here," he said. "It's only by the water it's so soft. Come on, let's get under cover before these goddamn mosquitoes eat us alive."

Rico followed him along a path bordered each side by dense thickets of custard apple. He could hear the steady pounding of the dredging machine distinctly now. It sounded close.

After walking some distance through the thicket, they came upon a small wooden cabin in what had once been a clearing, but which was now almost overgrown. Big cypress trees obscured the light around the cabin, but Rico was thankful to be out of the direct sunlight that had been scorching him during the trip up river.

"This is it," Baird said, pushing open the cabin door. "Not much of a place, but it'll do. I found it when I came down to look over the ground. I've fixed it up pretty well. There're mosquito nets, food and all the stuff we want for a couple of days. Come on in and take a look."

Rico entered the cabin and looked around the one big room.

"Doesn't anyone come here?" he asked uneasily.

Baird shook his head.

"No. Used to belong to the overseer of the dredging gang, but now they've moved up the river, he's got another place. Noddy said he'd keep an eye on the stuff I left here." Baird went over to a pile of canned food, two wooden cases, blankets and mosquito netting stacked in a corner. "It seems to be all here."

"Noddy?" Rico repeated. "Who's he?"

Baird pulled a blanket from the pile, tossed it on the floor and sat down on it.

"The guy who's helping us," he said, looking at Rico, his pale eyes expressionless. "Can't do the job without inside help."

Rico got himself a blanket and sat down. His head ached from the heat, and his feet felt too big for his shoes. He pulled off his shoes with a grunt of relief, and sat back against the wall, wiping the sweat from his face. Roughing it in a swamp wasn't his idea of enjoying life, and he thought wistfully of the quiet and luxury of his apartment, the ice drinks and an understanding woman to amuse him. He would gladly have given up his share of the half million if he could turn the clock back and pick up his life again before Zoe died.

"Noddy," he said, looking questioningly at Baird. "Who is he? Can we trust him?"

"We've got to trust him," Baird said curtly. "We can't pull this without him. He's one of the guys working the dredge. The gang is made up of three experts who direct the dredging operations, five guys who handle the dredge. Noddy's one of them. Then there're around fifty convicts handling the truck and bulldozers, and doing the dirty work. There're five guards on duty the whole time; armed with automatic rifles and a bunch of trained dogs." He stretched and yawned, went on, "I met Noddy in Astora. He goes in there every week for supplies. We got talking. He agreed to help get Hater out."

"What are you paying him?" Rico asked suspiciously.

"Five grand," Baird said. "Half tonight when he comes here to go over the plan, and half when we've got Hater."

"Five grand?" Rico repeated, staring. "Now, wait a minute ... five grand! That'll come out of our share."

"What's the matter with you?" Baird said. "How do you imagine we can get Hater without inside help?" He grinned slyly at Rico. "Maybe he won't collect the dough. He might run into trouble. This job's not going to be a picnic."

He got up and began to prepare a meal. Rico sat watching him, brooding. He was surprised to see how efficient Baird was. He had a meal cooked on a small primus stove in a very short time. After Rico had eaten and washed the meal down with several whiskies, he felt less worried.

They sat outside the cabin, smoking, until the light began to fade, then Baird lit a paraffin lamp and put it in the window, and they made themselves as comfortable as they could on the blankets and waited for Noddy to show up.

He came when it was dark. They saw the beam of his flashlight some time before he reached the cabin. He pushed open the door and came in: a tall, thin man with a pinched, sallow face, lank black hair and stubble on his chin. He was wearing soiled duck trousers and a singlet, and carried a .45 Smith and Wesson in a pistol holster at his hip. A battered panama hat rested at the back of his head.

Rico didn't like the look of him. Not a man to be trusted, he thought uneasily: like a ferret.

"So you got here," Noddy said, closing the door. "I've been in two or three times. No one's been near."

Baird waved his hand to Rico.

"This is Ralph Rico. He's working with me."

Noddy gave Rico a sharp, inquisitive stare, and then came and sat down on the blanket. They lit cigarettes, and no one spoke until Baird had poured out three whiskies.

"Hater okay?" Baird asked abruptly.

"Sure. The guy's nuts, but he's harmless," Noddy said indifferently. "Keeps to himself. I don't reckon he ever opens his mouth. The other guys hate him."

"What's the matter with him?" Rico asked.

"Stir-crazy, I guess," Noddy said. "Been in too long. He's got something on his mind. You might have trouble with him." He paused to take a long pull at his glass, went on, "You didn't make it clear why you wanted him." He was looking at Baird. "Or ain't it my business?"

"That's right," Baird said, and yawned. "Five grand should take care of your curiosity."

"It does," Noddy said, grinning. "I plan to buy me a turkey farm. I'm about sick to the guts working in this goddamn swamp. Five grand'll be a life saver."

"Make sure you earn it," Baird said softly.

"Sure," Noddy said carelessly, but his eyes went shifty. "When does the balloon go up?"

"Tomorrow, midday," Baird said. "Let's get this straight. Each of us has his own special job: I take care of the guards.

Rico creates a diversion. You grab Hater and bring him to us. Okay?"

"Sure," Noddy said. "That's the way it was arranged."

"What diversion?" Rico said, alarmed.

"Smoke bombs," Baird said. "All you have to do is to toss the bombs at the big dredge. As soon as we have a blanket of smoke you make your way back here. Noddy and I will join up and bring Hater here. Noddy goes back to the dredge with his dough. You and I and Hater will take the boat and get the hell out of it. That's the set-up."

Rico immediately saw a number of snags to this. How could he be sure Baird and Noddy would come to the cabin? Suppose they planned to double-cross him? They could make for the boat and leave him to get out the best way he could. Suppose Hater resisted? How could they hope to control a struggling man in such a frail boat?

"How far do you think we'll get if they come after us?" he asked, looking uneasily at Baird.

"We don't reckon they'll come after us. That's why we're coming back here," Baird said. "If you do your job right, there'll be a heavy smokescreen that'll blanket out everyone in sight. I reckon all the convicts will make a break. I'm relying on it. They're certain to stampede. There are only three routes out of the swamp if you haven't got a boat. These guys won't have boats. They'll make for the three routes in small parties. The guards and the dogs will know they must be going by the paths and not by the river. We'll come here to give the guards time to take to the paths, then we go down to the boat and get clear."

Rico looked a little less uneasy.

"But if Hater resists? He'll upset the boat."

Baird looked at him steadily, his pale eyes gleaming.

"He won't be given the chance to resist. I'll handle him."

Noddy said, "He won't be hard to handle. He ain't got the strength of a mouse. When I've got him where do I find you?"

"About seventy yards from where you're working there's a big oak. I'll be up in that where I can get a clear view of the guards," Baird said. "As soon as the smoke gets going I'll come down. Meet me there. We'll take Hater along the path, then through the thickets to here. I'll pay you off. Rico and me will take over Hater, and you'll get back the way you came. If you're spotted, you were going after one of the convicts, but he got away. Stall them so we can get clear. Okay?"

"Sure," Noddy said, and rubbed his sweating hands on his knees. "I guess that takes care of it. At twelve tomorrow?"

"Yeah," Baird said. "Hater will be where you can get to him?"

"He's working on my shift. I won't make a move until the smoke starts. Then I'll grab him as if I thought he was trying to escape. As soon as the smoke gets thick I'll rush him to you. You'll have to handle him after that."

"If he gets tough, clip him and carry him. Think you can do it?"

Noddy grinned, showing tobacco-stained teeth.

"For five grand I could push over the Woolworth building," he said. "I'll get him to you if I have to take him on my back."

"Right," Baird said. "I guess I owe you some dough."

Noddy's eyes glistened.

"That was the arrangement."

"Give him twenty-five Cs," Baird said to Rico. "You'll get the rest tomorrow."

Reluctantly, Rico went to his suitcase, opened it and counted out the money. He handed it to Noddy, who checked it, his breath whistling through his nostrils with suppressed excitement.

"Gee! I've never seen so much dough all in one heap," he said, stuffing the money in his hip pocket. He patted the bulge, grinning. "There lies half a turkey farm."

Baird lit a cigarette. He held the flame of the match so it lit up his face. His eyes were like stones, and his expression menacing.

"Maybe I'd better warn you not to try any tricks with me," he said softly. "Make sure you pull this job off or you won't be interested in even half a turkey farm."

Noddy flinched from the implied threat, but he managed an uneasy laugh.

"Sure, sure," he said. "You can rely on me. You'll have Hater by tomorrow morning."

When he had gone, Rico said uneasily, "I don't trust that guy."

Baird was settling down for the night. He pulled a blanket over him as he glanced up to stare at Rico.

"What makes you think I do?" he said curtly, and turned out the lamp.

II

From his lofty perch in the oak tree, Baird had a clear view of the large dipper dredge, operating a steam shovel that deposited its load in a waiting truck, parked on the concrete path constructed along the bank. Fifty yards farther upstream was a hydraulic dredge, driven by a diesel engine, that was removing the far side grass bank, widening the river.

Baird sat astride a thick branch, his back braced against the trunk, some thirty feet above ground. Across his knees lay a .22 Winchester repeater, fitted with a telescopic sight and silencer. He was wearing a loose jacket and trousers of green and yellow camouflage: the kind of kit the US Army issued for jungle fighting. He had smeared burnt cork over his face. No one looking up at the tree, even with the aid of field glasses, could spot him.

Below him, also astride a branch and similarly dressed, Rico sat and sweated. Slung over his shoulder was a canvas sack which contained a dozen smoke bombs Baird had given him.

They could see the convicts working in the blazing sunshine, manhandling the mud as it poured from the steam shovel into the trucks; sweat poured off them as they toiled. They worked stripped to the waist; old, battered straw hats shielded their shaven heads from the sun.

Baird surveyed the scene through a powerful pair of glasses. Up to now he had counted three guards, and was trying to locate the other two. Two of the guards were on the bridge house of the dipper dredge. One of them had an automatic rifle under his arm; the other appeared to have only a pistol at his hip. The third guard walked slowly up and down on the narrow deck of the hydraulic dredge. He was armed with an automatic rifle and a .45 Smith and Wesson.

Baird shifted his glasses to a building made of logs and thatched with sawgrass that stood in a clearing away from the bank. He spotted another guard sitting in the shade, astride a Browning machine-gun, covering the road that led out of the swamp.

The machine-gun startled Baird. Noddy hadn't said anything about a machine-gun.

"Take a look at that guy in front of the hut," he said in a low voice to Rico. "He's the one I've got to take care of."

Rico raised his glasses and nearly dropped them when he saw the Browning.

"He goes first," Baird went on. "There should be one more guard, but I can't spot him. What's the time?"

"Six minutes to twelve," Rico said, through dry lips.

Baird grunted. He began to search the bush with his glasses, but he couldn't spot the fifth guard.

"Maybe he's in the hut or somewhere with the dogs," he said, slipping the glasses into their case. He raised the Winchester and squinted through the telescopic sight. "I wish I'd had a little more practice with this gun," he muttered under his breath. He cradled the barrel in a fork of a branch. After shifting the gun a little he got the guard's head in the exact centre of the crosspiece in the sight. He grunted, satisfied, and lowered the gun. "Seen Noddy?"

"He's by the truck with the red disc on it," Rico said, looking through his glasses. "That must be Hater near him."

Baird took his glasses from the case and focused them on the truck. He spotted Noddy, standing by the truck, a cigarette in his mouth. His battered panama hat shielded his face, but Baird recognized him by his pigeon chest and tall, stooping figure.

Hater was shovelling liquid mud off the steam shovel into the truck. He was standing up to his knees in the heavy wet muck, and Baird recognized him immediately by his balding head and beetling eyebrows. He was the only convict in the gang who was bareheaded. He worked slowly and listlessly, stripped to the waist, his emaciated body burned brown by the sun.

"That's Hater," Baird said, nodding. "You'd better get down now and take up your position. Lob the first bomb on to the deck of the big dredge. Make sure every bomb you throw falls on something hard. They won't go off if they hit mud."

Rico muttered something. Sweat ran into his eyes, making them smart. He was trembling so badly he was afraid to let go of the branch he was clinging to.

"Make a job of it," Baird went on, watching him. "If you throw them high in the air, they won't spot where they're coming from." He looked at his watch. "Get going. We've got half a minute to twelve."

Rico began to climb down the tree. His breath was laboured, and once or twice he had to stop while he tried to control his trembling. Baird watched him, his face set.

"Get on with it!" he snarled. "What are you scared about? Nothing's going to happen to you."

Rico finally reached the ground. He leaned against the tree trunk, his legs buckling under him, then he made an effort, and began to move forward, completely screened by the tall sawgrass.

From his perch Baird could watch his progress through the bush, but the guard on the bridge of the dredge was not in a high enough position to see him. From time to time Rico stopped and looked up at Baird to get his direction. Baird waved him on, and he turned and continued through the sawgrass, stumbling over the swampy ground until he was within thirty yards of the big dredge. Baird signalled him to slow down. He focused his glasses on Rico's face.

"The little rat's nearly dead with fright," he muttered to himself. "If he falls down on this, we're all sunk."

Rico again looked over his shoulder. Baird made a signal telling him to go on more slowly still. Another ten yards brought Rico to the edge of the sawgrass. He could see the bridge of the dredge now, and he hurriedly ducked back, dropping on one knee.

He and Baird had rehearsed what he had to do again and again during the morning. He had to remain just out of sight until Baird gave him the signal to throw the bombs. He opened the canvas sack and took out one of the bombs. It immediately became slippery in his sweating hands and he put it back and wiped his hands on his handkerchief.

He looked up at Baird. He had to stare for some seconds before he could see him. Baird was aiming the Winchester now, covering the guard at the machine-gun.

Baird felt completely impersonal as he squinted through the telescopic sights at the guard. The big, fat, red-faced man he could see in the sights was no more human to him than the close-up of a movie star on a cinema screen. Baird thumbed back the bolt, steadied the rifle and drew in a long, slow breath. The sights of the rifle were as if fixed to the guard's head. It wasn't a difficult shot: fifty yards, probably a little more, but everything depended on it. If he missed, the cat would be out of the bag, and the whole set-up ruined. His finger began to squeeze the trigger. The guard sat motionless. He seemed half asleep. His hands rested on his knees, his head was lowered. Slowly and steadily Baird continued to put pressure on the trigger: then suddenly the gun went off: making a sharp plopping sound which was drowned by the steady thump-thump-thump of the diesel engine.

The guard slumped forward very slowly over the machine-gun, as if he had fallen asleep. His hat fell off and rolled away in the dust. His head rested on the barrel of the gun, and blood ran from his right ear in a quick, steady stream on to his trouser cuff and shoe.

Baird looked quickly at the dredge. Neither of the guards was looking towards the hut; neither of them appeared to have noticed that anything had happened.

Baird signalled to Rico. He watched Rico take a bomb from the sack. Rico seemed to be having difficulty in holding it, and it nearly slipped out of his hand. Baird held his breath as he watched Rico set himself and toss the bomb high up in the air. It was a wild, panicky throw, and Baird could see it was going to be wide and short of the dredge, and he cursed.

He watched the flight of the bomb. It seemed to hang in the hot, still air, sharply outlined against the blue sky. Neither of the guards noticed it, but out of the corner of his eye Baird saw Noddy had stiffened and was watching the bomb as it fell.

It landed with a loud splash in the river. Immediately both guards looked in the direction of the sound. The one with the automatic rifle swung up the rifle, looking for something to shoot at. They both stared at the circle of ripples forming on the still water of the river. Then one of them looked across at the hut. He stared, shading his eyes, then pulled out a pair of field glasses from a case slung around his neck and lifted them to his eyes.

Baird signalled frantically to Rico to throw more bombs, but Rico's nerve had gone. He crouched down in the swampy mud, bunching his shoulders, waiting for the shooting to start.

Baird's waving hand attracted the attention of the guard with the automatic rifle. He threw the rifle up to his shoulder. Baird saw him in the nick of time, and fell forward on to the branch, nearly losing his Winchester as he did so.

The automatic rifle cracked three times. Slugs hummed dangerously close to Baird.

Realizing no one was shooting at him, Rico managed to get to his feet. Feverishly he began to lob bombs towards the dredge, not looking where they were falling. It was entirely due to luck that two of them landed on the deck of the dredge. They burst, throwing out a mass of white smoke that enveloped the deck and the bridge before the guard could fire a fourth time.

A siren started up.

The guard on the hydraulic dredge began to shoot into the sawgrass.

Two men in white duck trousers and singlets appeared on the bridge of the smaller deck, revolvers in hand. They began to shoot at the oak tree as Baird slithered down it. A slug passed so close to his face he felt a burning sensation against his cheek. He let go of the branch he was clinging to and dropped heavily to the ground.

He ran through the sawgrass towards Rico. The three men on the small dredge could see the top of the grass sway violently as Baird forced his way through it, and they concentrated their fire on the moving grass.

Slugs hummed past Baird. He kept on, expecting to be hit at any second, his face set and hard, his breath whistling through his open mouth.

He came upon Rico, crouching in the mud, holding his hands over his head.

"Get up, you yellow sonofabitch!" Baird snarled, and kicked Rico to his feet. "Give me those bombs!" He snatched the sack from Rico, dropped the Winchester, jerked out his Colt and moved towards the bank where he could get a view of the small dredge.

Cautiously he reached the edge of the sawgrass and lay flat, looking towards the dredge. He could see the guard standing on the deck, his rifle thrust forward, staring uncertainly ahead. Baird lifted the .45 and shot the guard through the head. The guard sprang into the air and fell with a splash into the water. The automatic rifle hit the deck and went off.

Baird began to plaster the smaller dredge with smoke bombs. The scene before him was quickly blotted out in white smoke. He could hear a lot of shouting and rifle firing. The siren continued to scream its warning.

Grabbing Rico by his arm, Baird dragged him through the tall grass to the oak tree.

"Get back to the hut!" he said, "and hurry. If I don't join you in a quarter of an hour, I shan't be coming."

"What about the boat?" Rico panted. He looked as if he were going to faint. Sweat ran down his ashen face and his knees were buckling.

"Never mind the boat – get going!"

Baird gave him a shove that sent him reeling, then swung himself up on an overhanging branch of the oak tree and climbed just high enough to look over the sawgrass.

The two dredges and the trucks were wiped out by the mass of white smoke. The hut was still visible, and as Baird looked he saw a guard come running out of the smoke, pull the dead guard out of the way and sit astride the machine-gun.

Baird knew it was too long a shot for his Colt, but he thought he might drop a bomb near enough to make the gun useless.

He pulled a bomb from his pocket as the guard swivelled the Browning around on its mounting to cover the tree and that part of the swamp where Rico was.

Baird threw the bomb with all his great strength. As it whistled through the air, the guard opened up with the machine-gun. Splinters flew off the trunk of the tree ten feet above Baird's head. He saw the bomb drop on to the concrete path about fifteen feet from the gun and explode. He didn't wait to see what the result of the smoke would be. The hail of lead smashing through the leaves of the tree so close to him shook even his iron nerve, and he dropped to the ground.

The gun kept on for a second or so, then stopped. Away in the distance Baird could now hear the sharp barking of dogs. As he wiped the sweat from his face, he wondered if the convicts had made a break.

Where was Noddy? What the hell had he been doing while all this had been going on?

The sound of the siren was deafening. Baird knew it would warn the guards at the prison some five miles away that there was trouble at the river, and it wouldn't be long before reinforcements arrived.

Then he heard running feet and the sound of someone coming through the sawgrass. He got quickly behind the tree, his Colt ready, and waited.

Noddy and Hater came into the clearing. Noddy was pulling Hater along by his arm. Noddy looked scared. His eyes were bolting out of his head, and he was panting. Hater appeared to be dazed, and he let Noddy drag him along without protest.

Baird stepped out behind the tree.

Immediately Hater saw him, he seemed to come alive. He snatched his arm free from Noddy's grasp, spun around on his heel and darted back into the thick sawgrass.

Both Noddy and Baird were so startled they didn't move for a second. Then seeing Hater was escaping the way he had come, they both rushed forward, smashing their way through the bush, trying to head Hater off before he reached the smoke screen that was drifting towards them in the slight breeze that came off the river.

Baird was the first to overtake Hater. He grabbed at Hater's naked shoulder. Hater squirmed away from him, twisted to his right and ran slap into Noddy, who closed with him.

"What are you playing at?" Noddy panted as Hater began to struggle like a madman. If Baird hadn't grabbed his arm he would have broken loose again.

"Get his other arm," Baird snarled to Noddy. "Come on; if they come this way ..."

Feeling himself powerless to break free, Hater suddenly began to scream. The sound that came from his mouth was shrill, loud and horrifying. It was the sound of an animal caught in a trap. It made Baird's nerves creep. It did more than that to Noddy. It scared him so badly he let go of Hater and hurriedly stepped back.

Hater slashed at Baird's face with hooked fingernails. Baird managed to jerk his head aside and save his eyes, but the short, sharp nails ploughed down his cheek, leaving deep, bloody ruts in his flesh.

Baird let go of Hater, but as Hater turned to run, Baird jerked out his gun and hit Hater on the top of his balding head with the gun butt. He was careful not to hit hard. The force of the blow drove Hater to his knees. He began to scream again as he struggled desperately to get to his feet.

"Hit him! Hit him!" Noddy cried, unnerved. "Stop his noise!"

Baird hesitated. He felt a murderous urge to shoot Hater, and he had to struggle against emptying his gun into the brown, emaciated body. As he hesitated, Hater got to his feet and began to run unsteadily across the clearing towards the sawgrass.

Baird went after him, caught up with him in three long strides and spun him around.

Hater looked at him. His face was working with fear: the facial muscles, the thin skin over the bone structure moved like water disturbed by a sudden wind. The vacant, dark eyes glared horribly. The thin, cracked lips drew off his teeth in a snarl of defiance.

Baird brushed aside Hater's upraised arms as he stepped in close. The gun butt smashed down on Hater's bleeding scalp. Hater's eyes went blind. He gave a dry little groan and crumpled at Baird's feet.

Baird stepped back. Blood and sweat ran down his face. His eyes were a little wild, and he felt a sick uneasiness he had never known before.

"Get him up," he said, without looking at Noddy. "You carry him. Get him to the hut as fast as you can. I'll be right behind."

"He's crazy!" Noddy said, bending over the still body. "I told you we'd have trouble with him."

"Get on with it!" Baird snarled, as he wiped his face with his handkerchief. The deep scratches were bleeding badly. He could feel blood running down inside his shirt and across his chest.

Noddy got Hater across his shoulders and began a slow jogtrot towards the hut.

Baird went back for the Winchester. He had trouble finding it as the smoke screen had drifted over the sawgrass, but finally he located it. He couldn't see the river now. The dense smoke had blotted out the dredges and the water. The firing had died down. Away to his right he could hear men shouting, but couldn't make out what they were saying.

He ran after Noddy, and caught up with him a quarter of a mile or so from the hut.

Noddy was leaning against a tree, trying to get his breath back. Hater lay at his feet.

"Come on! Come on!" Baird said. "Do you want them to catch up with you?"

"I'm beat," Noddy panted. "I can't carry him any farther."

Baird thrust the Winchester into Noddy's hand, bent and pulled Hater up and across his broad shoulders.

"Come on!" he said. "You go ahead."

Noddy went forward, still gasping for breath.

By the time Baird reached the hut, he was breathing heavily. Hater was heavier than he looked, and the heat in the swamp seemed to drain all Baird's strength.

Rico came to the door. He was trembling and his white face looked ghastly.

"Are they coming this way?" he asked fearfully.

Baird shoved him aside and entered the hut. He let Hater slide off his shoulder on to the floor.

Both Rico and Noddy followed him in. Noddy stood by the window, looking down the path and the way they had come.

"Give Noddy the money," Baird said to Rico. "Twenty-five Cs. Snap it up! We've got to get to the boat."

Rico stared at him.

"Aren't you going to wait here, like we planned?" he asked.

"If you'd done your job like I told you," Baird said furiously, "we could have waited. But now those guys know we've come this way. We've got to get out quick."

"I couldn't help it ..." Rico said, wringing his hands.

"Shut up!" Baird exclaimed. "Get the money!"

Rico staggered over to his suitcase. As he fumbled with the locks, Noddy said sharply, "Hold it! Leave it alone! I'll take it as it is." He had a gun in his hand, and it pointed at Baird. "I'm going to have more than five grand for this job. Make a move, and I'll give it to you in the guts!"

III

Rico remained like a statue, looking helplessly at Baird. There were seven thousand dollars in cash in the suitcase: every nickel he owned. His hand gripped the handle of the case convulsively. He had warned Baird, and now this pigeon-chested double-crosser would take the money and shoot them.

Baird stood very still, his eyes on Noddy's gun. His face was expressionless, but the muscle below his right eye was twitching.

"Turn around," Noddy said, "then shed your rod. Drop it on the floor. Don't try anything funny. I'm a dead shot at this range. Go on! Turn around!"

Baird turned. Slowly his right hand went inside his coat and pulled out the Colt. Rico saw him softly thumb back the safety catch.

Noddy said, "This is where you get yours, pal. I'll get a pat on the back for rubbing you two out and capturing Hater. Drop that rod!"

It happened so quickly Rico had no idea how Baird did it.

Baird jumped to the right and turned at the same time. Noddy fired and missed. Baird's gun exploded three times; the gun flashes lit up the dark hut. Noddy dropped his gun, clutched his stomach with both hands and bent forward as if he had a hinge to his spine. He stood like that for a second or so, then his knees buckled and he fell forward on his face.

Baird stood over him.

Shuddering with relief, Rico came over and peered down at Noddy. All he could think of was that the money was safe.

"The mug," Baird said softly, and stirred Noddy with his foot. "To have tried to pull that ancient gag on me."

Noddy groaned. He looked up at Baird, his breath whistling in his throat.

Baird knelt by his side and ran his hands over his clothes. He found the roll of bills he had given Noddy the previous night.

"He won't need his turkey farm now," Baird said, and put the money in his hip pocket. "Come on! It's time we moved. Give me a hand with Hater. Where's that bandage?"

Rico found the wide roll of adhesive bandage, and together they strapped Hater's hands and ankles together. Baird strapped up Hater's mouth.

"I'll carry him. You bring the case and the Winchester," Baird went on. "They're certain to have heard the shots."

While Rico went over to pick up the case, Baird again bent over Noddy. He had stopped breathing. Baird touched the artery in his throat. Then he straightened with a little grunt.

"He won't double-cross anyone again," he muttered.

Then he hauled the unconscious Hater across his shoulder and moved to the door.

Rico followed him down the path, carrying the case and the Winchester.

Rico's mind was in a whirl. They had got Hater, but they had still to get out of this awful swamp. They had still a twelve-hour paddle down the river ahead of them before they reached the place where the getaway car was hidden.

Even if they got Hater away, there was still the complex business of getting the money from Kile. The whole scheme now seemed to Rico to be a madman's pipe dream.

A distant sound suddenly brought him to a standstill as if he had run against a brick wall. Baird had heard it too, and had also stopped. Both of them looked back along the path. Baird had his gun out.

Away in the distance they could hear the barking of dogs. Even as they listened the barking got nearer.

"Snap it up!" Baird exclaimed. "They've got our scent."

He turned and began to jogtrot down the path, while Rico blundered after him. Hater's weight made it impossible for Baird to move fast. He had still some distance to cover before he reached the boat, and he knew he had to conserve his strength for a final burst.

The barking grew louder, and they could hear men shouting to each other. They kept on. Baird even managed to increase his speed a little, but he was already beginning to pant. Rico was so scared he scarcely knew what he was doing as he stumbled blindly along behind Baird.

With every yard of ground covered, the sound of the dogs became louder. Baird was gasping for breath when he saw the river ahead of him. He stepped off the path and dumped Hater in the undergrowth.

Rico came up panting. He kept looking over his shoulder, his eyes rolling. He was hysterical with exhaustion and fear.

Baird grabbed him and pulled him off the path.

"We've got to nail those dogs," he said. "If they guess we've got a boat we're sunk. They'll come after us in a motor launch. We wouldn't stand a chance."

"What are you going to do?" Rico sobbed, lying on his side and looking helplessly up at Baird.

Baird grabbed up the Winchester.

"It's a lucky break I went back for this. They won't hear the shooting, and maybe I can wipe them out before they know what's hit them."

A sudden crackling of undergrowth made Baird swing around. He caught sight of a prison guard coming down the path. He had a revolver in one hand and in his other hand he held a chain that restrained a massive Alsatian dog that was dragging the guard down the path.

Baird hadn't time for any fancy shooting. He got the rifle to his shoulder as the guard saw him. If the guard hadn't been pulled off balance by the dog he would have got Baird, but Baird fired a fraction of a second before the guard could get his gun sight on Baird. The rifle slug hit the guard in the centre of his forehead. He dropped in his tracks, his dying fingers releasing the chain.

The dog didn't hesitate. It came down the path like a black streak of lightning. Baird hurriedly levered another slug into the breech and fired again, but the dog was coming too fast for accurate shooting. Baird's shot went wide, and before he could fire once more, the dog was on him.

Baird stabbed at its massive chest with the barrel of the gun, but force of the dog's charge sent the rifle out of his hands. Baird grabbed hold of the dog by its throat, throwing back his head to avoid the white fangs that slashed at him.

Man and dog rolled over and over, down the path towards the river bank. It was all Baird could do to keep the brute away from his throat. He screwed his fingers into the loose skin around the dog's throat and hung on, while the dog clawed at his chest with its front paws and tried to get close enough to snap.

Rico lay motionless, sick with horror. He knew he should go to Baird's help, but he hadn't the will to move.

Baird tried to choke the dog, but its heavy, brass-studded collar protected its throat. He rolled over, dragging the dog with him, not daring to release his grip for a second. The dog was incredibly strong: it was like holding on to a tiger. Baird realized his grip was slipping. The white fangs were now snapping within inches of his face. He made a tremendous effort, half reared up and threw himself and the dog into the river.

The warm, muddy water closed over his head. One of his hands lost its grip, but the dog was under the water too, and was more anxious to get to the surface than to snap at Baird. They both came to the surface together, and as Baird found his feet, he grabbed the dog by its collar with both hands and shoved it under the water again.

The struggling animal churned up the water into foam. It was as much as Baird could do to hold it. Just when he thought it was beginning to weaken, it managed to break surface and get some air before Baird forced it under again.

Rico had got to his feet and had come down to the bank. He watched the struggle with fascinated horror, unaware of the approaching sounds of more dogs.

The dog finally began to weaken and gave Baird the chance of freeing one hand. He snatched out his Colt and hit the dog on the top of its skull. The dog made a convulsive movement, snapped at Baird's wrist, and Baird felt white-hot pain shoot up his arm as the dog's teeth sank into his flesh. He hit it again and again until the teeth released their grip on his wrist and the dog, kicking and twitching, went limp. Gasping, Baird let go of it, and it sank slowly out of sight in the muddy, churned-up water.

Baird came staggering out of the water to the bank. "Get the boat!" he panted, as he toiled up the steep slope of the bank, blood running down his fingers. "Hurry!"

Rico floundered up to his knees in water and mud as he made for the place where the boat was hidden. He started to drag it from its hiding place of bush and saw grass as Baird came up with Hater across his shoulder.

"Okay," Baird said, "get the case and rifle."

Rico floundered back to the bank and returned with the case and the Winchester. Baird had got Hater into the boat and held the boat steady while Rico got in. Then he climbed in himself, took the paddle and pushed off, turning the nose of the boat upstream.

He paddled hard for some minutes, sending the boat along at a good pace, keeping close to the tangled shrub and bush that made an impenetrable screen along the bank. After he had gone some hundred yards, he steered the boat under the branches of an overhanging tree, and drew up by the bank.

The boat was well hidden from the opposite bank. They could hear the barking of dogs dangerously close now, and Rico looked appealingly at Baird.

"Hadn't we better get on?" he whispered. "Those dogs will find us!"

"Shut up!" Baird said. "Give me the case."

Rico pushed the suitcase to him, and Baird opened it and took out the first-aid box. He carefully washed his torn wrist in the river water and strapped it up. Then he took off his wet jacket and washed the scratches on his face, dabbing iodine on them after he had dried his face on a towel. He put away the first-aid box and took out the gun-cleaning outfit. He hurriedly cleaned the Colt and reloaded it. Then he cleaned the Winchester and added four more slugs to the magazine.

"That's better," he muttered, laying the Winchester in the bottom of the boat where he could get at it quickly. "Phew! I don't want to meet any more damned dogs." He glanced over at Rico. "Keep an eye on Hater. If he comes to the surface, he may try to overturn the boat. Hit him over the head if he looks like making trouble."

Rico gulped. He fingered the .38 which he wasn't sure how to use, and looked doubtfully at the still body lying at his feet.

"There they are," Baird whispered suddenly, and pointed.

Rico looked in the direction. He caught a glimpse of three guards standing half hidden by the bush on the opposite side of the river, looking to right and left. Each man carried a Thompson riot gun, and they all looked as if they could use the gun. They were talking, and one of them pointed downstream.

Then a man's voice called out so close to the hidden boat that Baird and Rico started violently and grabbed at their guns.

"This is the way they came," the man shouted. They couldn't see him as he was on the same side of the river as they were, but the other guards could see him. "They've killed Ben. The bastards have got a rifle."

"Think they've got a boat?" one of the guards called back.

"Don't see how, unless they're getting outside help. It's my bet they've swum over to your side."

"The dogs won't be long," the guard on the far side of the river said. "We'll soon pick up their scent. Have you checked the old cabin? Maybe some of them have holed up there."

"Jed's doing that. I'm staying with Ben until they get a stretcher down to him."

The three guards waved and moved off downstream.

"We stay right here," Baird whispered. "The dogs can't get through the bush, and as long as we're on the water they won't get our scent. We'll give them a couple of hours to cool off, then we'll try and make a break."

He took off his wet trousers, and sitting naked in the bottom of the boat dried himself carefully. He hung the jacket and trousers over a branch to dry, then uncorked a bottle of whisky and took a couple of shots.

Rico sat motionless, staring with frightened eyes at the opposite bank. He could hear the distant barking of dogs and men shouting. There was a lot of activity going on in the bush.

"Here, have some of this," Baird said, offering him the bottle.

Rico took a long drink. The spirit helped him a little, but he still couldn't control his trembling.

"Think we'll get out of this?" he asked suddenly.

"Yeah," Baird said, "I guess so. They won't waste too much time here. They've got fifty convicts to round up."

He made himself as comfortable as he could on a blanket and took another drink.

"Wish I could smoke," he said, half to himself, "but the dogs might smell it." He glanced at Hater. "Is he okay?"

Rico could see Hater's thin chest moving as he breathed.

"He's still breathing."

"That's something," Baird said, and grinned sourly. "He must have a skull like granite."

"He's crazy," Rico said uneasily. "There's something about his face ..."

"You should take a look at yourself," Baird said. "You look a little nuts, too. Maybe I do. That dog nearly had me."

Rico shivered.

"You've been a big help," Baird went on. "I must have been soft in the head to have picked on you for a caper like this. If you'd hit the dredge with your first shot they wouldn't have known where to look for us. We'd have been the hell out of this by now."

Rico didn't say anything. He was thinking he must have been soft in the head to have got mixed up with Baird in the first place.

"Maybe we'd better take it in turns to sleep," Baird said, yawning. "Hell! My wrist hurts. We may have to paddle all night. I'll take the first nap. Keep your eye on Hater. Wake me if he shows any sign of coming to the surface."

He stretched and closed his eyes. Rico watched him, fascinated. To be able to contemplate sleep at such a time! He had always known Baird had nerves of steel, and looking at him, a naked giant of solid bone and muscle, already dozing, Rico felt suddenly more hopeful. If there was a way out of this jam, Baird would find it. If they did get out of the swamp there was a quarter of a million dollars waiting for him.

An hour dragged by. Every now and then the sound of voices and the barking of dogs seemed unpleasantly close. Once Rico caught sight of some guards moving slowly along the opposite bank. They passed without even looking across the river.

Hater showed no signs of recovering consciousness, and Rico wondered uneasily if he were going to die. He rigged up some shading for Hater by draping a blanket over the suitcase. It was very hot in the boat, and Rico longed for an iced highball.

He knew he wouldn't be able to sleep, so he made no attempt to wake Baird. He sat in the prow of the boat, his ears and eyes missing nothing, while the hours dragged by.

By four o'clock the sounds of men and dogs had died away. The silence was broken now only by the drone of mosquitoes and the lapping of the water against the side of the boat.

A river snake slid from under the boat and went swimming swiftly downstream, startling Rico. He took another drink from the whisky bottle, then reached over and shook Baird.

"What's up?" Baird asked, instantly awake. His hand automatically reached for the Winchester.

"Isn't it time we did something?" Rico asked uneasily. "It's after four o'clock."

Baird sat up slowly and stretched. He touched his wrist with a grimace and shook his head.

"I guess you'll have to do some work. This wrist of mine doesn't feel so good. I doubt if I can use the paddle." He looked towards the opposite bank. "Seen anything?"

"Nothing for the past hour. I haven't heard anything, either."

Baird took a drink from the whisky bottle, then lit a cigarette.

"We'd better stay here until it's dark," he said. "We might run into them on their way back. Now we've got so far, it'd be crazy to take any more risks than we have to."

Rico shrugged. He wanted to get moving, but he realized what Baird said made sense.

"How's Hater?" Baird went on.

They both looked at the still body lying at the bottom of the boat. They were startled to see the dark eyes were open and watching them.

Baird shifted over to Hater and knelt at his side. "Take it easy," he said. "You're okay now." Hater made a soft, moaning noise, but he kept still. Rico leaned forward to stare down at him. Could this frail, odd little man, with his beetling eyebrows, his thin, emaciated face and body, his wild, staring eyes, be Paul Hater, the internationally renowned jewel operator? It didn't seem possible, until Rico remembered Hater had been inside for fifteen years: probably been working in this ghastly heat and swamp for most of that time. He shuddered at the thought, wondering what he himself would look like if he had been through what Hater had had to face.

Baird undid the gag and lifted Hater's head. "Have a drink, pal," he said, and offered the whisky bottle.

"Who are you?" Hater asked in a hoarse whisper. "What do you want with me?"

"We're getting you out of here," Baird said. "You've got friends on the outside rooting for you."

Hater licked his lips. His eyes went from Baird's hard, expressionless face to Rico.

"I haven't any friends," he said.

"Sure, you have," Baird returned. "You take it easy. You've got nothing to worry about now."

Hater closed his eyes.

"I know what you're after," he muttered. "But you're not going to get it. No one's going to get it."

"Don't get excited," Baird said. "Well talk about who's going to get what when we're out of here."

Hater started to say something, but the effort was too much for him. His face went slack, and he seemed to drift off once more into unconsciousness.

After watching him for a while, Baird returned to his blanket. He sat down and began to pull on his camouflage jacket and trousers. When he had finished dressing he told Rico to go to sleep.

"We'll get going as soon as it's dark. Get some rest. You'll have to do most of the paddling."

Rico was still watching Hater.

"Did you hear what he said? Suppose he doesn't tell Kile where he's cached the stuff? The cops must have tried to make him spill it. If they couldn't do it, how does Kile think he'll get him to talk?"

Baird shrugged.

"That's not my headache. If Kile can't make him talk, maybe I'll take charge of him." He stared at Rico for a long second. "I could make him spill it. A half a million's worth taking a little trouble for. I don't say it'd be easy, but in the end he'd come clean."

"Why don't you do it now?" Rico asked anxiously. "Why hand him over to Kile at all?"

"Suppose we did know where the stuff was hidden? What good would it do us? We couldn't get rid of it. Talk sense. Kile's got an in with this Rajah guy; we haven't."

Rico lay down in the boat. His feet were close to Hater's head.

"If we don't pull this off I'm ruined," he said miserably. "I don't know what I shall do."

"Aw, shut up!" Baird snapped. "Go to sleep. I don't want to listen to your bellyaching."

Rico closed his eyes, but he knew he wasn't going to sleep. He watched Baird through his eyelashes.

Baird stared thoughtfully at Hater while he nursed his aching wrist. His mind made plans.

IV

Around nine o'clock the light began to go quickly. For five hours the three men had lain in the boat, sweltering in the tropical heat, tormented by mosquitoes that buzzed above their heads in a thick cloud.

Only twice during the long wait for darkness had Hater moved. He seemed to hover on the edge of consciousness, but the slightest movement or effort to open his eyes drove him back again into a coma that made Rico nervous.

If Hater should die before he could be persuaded to talk! Rico kept thinking. This nightmare he was enduring would be for nothing. If he didn't get that money his future would be something he dared not contemplate.

Rico had scarcely noticed the heat or the mosquitoes so engrossed was he in worrying about Hater. Every now and then he would reach forward and touch Hater's pulse to reassure himself that Hater was still alive. This bundle of skin and bones represented Rico's future. There was nothing Rico wouldn't have done for him if there had been anything to do. He kept urging Baird to get moving. Hater should see a doctor, he told Baird repeatedly. It was madness to let him lie in this awful heat without proper attention.

Baird wouldn't listen. He lay in the stern of the boat, nursing his wrist. Rico was so busy fussing over Hater that he hadn't noticed how red and angry looking Baird's left arm had become. Long red streaks came from under the bandage and reached up as far as Baird's elbow. Every so often Baird hung his arm over the side of the boat, keeping his burning forearm in the water.

He was worried about his arm. He knew it was infected, and he knew, too, he was growing feverish. His head felt hot, and he experienced hot and cold chills up and down his spine. To be ill at a time like this! he thought savagely. To have to rely on a useless sonofabitch like Rico! If he told Rico how he was feeling, Rico would promptly lose his head. Would the darkness never come? He needed a doctor far more urgently than Hater did.

Rico said sullenly, "It's dark enough now, isn't it? It's nearly nine."

The sun had gone down behind the trees, but they could still see the far bank quite clearly. Sick of doing nothing and tormented by the pain in his arm, Baird decided to take the risk.

"Yeah," he said, "let's go. Think you can handle this tub?"

Rico looked startled.

"Isn't your arm all right now?"

"It's stiff," Baird said. "Maybe I'll take over in a while. We're going with the stream. It won't be hard work."

Rico picked up the paddle. He shoved the boat away from the bank and began to paddle into midstream. The boat zigzagged through the water under his uneven strokes.

"Keep by the bank," Baird said, "and don't try so hard." After a few minutes Rico got the hang of the paddle, and managed to keep the boat fairly straight.

"Should be dark in about ten minutes," Baird said, staring up at the cloudless sky. "There'll be a big moon in an hour, I'd say."

It was almost dark when they heard the sound of an aircraft. Rico had allowed the boat to drift away from the bank, and they were away from the shelter of the overhanging trees.

Baird had been dozing. He was lying down in the boat now, his arm hanging over the side. The cool water made the throbbing and burning bearable. He opened his eyes and half sat up. Rico was staring up at the sky. Then realizing the plane was heading towards them, he tried desperately to paddle the boat to the shelter of the trees. He got in such a panic he nearly capsized the boat, churning up the water and scooping water on to his legs and into the boat.

"Steady, you crazy punk!" Baird snarled, "or you'll have us over!"

Rico controlled himself and began to paddle more carefully. The boat swung towards the bank and the sheltering darkness of the trees. They were within three or four yards of cover when the aircraft went roaring overhead.

It was flying low, and the roar of its engine and the rush of wind from its slipstream made both men duck. It was gone as quickly as it had come.

"Hell!" Baird exclaimed. "Think they were looking for us?"

Rico wiped the sweat from his face with the back of his hand.

"They couldn't have seen us," he said uneasily. "It's nearly dark, and at that speed ..."

"Better get going," Baird said. "Keep nearer to the bank, and put your back into it."

Rico drove the boat forward. He was rapidly tiring. It was years since he had taken any exercise, and paddling the boat as heavy as this made his arms ache.

"I can't keep this up much longer," he panted. "Can't you take a turn?"

"You're damn well going to," Baird said. "Take a look at this," and he thrust his swollen arm at Rico. In the failing light Rico could see the angry red streaks, and the flesh turning blue around the bandage. The sight horrified him.

"That's poisoned," he said. "Hadn't you better do something about it?"

"What the hell do you think I can do, you dope?" Baird said, exasperated. "Keep going, and make it fast!"

Rico continued to paddle. He kept glancing at Baird uneasily. Baird looked bad. Sweat beaded his face and his eyes seemed to have sunk into their sockets. He kept passing his hand across his forehead, and every now and then he swayed as if he were going to topple out of the boat.

"Better lie down," Rico said feverishly. "You look bad."

"Aw, shut up!" Baird said, but his voice lacked its usual snap. After a moment or so, he did lie down.

Rico was paddling more slowly now. There was a burning ache in his shoulders, and he could feel blisters forming on the palms of his hands. He kept digging the paddle into the water, but their progress was slow.

"How much farther do you reckon we've got to go?" he asked, after a long silence.

Baird grunted.

"Another three or four hours at this rate. Can't you go faster? We want to be miles from the river before dawn."

Rico made the effort and slightly increased his stroke. He groaned softly to himself. Baird had said they would earn every nickel of that half million. He hadn't believed him at the time, but he believed him now.

An hour crawled by. Rico was so tired he scarcely did more than make the motions of paddling. The boat moved sluggishly along with the stream. It had become almost dark since the plane had passed. But now Rico was aware of more light, and he could see the outlines of the trees against the night sky. The moon was coming up, he thought thankfully. This drifting in the darkness was beginning to get on his nerves.

He increased his rate of paddling slightly. His hands were so sore it was an effort to hold the paddle tightly. Would this nightmare journey never end? he asked himself. It was too dark to see how Hater was. For all Rico knew Hater might have died. He could hear Baird muttering to himself as he dozed. How was he going to manage Hater as well as Baird? Rico thought wildly. There was a five-hour car drive to the shooting lodge yet to be tackled.

Suddenly he imagined he heard a sound and he stopped paddling to listen, letting the boat drift. Far away he thought he could hear a faint throbbing of an engine. Was the aircraft coming back?

He looked towards the bank, and turned the nose of the boat so that he could get under cover if the plane was returning.

"Baird! Wake up!" he called anxiously.

"What's the matter now?" Baird asked harshly, sitting up.

"Listen!"

The pulse in Baird's head drummed violently, and his arm was a blaze of fire. Cursing softly, he leaned out of the boat, bringing his head closer to the water. He picked up the sound that Rico had heard.

"It's a motor boat!" he said, swinging upright. "That goddamn plane spotted us!"

Rico went cold with panic. He began to paddle furiously until Baird snarled at him to stop.

"We don't stand a chance of racing them, you fool! Get over to the bank!"

Rico paddled the boat to the bank.

"Shall we get out?" he asked.

"Yeah," Baird said. "Those boys will be carrying a machine-gun."

He hauled himself out of the boat on to the bank, surprised to find how weak his legs were.

"Get Hater up here, and snap it up."

Rico struggled with Hater. He managed to get him from the boat to the bank, nearly upsetting the boat as he did so. Baird reached down and dragged Hater to higher ground.

"Get the Thompson and the Winchester," he said. "Better bring the suitcase, too."

Rico floundered up to his knees in the water as he got the guns and case. He climbed up the bank and joined Baird. They lay down in the darkness.

"The chances are they'll miss the boat in the darkness," Baird said, "but if they don't we've got to nail them somehow. They'll probably have a radio on board ..." He broke off as a light appeared on the river.

A white motor launch came around the river bend with a big searchlight mounted on the bridge. They could make out three figures on the bridge and two others kneeling in the prow with a machine-gun between them. The light was sweeping both banks, and Baird could see at once that the police couldn't fail to spot the boat.

"Split up!" he said urgently. "Quick! You go to the left. Use your gun if they start shooting."

Bending double he ran from where their boat was moored and took shelter behind a tree.

Rico was too scared to move. He flattened down in the long grass and lay still. His hands covered his head.

The beam of the searchlight crept along the bank, reached the boat and then passed on. For a moment Baird thought they had missed the boat, but as he began to relax he heard someone shout from the bridge and the searchlight swung around and focused on the boat. There was a clanging of a bell and the motor launch went about in a tight circle.

Baird didn't wait for the police to take action. He opened up with the Thompson. He saw splinters fly from the deck, shifted his aim a little higher. The two men at the machine-gun were blasted off the deck into the river.

Answering fire came from the bridge. Baird again shifted his aim, but the three men had ducked down below the armour of the bridge, and the launch went on at full speed downstream.

Baird stood up and watched it. As soon as it was out of range, it turned. The searchlight had gone out, smashed by Baird's fire. He guessed they'd man the machine-gun again and sweep the bank on the return trip.

He took cover behind the tree and waited. His turn would come when the launch went about.

The launch came on. They had got the machine-gun on the bridge now. When it was almost abreast of Baird's boat the gun opened up. A hail of bullets churned up the bank, smashed through the trees, sending splinters of wood flying like shrapnel, and hammered the boat to pieces.

Baird lay flat behind the tree, waiting for his chance to return the murderous fire.

Rico could hear the slugs zipping through the bush, and he squirmed down farther into the soft ground. Then the launch passed by him, and he came under the direct fire of the gun. A deluge of lead threw mud and water over him. The noise drove him crazy with fear. Not knowing what he was doing, he sprang up wildly and began to run into the bush. He had only taken a few steps when something bit into his leg, bringing him face down in the swamp.

Baird had seen Rico panic, and he cursed softly. No one could stand up in that hail of lead and survive. He might have guessed Rico would have done that, the useless punk! Just when he was wanted he had to get himself killed.

Baird swung up the Thompson. The launch was turning, and for the moment the machine-gun was out of action. He sprayed the bridge with a long burst. There came a smashing of glass and the launch suddenly wheeled sharply round. Baird caught sight of a man wrestling with the wheel, and he fired again.

The steersman threw up his hands and disappeared. The launch headed straight for the bank close to where Baird was standing, and drove its prow into the soft mud. The launch swung half round, its engines still running, its propellers churning up the water.

From his hiding place Baird could look into the bridge. Two of the guards lay face down, while the remaining guard sat propped up against the wall, his head down on his chest.

Baird didn't hesitate. He dropped the Thompson, snatched out his Colt and jumped from the bank to the deck.

He entered the bridge house cautiously. The guard against the wall raised his head. Blood ran down the side of his mouth. He stared at Baird, then made an effort to lift the gun that lay across his knees.

Baird shot him through the head before he could get the gun up.

As the guard slumped over, Baird ran over to the controls, throttled back the engine, put it in reverse, then opened the throttle slowly. The launch pulled out of the soft mud into deeper water. Baird half closed the throttle, and brought the launch alongside the bank.

Every movement he had to make was by sheer effort of will. His head was expanding and contracting, and it was as much as he could do to stand upright. He drove himself ruthlessly. Here was a chance of escape. If he could get Hater on board, most of his troubles would be over.

He slid overboard into the warm, muddy water, climbed up the bank and hunted around for Hater. He found him still lying motionless where he had left him. He made sure he was still alive, then began to drag him through the bush to the bank.

It took him a long time to get Hater on board. He was so exhausted by the time he had rolled Hater on to the deck that he flopped down in the shallow water, holding his head between his hands, only half conscious.

He sat there for some minutes. Conscious he was wasting time, he finally made an effort and stood up. He got back on the bank and began to search for the suitcase and the Winchester. He found them with difficulty, and as he picked them up he heard Rico calling.

He stood looking in the direction of the shouts, surprised that Rico was still alive. Leaving the case and the gun, he staggered into the bush in search of Rico.

By now the moon had swung up into the sky. Baird came upon Rico lying on his back, his white, sweating face agonized with pain.

"I thought you'd forgotten me," Rico gasped, and began to sob with relief. "I thought you were going to leave me here to die."

"Get up, you rat!" Baird snarled. "What do you think you're doing, lying there?"

Rico groaned.

"It's my leg. It's broken. It's bleeding. Help me, Baird."

Baird stood over him. He could scarcely keep his feet.

"You asked for it," he said, his breath coming in great laboured gasps. "Why didn't you keep down?"

"Help me," Rico said, reaching out a shaking hand. "Don't leave me here to die."

Why not leave him here? Baird asked himself. All along Rico had been useless. Now with a broken leg he'd be worse than useless. Baird had already exhausted himself getting Hater on board. The thought of having to go through that all over again with Rico decided him.

"Take it easy," he said. "I'll be back. I've got to find Hater."

Rico knew at once he was lying.

"You can't leave me like this!" he cried, half sitting up. "I'm bleeding! Baird! You can't do it!"

"Aw, shut up!" Baird said, and staggered back to where he had left the gun and the suitcase.

Rico shouted after him, but Baird didn't look back. Sure now Baird was going to leave him, Rico started to crawl after him, dragging his broken leg behind him. His body was torn with pain, but somehow he managed to keep moving, digging his fingers into the soft ground to pull himself forward.

"Baird!" he shouted. "Wait for me!"

Baird looked over his shoulder. He saw Rico crawling after him, and he was tempted to put him out of his misery, but he decided not to risk a shot. The guards might still be near at hand looking for him for all he knew.

He slid down the bank into the water, hoisted the Winchester, then the suitcase on board and heaved himself over the gunwale.

Rico made a desperate effort to increase his speed. He was half out of his mind with pain and fear, and he began to scream at Baird.

"Come back! Come back!"

Baird dragged himself to the bridge, eased open the throttle and the launch began to edge away from the bank.

Rico pulled out his gun.

"Come back, Baird!" he yelled. "I'll kill you if you don't come back!"

Baird spun the wheel and the launch headed out to midstream. Already he was fifty yards or so from the bank. He wasn't even listening to Rico's frantic cries.

Rico pulled the trigger, but nothing happened. He tried to thumb back the safety catch, but the gun slipped out of his hands and fell with a splash into the river. He made a frantic effort to save it, overbalanced and toppled over into the shallow water.

His broken leg twisted under him, and for a moment he lost consciousness, engulfed by pain. The water, closing over his head, brought him round and he struggled to the bank, where he lay half in and half out of the water.

With sick horror, he watched the dim shape of the launch gathering speed, and disappearing down the river into the darkness.

He dropped back, sobbing wildly. He could feel blood coming from his wound. In the bright light of the moon he saw the water around him was turning red.

Even then he wouldn't believe he was going to die. The police would find him, he told himself frantically. Another launch would come in search of the first one, and they would find and save him.

He closed his eyes and began to pray: words coming from his mouth without meaning.

He didn't see a dark, log-like shape slither down the opposite bank and take to the water. The scent of his blood drifted across the river: it was an irresistible invitation the alligator accepted with alacrity.

The dark silent shape came through the water with surprising speed, only its scaly snout showing; as dangerous and as menacing as the half-hidden periscope of a submarine.

Rico felt a movement of water against his face. He opened his eyes. A few yards away from him he saw a steady ripple on the water that was advancing towards him. He stared at it, wondering what it could be. Pain had dulled his fears. The ripple didn't frighten him. He watched it, puzzled.

He only realized what it was when it was too late even to cry out.

PART FIVE

Rain ran in the gutters and dripped from the trees that lined the broad Roosevelt Boulevard. The street lamps made wet pools on the glistening sidewalk. An occasional car swished past, its headlamps lighting up the driving rain.

Adam Gillis stood under a tree, his hands thrust deep into the pockets of his shabby mackintosh, his soggy felt hat pulled down over his eyes.

He didn't appear to notice the heavy rain or the fact that he was soaked to the skin. He was concentrating on Kile's house, a big, double-fronted mansion, its lower windows ablaze with light.

They won't be much longer, he told himself. Nothing like a policeman for getting some fast action. A little too fast, if anything, he thought, as he remembered he had only just left the pay booth and had taken cover in a dark doorway before a couple of prowl boys had arrived. Lieutenant Olin certainly knew his business. He had tried to keep him talking while he had sent his men to pick him up.

When the prowl car had gone, Gillis had taken a taxi to Roosevelt Boulevard hoping to be there in time to see the result of his anonymous call to Olin.

He had had to wait longer than he expected. He wasn't to know Olin had had difficulty in finding a judge to sign the necessary search warrant at that time of night.

Gillis had twenty minutes to wait in the rain before he saw the red light of a police car coming swiftly up the boulevard.

He drew back out of sight as the car pulled up outside Kile's house. He watched Olin and two detectives mount the steps and ring on the front door bell. He saw them admitted, and the door close behind them.

The driver of the police car remained with the car, and prevented Gillis from getting nearer to the house in the hope of looking through a window to see what was going on. He had to content himself with waiting in the rain. He didn't have long to wait. The front door suddenly opened, and Olin came out, followed by Kile, then by the two detectives.

Kile had on a hat and coat. He walked unsteadily, his head held low. One of the detectives had to help him into the car. Olin got in beside him and the detective got in beside the driver. The car moved off, leaving the remaining detective to return to the house.

Gillis had a good view of Kile as the car went past. Kile's face was white, and his eyes stared fixedly at the back of the driver's head. He seemed suddenly to have become an old man.

Gillis felt a wave of satisfaction run through him as he watched the car turn the bend and disappear. Well, at least, he thought, that's one untidy end snipped off.

He had spent his last dollar on the taxi fare to Kile's house, but he wasn't despondent. He knew Eve had money at her apartment, and it would be easy enough to get it out of her. It was a long walk to Roxborough Avenue, but he was in a jovial mood and he strode along briskly. Maybe tonight would be the last time he would have to walk anywhere. From now on, if his luck held, it would be taxis until he got his own car.

He entered Eve's apartment block, rode up in the elevator and rang the front door bell. Water dripped from his sodden mackintosh on to the mat, and squelched in his shoes, but he didn't care. With his mind full of his future plans, he had never felt better in his life.

Eve came to the door. She started violently when she saw him, alarm jumping into her eyes.

"Oh, Adam! What are you doing here? How wet you are!" she exclaimed. "I suppose you'd better come in."

"I was going to suggest it," Gillis said, with his most charming smile. "It's raining Great Danes and Ginger Toms, and I couldn't find a taxi."

He entered the cosy sitting-room and took off his hat and coat.

"I'm afraid I'm going to make a bit of a mess," he said apologetically. "Shall I take these things into the bathroom?"

"I don't think you'd better, Adam. I'm expecting Preston," Eve said uneasily. "He phoned this evening to say he was coming. I thought it was he when you rang."

Gillis smiled.

"You don't have to worry about Preston. He won't be coming. He has a much more pressing appointment." He crossed the room to the door leading to the bathroom. "I think I'll take a bath. I don't want to catch cold."

"How do you know Preston won't come?" Eve asked sharply.

"I'll tell you all about it when I've had a bath," Gillis said. "There's plenty of time."

He went into the bathroom and locked himself in. He took a bath, lying in the hot water for some time, enjoying the luxury of it. Then he shaved, using Kile's razor, and put on the dark-blue, quilted dressing gown that Eve had left outside the door, and re-entered the sitting-room.

"That's much better," he said, going over to the electric fire Eve had turned on. He sat in an easy chair before the fire. "A whisky and soda would be welcome if you can run to it."

Eve brought him the drink and sat opposite him. Her face was white and strained, and she looked searchingly at him.

"What has happened to Preston?" she asked.

"I'm afraid he's in trouble," Gillis said. He drank some of the whisky. "Good stuff this." He leaned forward to read the label on the bottle. "I must get some for myself."

"Adam! What has happened to Preston?"

He looked at her, smiling.

"I told you: he's in trouble. I think it's very unlikely you'll be bothered with him again."

"But what happened?" Her vice was sharp-edged as she leaned forward. "Why is he in trouble?"

"The police found out about the bracelet," he said, shrugging. "They arrested him about half an hour ago."

"Adam! You told them about it!"

"As a matter of fact, I didn't," Gillis lied. "I must admit I've been tempted to do so several times, but in view of what's just happened, I'm glad I didn't."

"What will they do with him?"

"I imagine he'll get ten years. Why should you care? He'll be out of the way for some time," Gillis said, finished his drink and offered the glass to her. "Would you like to mix me another? And if you have a cigarette?"

She made another drink, gave it to him, and put a box of cigarettes where he could reach them. He lit up, stretched out his long legs and sighed contentedly.

"This is the life, pet," he said. "You're lucky. You may not believe it, but I often wish I had been a girl. I'd have enjoyed being some old fool's kept darling."

Eve shuddered, but she didn't say anything.

"By the way, did Preston tell you what happened at the shooting lodge?" Gillis asked, after a long pause.

"He didn't go into details," she said, looking down at her hands. "He said he hadn't been successful."

"That's rather an understatement," Gillis said. "The whole thing was a complete flop."

She didn't say anything or look at him.

"You don't seem particularly concerned," Gillis said, watching her narrowly. "After all, you've lost a quarter of a million, haven't you?"

"Have I?" she asked, and looked up to meet his eyes. "I didn't count on getting it, Adam. Come to that, you don't seem particularly concerned, either."

"You wouldn't have said that the night before last," Gillis said, and laughed. "I don't think I've ever been in such a rage. I had everything so well worked out. Preston was marching up and down outside the lodge in a perfect fever, and I was crouching behind a bush, also in a fever. We waited hours, and nothing happened. Then Preston turned on the radio, and we heard the details of the escape. They said Hater had stolen a police launch. We waited and waited, but Baird didn't show up. I nearly tore my hair out I was so angry."

Eve got up and began to move around the room aimlessly. Her silence irritated Gillis.

"You don't seem very interested," he said sharply. "After all, we were working on this together."

"We weren't working together, Adam. I behaved like a weak fool and did what you told me to do. All along I thought the idea was crazy, and I'm glad it didn't come off."

Gillis shrugged.

"You're a funny girl," he said, blowing smoke to the ceiling. "We could have snapped our fingers at the world with half a million in our pockets. You don't seem to realize what you've lost."

"I think I do, but I've gained much more."

"Nice to have such a placid philosophy. Well, I wasn't wrong about Baird. I told you he could do anything if he put his mind to it."

"Eight men lost their lives through him. Doesn't that mean anything to you?"

"Should it?" he said, mildly surprised. "It's what they were paid for. If a man's mug enough to be a prison guard, he must expect to run risks."

"What do you think has happened to Hater?" she asked, turning away so he shouldn't see her disgust.

"I imagine Baird's hanging on to him," Gillis said, frowning. "There was always the possibility that Baird would deal direct with the Rajah. I'm afraid that's what he's going to do. It won't be easy for him. The police are hunting for him for Zoe Norton's murder. But if he can get to the Rajah, the Rajah will do a deal with him."

"When you found out that Baird had tricked you," Eve said quietly, "I suppose you decided Preston was of no further use, and you gave him away to the police?"

Gillis looked at her, his eyes cynically amused.

"Do you really want to know, pet? Wouldn't your silly conscience be happier if you didn't know?"

"I want to know."

"Then you shall. You're quite right. You've said all along you want to be rid of Kile. I phoned Olin and told him he'd find Jean Bruce's bracelet in Kile's safe. He went along and found it. So now you don't have to worry about Kile any more."

"So I'm to blame, really?"

"Well, I suppose you are," Gillis said, and laughed. "I certainly wouldn't have bothered to phone Olin if you were still anxious to remain Kile's mistress. But as you aren't, I thought I'd better do something about it. After all, Eve, you've helped me in the past. The least I could do was to help you when the opportunity arose."

"Are you sure it wasn't because Baird tricked you?" Eve said quietly. "Are you sure you didn't round on Kile in a moment of spite because you had to work off your temper on someone, and he was the least likely to hit back?"

For a moment Gillis' face hardened, but he quickly controlled himself, and burst out laughing.

"You certainly know me, don't you, Eve? You're absolutely right. I was livid at the time. Everything was going so well. Yes, I underestimated that sonofabitch. I thought he was a gun-happy thug without any brains. But he beat me to it. I admit it. He even got paid to get Hater out of the swamp, and then he calmly walked off with him, and will probably do a deal with the Rajah and pocket the half million. Well, I've got over it now. I've other ideas: not quite so lucrative, but definitely more promising."

It had always been the same, Eve thought bitterly. He was forever working on some new idea to get rich quickly. Nothing discouraged him. As soon as one idea petered out, he began working on another. He would go to endless trouble to try to make money out of his crackpot schemes, although he wouldn't stir a finger to get himself a job that would bring him in a legitimate income.

"I think I'll go to bed now," she said abruptly. "I'm tired. You can stay here for the night if you want to."

"I was going to suggest it," he said, smiling. "But don't run away just yet. I want to talk to you about my new idea. By the way, pet, how are you off for money?"

"How much do you want?"

He sat up, his face suddenly ugly with rage.

"Don't keep assuming I'm going to sponge on you, damn you!" he said. "I'm asking you how much longer you can keep this apartment on now you haven't Kile to pay the bills?"

"I shall go back to the Follies," she said. "I shan't stay here. If you want any money, I can let you have fifty dollars."

"I don't want your money," he said shortly. "Now look, let's be sensible about this. There's no point in going back to the Follies. Besides, you don't know if they'll have you back." He got up and poured himself another whisky. "As a matter of fact, the Rajah has taken a fancy to you."

Eve stood motionless, looking at Gillis.

"What did you say?"

"The Rajah's taken a fancy to you," Gillis said, his smile becoming fixed. "He would like you to go back with him to Chittabad. I promised to talk it over with you."

Eve went a shade paler.

"I don't understand. Do you know him? How did you come to meet him?"

Gillis waved an airy hand.

"Why, of course I know him. I met him in India. As a matter of fact, I did him one or two little services: nothing very grand, but he was impressed by my usefulness."

"You mean you introduced him to some white women who were accommodating?"

Gillis lost his smile.

"There's no need to be sarcastic," he said curtly. "I just happened to be useful. I forget what I did. We became friendly and he told me about the collection. Between us we engineered the plan to get hold of Hater."

"Oh, I see. Then why did you bring Preston and me into it? I always thought it was odd the Rajah saw me so easily. You had arranged all that before you told me to go and see him?"

"Of course," Gillis said, poured whisky into his glass and sipped it. "We decided it would be safer to have a stooge in case things went sour on us. That's why we picked on Kile. We were just safeguarding ourselves. That's all."

"I see." She began to move around the room again. "You didn't bother about what would happen to me if things went sour, as you call it."

"Oh, rot! Nothing was likely to happen to you. We knew that. The police wouldn't he interested in you."

"If Preston had told them it was my idea – as he thought it was – they might have been," Eve said, going to the window and pushing back the curtain to look down at the rain-soaked street.

"I knew Kile was too much of a gentleman to implicate you," Gillis said easily. "I had it all planned pretty neatly. It was just bad luck it flopped. Anyway, that's all ancient history now. You've got your future to think of. The Rajah will make you a settlement."

She didn't say anything or look round.

"Did you hear what I said?" Gillis demanded, raising his voice.

"Yes."

"I've persuaded him to be pretty generous. Of course he's not as rich as he was, and this Hater business has rather put a spoke in his wheel, but he's still got plenty," Gillis went on. "You'll like the life out there. Of course women don't get quite so much freedom as here, but there are other compensations. He's got a magnificent palace, and he still owns a lot of diamonds and jewellery. He'll want you to wear them."

"I was under the impression he was married," Eve said, still with her back turned.

Gillis laughed.

"Well, you know what these Rajahs are," he said. "It won't make any difference to you. They look on these things differently out there. There's nothing for you to worry about. Anyway, his present wife's not a patch on you."

She didn't say anything.

"He's going to stay here for one more week in the hope Baird'll get in touch with him. He'll be sailing on the 30th. We'll travel with him. You'll enjoy it, Eve. Everything first class, and he'll give you a pretty substantial cheque for an outfit. He likes his women to look smart."

"He is giving you a job, then, Adam?"

"Well, of course. I'm going to be his confidential secretary. The pickings should be pretty good. You'll find that out, too. Of course it won't be a permanent thing. I don't think the chap will last much more than five or six years at the rate he's spending his money. But you and I will be able to feather our nests pretty well by then."

"I'm glad you've got a job, Adam. I hope you'll be very successful, and have a lot of pickings."

He looked at her slim back suspiciously.

"I'll take good care I am successful," he said shortly. "But never mind about me. I told him you'd call at his hotel tomorrow and have lunch with him. Naturally he's anxious to get to know you as soon as possible."

"I'm sorry to disappoint him, but I won't be able to go," Eve said, still with her back turned.

"But you can't have anything more important to do than to see him," Gillis said sharply. "You must go."

She turned then, and he was startled to see how white she was, and how her eyes glittered.

"Do you realize what you are suggesting?" she asked, in a cold, levelled voice. "Do you realize this man's coloured?"

"Now, please don't be ridiculous," Gillis said. "The Rajah's a high-born gentleman. He was educated at Eton and Cambridge."

"That doesn't make the slightest difference to me. Anyway, even if he wasn't coloured, the answer's still no. I'm going back to the Follies. I've had enough of this kind of life."

"My dear girl, I doubt if the Follies would have you. There'll be a hell of a scandal when the press hear Kile's been arrested. I can't imagine the Follies will want the discarded mistress of a jailbird decorating their theatre."

She looked away, biting her lip, her hands clenched into tight fists.

"Now, look, do be sensible, Eve," Gillis said, pressing his advantage. "See the Rajah tomorrow. He's got a lot of charm. He won't rush you. Maybe on the boat you'll be expected to do your job, but certainly not until you get on the boat."

"You'd better go, Adam," she said, without looking at him.

He stared at her, startled.

"What do you mean?"

"What I say. I don't want to see you again. I've been trying to make up my mind to end our sordid association for weeks, but I've never had the courage. But I have now. There was a time, Adam, when I loved you. I was ready to do anything for you, but you've killed all that. Looking at you now, I can't understand why I have been such an utter fool. Well, I'm glad you've got a job. I'm glad you're going to India. We needn't meet again. I sincerely hope we don't." She turned back to the window. "Please go now."

"Don't be ridiculous, Eve," Gillis said, with an uneasy laugh. "You don't mean it. As soon as I get home you'll call me up as you always do. Let's get down to earth. This is a chance of a lifetime for both of us."

"Will you please go?"

There was something in her voice that made him realize suddenly that she meant what she said. He experienced a sick, empty feeling of rage.

"Now, look here, Eve," he said, his voice sharpening, "this has gone far enough! You can't do this to me! You've just got to do what I tell you. I won't get the job if you don't. It is because the Rajah wants you, he's giving me the job. Don't you understand? I don't mind telling you he was livid with me because I let Baird trick me. He wouldn't believe it wasn't my fault. If I hadn't thought of you, he was going to prosecute me. I've signed one or two of his blasted cheques, and he's found out. He could send me to jail, Eve! Don't you understand? It was only because I promised you'd be nice to him, he's withdrawn the charges. You've got to ..."

"Get out!" Eve said, turning. "I never want to see you again!"

"Oh, no!" Gillis said, his face flushing, "you're not going to talk to me like this. I'll go when I damn well want to. You're going to listen to me or you'll be sorry!"

"If you don't get out I'll call the janitor and have you thrown out!"

"You won't!" Gillis snarled, turning from red to white. "What you want is a damn good hiding! You'll get it too if you don't do what I tell you. I'm not going to lose a perfectly good job because you're suddenly squeamish about the colour of a man's skin. That cat won't jump."

"There's a name they call men like you," Eve said quietly, "and it isn't a pretty one." She walked over to the telephone. "Are you going?"

"No, I'm not!" Gillis said, and started around the table towards her. "I've warned you. Put that phone down or you'll be sorry."

Eve hurriedly began to dial the janitor's number. Gillis reached her and wrenched the phone out of her hand. She gave him a violent and heavy slap across his face.

Not knowing quite what he was doing, but too viciously furious to think or care, Gillis snatched up the whisky bottle and smashed it down on top of her head.

II

Baird sat at the wheel of the Packard, driving with one hand. His left arm hung uselessly at his side. It was swollen now to twice its normal size, and the forearm was black and green.

Sweat ran off him as if he had had a sponge of water squeezed over him. His body shook with extreme rigour, and every muscle ached. He drove the car automatically along the broad highway. Only his will-power kept him upright at the wheel.

At that hour – it was three o'clock in the morning – there was no traffic on the road, and he could keep the car moving without having to slow down or manipulate the gears.

He had long lost all sense of time. He knew he was dangerously ill. He knew, too, his arm was so badly infected that he would probably lose it. He had decided to die rather than stop and seek help.

Somehow he had managed to carry Hater from the police launch to where he and Rico had hidden the car. He had dumped Hater on the floor of the car, behind the driving seat, and had covered him with a blanket. Then he had changed his wet camouflage suit, taking a change of dry clothes from the suitcase. He now wore his jacket slung cape-wise over his shoulders, as he had found it impossible to get his coat sleeve over his swollen arm.

He had set out for the long drive to the shooting lodge. It was during the drive the fever that had taken hold of him became worse. He felt hot and cold in turns, and he began to shiver violently. When it came to the time to turn off the highway to the back roads that would take him to the shooting lodge, his mind couldn't cope with the change of direction. The broad highway out of Louisiana seemed now so uncomplicated and easy to drive on that he gave up the idea of going to the shooting lodge.

It suddenly occurred to him that he was dying, and he was seized by an obsession to see Anita Jackson before he died. The attraction he had felt for the girl now dominated his mind, and it was this obsession to see her again that gave him the strength to stay at the wheel.

Hour after hour passed. He stopped only for gas, pulling up at isolated service stations, and getting away again as soon as the tank was filled, without leaving the car.

He was beyond noticing the curious looks the service station attendants gave him. Those who were able to get a good look at him were startled by his ravaged face and sickened by the putrefying stench that came from his arm. They stared after the car, wondering if they should report what they had seen to the police, but finally deciding it wasn't their business.

Baird had forgotten Hater. His mind was confused by his raging fever, and he couldn't remember what he was doing on this broad highway, or even how he had injured his arm. Anita's face floated before his eyes as he drove and sustained him, giving him the will to keep the car moving.

Seventeen hours of non-stop driving brought him to the City limits of Essex City. He was driving more slowly now, as he had difficulty in keeping his eyes properly focused.

Heavy rain clouds had brought darkness early. Although it was only just after eight o'clock, Baird had turned on his headlights. The highway seemed to him to be rising and falling in the beams of the headlights, and he had a crazy idea that the road must be floating on a rough sea. Every so often he was startled to find the car was wandering on to the wrong side of the road, and he hurriedly twisted the wheel to bring it straight. He only just averted an accident when a car overtook him and passed him with a furious blast of its horn.

He slowed down almost to a crawl. Sweat ran into his eyes, making them smart, and he was aware now of the smell from his arm, and it frightened him.

He kept going somehow. A few miles farther on, he vaguely remembered he had to turn right into the Paseo. Even at fifteen miles an hour he was having difficulty in keeping the car straight.

Behind him he suddenly heard the sharp note of a police siren. Immediately his confused and tired brain galvanized itself into life. This was the one sound that could jerk him out of his coma back to comparatively rational thinking. He looked quickly into his driving mirror. Behind him, coming up fast, was the large glaring headlamp of a motorcycle. A moment later a prowl cop drew level and signalled him to stop.

Baird pulled over to the grass verge. He braked, forgetting to throw out his clutch, and the car engine stalled. The car came to a wobbly stop, its offside wheels bumping up on to the grass.

The cop pulled up beside him.

"What the matter with you?" he demanded in a loud, bullying voice. "Been drinking?"

Baird groped down by his side. His fingers closed around the butt of the Colt. He leaned against the car door, peering up at the cop's red, angry face.

The cop flashed a light on Baird. He caught his breath sharply.

"Jeepers! What the hell's the matter with you? You ill?"

"Yeah," Baird gasped. "But I'll be all right. Just leave me alone, will you? I'm going to see a friend of mine. She'll take care of me."

"You ain't fit to drive," the cop said. "What's happened to you to get into this state?"

"Infected arm," Baird told him. "I'll be okay if you'll leave me alone."

"You're not going to drive another yard. Move over. I'm going to take you to hospital," the cop said, and pulled open the car door.

Baird, who was leaning against the door, nearly fell into the road, but the cop caught hold of him and lifted him upright. Baird pushed the Colt into the cop's stomach and pulled the trigger twice.

The roar of the gun hit Baird like a physical blow. He had to grab hold of the door to save himself from falling out of the car.

The cop reeled back, his hands pressing his belly. He fell slowly on his knees, then straightened out in the road.

In saving himself from falling, Baird dropped the Colt on to the grass verge. He had only a vague idea he had lost something that was important to him, but he couldn't remember what it was. He managed to slam the door shut, and somehow start the engine going again. With a clash of gears he sent the Packard lurching forward once more.

After he had been driving a few minutes, he completely forgot about the cop. It was as if the accident had never happened, and his fever-ridden mind returned to thinking about Anita.

He was on more familiar ground now. He turned off the Paseo on to Armour Boulevard, through to Broadway, up Summit Street, and across the Essex Avenue Bridge.

He was driving better now, although twice, without knowing it, he ran through a red traffic signal. The traffic was light at that hour and no car crossed his path.

He began to slow down as he reached the shabby, darkened street where Anita's apartment was.

The street was deserted. Only a few lights showed at the upper storey windows. As he pulled up opposite Anita's apartment house, rain began to fall from the heavy black clouds that had been piling up for the past hour.

He sat for some minutes looking up at the dark building. It was now twenty minutes to nine o'clock. Anita's window on the top floor was in darkness. It would be another hour and a half before she came home, he thought. Could he last out that time?

He rested his burning forehead against the car window. If he let go now, he knew he would slip off into a coma from which there would be no awakening. He decided to go up and wait outside her door. Anything would be better than sitting in the car in which he now seemed to have passed a lifetime.

He opened the car door. When his feet touched the road, he nearly fell, but caught hold of the door in time to steady himself. He had thought he had been pretty bad the first time he had come to this house, but that was nothing to what he was feeling now.

He stood still, gathering his strength. It seemed a long way across the street, and his mind recoiled from the thought of climbing all those stairs, but he was determined now to get to her room: nothing would stop him.

As he was about to close the car door, he saw the Thompson gun on the floor by the driving seat.

He picked it up instinctively and, holding it under his arm, he turned, leaving the car door open, and began a slow, staggering walk across the street.

A car coming around the corner avoided him with a scream of tortured tyres and a blast of the horn. Baird scarcely noticed it; his eyes were fixed on the front door of the apartment house, and he was oblivious to anything else.

Painfully he dragged himself up the steps. Every muscle in his body seemed to be on fire. He pushed open the door and walked into the dimly lit, airless lobby.

The flight of stairs faced him. He stood looking at them, swaying to and fro, only just keeping his balance. Then he moved forward, and began the nightmare climb that seemed to go on and on: a climb that wracked his body and forced his breath in great labouring gasps through his clenched teeth.

He reached the first floor landing, and stopped, his back against the banisters, sweat streaming down his face. He couldn't remember how many more stairs he had to climb, and he began to doubt if he could reach the fourth floor. But his will drove him on, and slowly he staggered and lurched down the passage to the next flight of stairs.

He climbed them somehow, pausing on every step before mounting to the next. As he went down the passage to the third flight, a woman opened the door of a room close by and stared at him.

He kept on, not seeing her, and horrified at the sight of the gun and his lurching, staggering gait, she hastily closed the door.

He went up the last flight of stairs on his hands and knees, dragging the gun with him. He lay face down on the landing, drawing in great gasps of breath.

Well, he had done it. An hour's wait, he thought, and he heard himself groan. He rolled over on his side and looked at the closed door a few feet from him.

He was going to see her again. She might have changed her mind about him. He wouldn't let go, now he had got so far. She had saved him before. She might even save him again.

Through his dazed and confused mind a gruesome joke filtered.

He thought, "I'll see her again if it kills me."

III

Lieutenant Olin was on the telephone when Dallas put his head around the door.

"I'm busy," Olin grunted. "Go away and bother someone else."

Dallas came into the small office, pulled up a chair and sat astride it. In the hard light of the desk lamp he looked tired and edgy. He made a face at Olin, took out a cigarette and pasted it on his lower lip.

Olin said into the phone, "Okay, check it for fingerprints and call me back." He hung up, pushed back his chair and scowled at Dallas. "What do you want? I'm busy."

"I heard you the first time," Dallas said. "Found Hater yet?"

"I'm not even looking for him," Olin returned. "What makes you think he's where I could find him?"

"It's my bet Baird engineered his escape."

"Baird?" Olin reached for a cigar, bit off the end and spat into his trash basket. "Are you making guesses or do you know something?"

"I know something," Dallas returned, paused to light his cigarette, then went on, "Kile hired Baird to get Hater out of jail. Hater was to tell Kile where he had cached the stuff. The idea was put to Kile by a guy named Adam Gillis, Eve Gillis' brother. He and Kile were going to hand the stuff over to the Rajah of Chittabad in return for a half million in cash."

"How long have you known this?" Olin said, his eyes suddenly hard.

"Purvis had an idea this was the set-up for weeks, but he hadn't any proof. As soon as I got proof, he told me to come down here and give you the dope."

"You mean you can prove it was Baird who got Hater out?"

"Yeah. Gillis has just been booked for attempted murder. He'll talk."

Olin put down his unlighted cigar.

"What's this? How do you know Gillis has been booked? Who's running this goddamn police force?"

"Take it easy, George," Dallas said soothingly. "I was on the spot when Gillis went for his sister. I guess if I hadn't broken in, he'd have killed her. As it is she's got a fractured skull, and may lose an eye. The punk hit her with a bottle."

Olin drew in a long, deep breath.

"Look, I'm busy," he said. "I've got a cop killing on my hands. This'll have to wait. You're sure Gillis has been booked?"

Dallas nodded.

"What's left of him," he said, and looked down at his skinned knuckles. "He tried to get tough with me, so I had to quieten him."

"You know we've picked up Kile?"

"Yeah. I saw you pick him up. Gillis tipped you. I was right behind him when he put the call through to you. I've been on his tail all the evening. Lucky for his sister I was."

The phone rang.

Olin snatched it up.

"What is it?" He listened, stiffened, half got up. "You sure? A blue Packard? Okay, I'll start something. Thanks, Bill," and he hung up. "My cop was shot by a .45 Colt with Baird's prints on it," he told Dallas. "A blue Packard was seen by a passing motorist heading away from the scene of the shooting, coming this way."

"Maybe he's got Hater with him," Dallas said, getting to his feet.

"I don't give a damn one way or the other. I want Baird."

Olin got up and went out of the office. Dallas could hear him shouting orders in the outer office. He came back after a while.

"Not much I can do until we get organized," he said. "They'll pick up the Packard fast enough if it's in town. Maybe I'd better take a look at Gillis."

"I've been thinking about him," Dallas said. "The set-up is a little delicate. It mightn't be such a bad idea if you didn't see him tonight. When you do see him, he's going to talk. He's going to tell you it was the Rajah's money that financed Hater's escape. Might be awkward to have to arrest the Rajah. He's a big shot in his own country."

Olin grunted.

"I couldn't care less if he was Gandhi himself."

"No, maybe you couldn't, but the State Department might." Dallas stubbed out his cigarette. "It would save complications if the Rajah was tipped off that trouble was heading his way. He might pack his trunks and return home. If he did, you'd be let out of a tricky situation."

"Are you working for this guy?" Olin demanded aggressively.

Dallas shook his head.

"I'm figuring it from your angle, George. I wouldn't like you to get in bad with the State Department."

Olin hesitated.

"I've got to see Gillis," he said obstinately.

"Did I tell you I broke his jaw? As soon as he was booked he was shipped off to hospital. He isn't fit enough to talk tonight."

Olin stared at Dallas, then suddenly grinned.

"I'm going downstairs for a moment," he said. "Maybe you'd like to talk to your friend the Rajah."

"Yeah, I might at that," Dallas said, and reached for the phone.

Olin went down to the information room.

"Lieutenant," the desk sergeant said, "a message's just come in. A blue Packard's been found in 25th Street. There's a body of a man in it."

Olin's eyes lit up.

"Who found it?"

"O'Brien, sir. It's on his beat. He's just phoned through."

"I'll go myself. Tell Morris to come on after me with the squad. I'll want ten uniformed men as well. Have 'em out there fast."

Olin went quickly down the steps to where his car was parked. He drove away fast, his siren blasting.

Three minutes later another police car, followed by an Emergency Squad truck, went tearing down the street after Olin.

Olin found the shabby 25th Street blocked either end by a big crowd of curious sightseers. There were three prowl cars drawn up by the sidewalk. The patrolmen were keeping the crowd well away from the big blue Packard that stood under a lamp standard, its driving door open.

Olin pushed his way through the crowd and walked down the street to the Packard.

O'Brien, a big, beefy man with greying hair and keen blue eyes, saluted.

"What have you got here, Tim?" Olin asked, pausing beside the Packard.

"I'm making a guess, Lieutenant," O'Brien said, "but it's my bet it's Hater."

"Hater?"

Olin moved forward and peered into the car.

"At the back, under the blanket," O'Brien said. "I left him how I found him."

Olin opened the rear door as more police sirens wailed through the night. He lifted the blanket, and O'Brien threw the beam of his powerful flashlight over Olin's shoulders.

They both stared at the emaciated, half-naked, mud-streaked body, and at the bluish-white face. The adhesive bandage across the mouth had cut deeply, and the flesh each side of it had swollen, giving the dead face a grotesque, horrifying appearance.

"What makes you think it's Hater?" Olin asked.

"I once worked at Bellmore Farm, Lieutenant," O'Brien explained. "That's their uniform," and he touched the mud-soaked trousers.

"Ever seen Hater?"

"I've seen pictures of him. Looks like him: same eyebrows."

"Yeah," Olin said, and stepped back. The stench in the car made him feel ill.

Morris came running up.

"It's Hater," Olin said.

"What do you know?" Morris gaped into the car. "He's got his hands tied."

"You'll be telling me he's dead next," Olin snapped. "Isn't that damned ambulance coming?"

"Yes, sir. Should be here any second now."

Olin looked up and down the shabby street.

"Isn't this the street we cornered Baird in last time?"

Morris nodded.

"Yeah, I guess it."

"Maybe he's still around." Olin looked up expectantly at the roofs of the buildings. "Get four men up there. The rest of them had better go from house to house and find out if anyone's seen Baird."

While Morris went off to get his men posted, the two interns, who had got off the newly arrived ambulance, carried Hater from the car to the sidewalk. They laid him on a stretcher, and one of them carefully removed the adhesive bandage from his mouth.

"What did he die of?" Olin asked, pulling fiercely on his cigar.

"Heart failure, from the look of him," the intern said. "I'd say he's been dead for two or three days."

"What's the stink in the car, for Gawd's sake?"

"Gangrene," the intern told him. "It's not from this guy."

Olin stroked his jaw.

"Pretty bad?"

"I'd say it was bad. Whoever owns that stench is about ready for a wreath."

A patrolman came up and saluted Olin.

"Lieutenant, there's a guy wanting to speak to you," he said. "Name of Dallas. Shall I let him through?"

Olin hesitated, then shrugged.

"Yeah, let him through."

Dallas joined Olin.

"What have you got?" he asked, looking at the body on the stretcher.

"Hater," Olin said. "Not much doubt about it. O'Brien here has seen a picture of him."

Dallas blew out his cheeks.

"That's sweet, isn't it? The only guy in the world who knows where the Chittabad collection is, and he has to croak. Think he told Baird where it was cached before he handed in his pail?"

Olin shrugged.

"Looks like Baird's badly hurt. Someone who's been in that car's got gangrene. He couldn't have got far."

Dallas looked thoughtfully down the street at the gaping crowd. Then he frowned, peered forward, stared, and turning, caught hold of Olin's arm.

"I think I can guess where Baird is," he said. "See that girl in the front row? The one with a scarf over her head."

Olin looked in the direction.

"What of her?"

"She's Baird's girl. She lives across the way. No. 30, on the top floor. It's my bet Baird's up there right now."

"How the hell do you know all this?" Olin snarled. "If you've been holding out on me ...!"

"Burns found out about her," Dallas explained. "I didn't know until tonight."

"There are a lot of things you didn't know until tonight," Olin said angrily. "You're sure that's Baird's girl?"

"Yeah."

Olin turned to O'Brien.

"That girl with the scarf on her head. Bring her over here."

"Miss Jackson?" O'Brien looked startled. "Excuse me, Lieutenant, you're sure you want her?"

Olin glared at him.

"That's what I said! What is she – untouchable or something?"

"Sorry, Lieutenant," O'Brien said uncomfortably. "I know most people on my beat, and she's a good girl. She works hard and keeps to herself. She's never been in any trouble, and that's saying something in this street."

"Well, she's in trouble now," Olin snapped. "Bring her here."

O'Brien saluted and walked stiffly down the street. He went up to Anita, said something, took her elbow and brought her back to Olin.

Anita's dark eyes were scared, but she didn't flinch from Olin's hard gaze.

"You know Verne Baird?" he snapped.

"I've met him," Anita said.

"Yeah? Didn't he hole up in your room about a month ago?" Olin demanded aggressively. "You'd better not lie. I've got a witness."

She looked quickly away from him, and her eyes took in the stretcher. The intern was dropping a blanket across Hater's dead face. She had a glimpse of the swollen, grotesque mask before the blanket hid it.

Her hands went to her breasts, and the colour drained out of her face. She looked appealingly at O'Brien, claiming his attention because he was a familiar stranger among unfamiliar ones.

"Who – who is it?" she asked.

"Did you hear what I said?" Olin barked. "I asked you ..."

"Who is that, please?" she repeated, looking at O'Brien, and pointed at the still figure on the stretcher.

"A guy named Hater," O'Brien told her. "But answer the Lieutenant's question."

"Hater? Is he dead?"

There was something about the way she was holding herself and the sudden horror in her eyes that stopped Olin from grabbing and shaking her. He glanced at O'Brien and nodded.

"Yes, he's dead. You don't have to worry about him," O'Brien said. "Tell the Lieutenant about Baird."

Slowly, as if she was sleepwalking, Anita walked over to the stretcher.

The intern, a young, red-faced fellow, looked up impatiently.

"Can I see him, please?" she asked.

Surprised, he looked across at Olin, who signalled to him.

"He's not pretty," the intern said grudgingly, as if he were jealous of sharing his world of horrors with any outsider.

He lifted the blanket.

Anita looked for a long moment at the dead, swollen face. She seemed to go suddenly limp, and O'Brien went quickly to her side, taking her arm. He turned her away, so her back was to the body on the stretcher.

"What happened to him?" she asked, her fingers digging into O'Brien's wrist. "He had only two more years to serve, he wouldn't have run away."

"What is this?" Olin said, exasperated.

As he made a move to go to her, Dallas pulled him back.

"Let me talk to her," he said urgently, and before Olin could stop him, he was at Anita's side.

"He was kidnapped from prison," he told her. "They wanted to find out where he had hidden the Chittabad collection. Baird was paid to get him out of jail. It was Baird who killed him."

She stiffened and pushed away from O'Brien.

"Baird did that?"

"That's right. Do you know Hater?"

She jerked up her head and looked defiantly at Dallas.

"Of course I know him. He was my father."

Before Dallas could collect his startled wits, a patrolman with an elderly woman came quickly across the street towards Olin.

"Lieutenant," the patrolman said, "this woman says she's seen Baird."

"Where?" Olin demanded, turning to the woman.

"He was going to the top floor of my house," the woman said excitedly. "A big man; he seemed ill, and he was carrying a gun."

"Where's your house?"

"No. 30. That's it over there," and she pointed.

"You say he had a gun: what kind of a gun?"

"I don't know: a sort of machine-gun."

"Okay," Olin said; he waved the patrolman and woman away. "Come on, boys, let's get him."

"Wait a minute," Dallas said, catching hold of Olin's arm. "You don't think you'll take him alive?"

"I don't care if he's alive or dead," Olin said. "Maybe he knows where the collection is. You've got to get him alive."

Olin stared at him.

"I don't give a damn about the collection. I'm getting him dead or alive."

"Can I quote you?" Dallas said. "The insurance companies will love to know the name of the officer who gypped them out of four million."

Olin threw his cigar butt in the street.

"Will you get out of my way! I've had about enough of you!"

"Without the gun you could take him alive," Dallas said, speaking quickly. "Let me go up there and try and get the gun. I can tell him I'm from Miss Jackson. He might listen to me."

Anita touched Olin's arm.

"I'll get his gun," she said quietly. "He won't hurt me. Then you can come up and take him."

"You don't know what you're saying. This guy's dangerous," Olin said, exasperated. "Will you two get out of my hair?"

"Let her do it," Dallas said. "You can be right behind her. If he starts blasting with that gun, he could kill half your men before you got him."

"I tell you she's not going up there ...!" Olin began.

Anita turned suddenly and began to run across the street towards the house.

As Olin opened his mouth to shout after her, Dallas stumbled against him, knocking him off balance.

"What the hell do you think you're doing?" Olin snarled, recovering himself. "Come on, you guys, get after that girl!"

IV

Baird, lying on his side, his head on his arm, his back against the wall, was suddenly galvanized from his coma by the sound of a police siren.

He lifted his head, listening. The wailing note of the siren floated up the stairs like the vanguard of death. With an effort that made him feel faint and sick, he dragged himself to a sitting position. His right hand went out and pulled the Thompson gun towards him. He rested the butt against his chest, the barrel covering the stairs.

How had they found him? he wondered. He had a vague idea that he had come in a car, but his mind was too dazed and sick with fever to remember what he had done with the car. Surely he couldn't have been so crazy as to have left it outside the house?

He looked over his shoulder along the passage. He could see the faint light of the moon coming through the skylight. If he remained in the passage, they would take him in the rear. Some of them would come up the stairs, the others would come through the skylight.

Slowly he dragged himself to Anita's door. He reached up and turned the handle, but the door was locked. The effort sent him into a half-conscious stupour, and he lay on his side, against the door, fighting off the feeling that he was about to slip off the edge of the world.

More sirens brought him alert again. He caught hold of the door handle and dragged himself to his feet. He set his back against the door. From this position he could watch both the skylight and the stairs.

He got the Thompson under his arm with the butt against the door, his finger curled around the trigger. It wouldn't last long, he told himself, but he'd take some of them with him. He remembered with startling clearness the same thing had happened to him in this very passage some five weeks ago. Then he had given himself up for lost, but she had saved him. It was still possible she might save him again.

Time hung in space. He waited with the patience of a wounded and trapped animal. Every now and then his head dropped to his chest, and his legs sagged, but each time he made the effort and stopped himself from sliding to the floor.

It was a long time before he heard footsteps on the stairs. He raised the gun, and waited.

Then he saw her. She was coming up the stairs, her hand on the banister rail, a red and blue scarf on her head, and her shabby overcoat dark with rain. She looked at him, white-faced, and her eyes big and frightened.

"Hello," he said huskily. "This is where we came in, isn't it?"

She didn't say anything. He saw her eyes shift from him to the gun. He realized he was still pointing it at her, and he hurriedly lowered the barrel.

"What are you doing here?" she asked, not moving.

"My arm's bad," he said. It was extraordinary how her presence had suddenly given him a new lease in life. The sight of her seemed to lift him above the fever that was devouring him. "Are the cops outside?"

"There's been an accident," she said. "A man died."

"Aren't they looking for me?"

"It's the accident," she repeated, and began to move slowly and warily up the stairs. "Do you want me to look at your arm?"

He tried to grin.

"It's past being looked at. It'll have to come off."

"Perhaps I can do something." She came within a yard of him and stopped, her eyes on the gun.

"Your door's locked. I tried to get in."

"I always keep it locked. Do you want to lie on the bed?"

"Maybe I'd better not. I don't want to get you into trouble. I may die on you." He closed his eyes for a moment. "Are you sure the cops aren't looking for me?"

"There was an accident," she said, refusing to lie to him. "They found a dead man in a car outside."

"A dead man? You're sure he's dead?"

"Yes."

"That's Hater," he said. "I remember now. He's dead, is he?"

She didn't say anything.

"Yeah, that's right," he said, his mind groping vaguely into the past. "I forgot about him. We tied him and hid him under a blanket, then my arm got bad and I forgot about him. I forgot about everything except you. I've driven over five hundred miles to see you."

Still she didn't say anything.

"Hater was quite a guy," Baird went on, half to himself. "You wouldn't believe it to look at him. He hid four million bucks worth of jewellery somewhere. Think of that! Now he's dead, and no one will ever find the stuff."

"You killed him," she said, in a cold, flat voice.

"No. If he's dead it's because it was coming to him. I forgot about him, that's all. You can't call that killing a man." He put his hand on the doorknob. "Aren't you going to open up?"

"Yes," she said, and moved closer to him. She touched the gun. "Shall I take this? You won't need it."

His fingers tightened on the gun.

"I might," he said. "I guess I can manage. Open the door, won't you?"

She put a key in the lock and pushed open the door.

"Remember the last time?" he asked, looking into the shadowy room, lit by the moonlight coming in through the window. "Take it." He pushed the Thompson into her hands. "When I woke up last time you had put my rod by my side. I haven't forgotten that. You're the only one I've ever met who I can trust." He sank down on the bed. "I've often thought about you and what you did for me. I've often thought what you said about kindness isn't something you buy from a grocery store. I guess you were right. You've got to have kindness in you."

She held the gun stiffly, the barrel pointing down at the floor.

"Paul Hater was my father," she said.

Baird rubbed his ravaged face with the back of his hand.

"What's that?"

"I said Paul Hater was my father."

He looked at her, then at the gun.

"Would you have told me that if I hadn't given you the gun?"

She shook her head.

"But he can't mean anything to you. You can't have seen him for fifteen years. You must have been about five when they took him away."

"My mother told me about him," she said quietly. "She told me how they tortured him. The only thing that kept him alive was the knowledge I'd be waiting for him when he came out."

"The only thing that kept him alive," Baird said, "was the thought of that stuff he had hidden away, and what he was going to do with it."

"No, that's what everyone thought," she said, coming to the foot of the bed and looking down at him. "When he was arrested, my mother took the collection. No one knew he was married. It was easy for her to get out of the country. The ship struck a reef. Only she and five others were rescued. The collection went down with the ship. For fifteen years my father suffered so my mother could go free. I never told him she found someone else. Then you had to come along and kill him when his suffering was nearly ended."

"I didn't kill him," Baird said obstinately.

"But you did. If you had left him alone, he would be alive now."

"You're feeling pretty bad about it, aren't you?" he said. "I guess I'm sorry. I wouldn't have done it if I'd known. I want you to believe that. I still owe you a lot. I could have squared our debt if I had known."

"I shouldn't have helped you the first time," she said. "That's where I went wrong. I only did it because I remembered what they did to him. If I had let them find you here, he would be alive now."

"I guess that's right," he said, and lay back on the pillow. "There's not much of me left. They can have what there is. Go ahead and call them."

"They're waiting now," she said.

"I wouldn't have done it if I'd known," he muttered. "I don't suppose you'll believe that."

"Does it matter now? It's a little late for regrets, isn't it? You did it, and he's dead. I blame myself, not you."

His despair was bitter as she went out of the room without looking at him. For the first time in his life he felt afraid, for he realized he was going to die as he had lived: uncared for and in loneliness.

Olin and two patrolmen, guns in hand, came into the room. Dallas followed them.

Baird lay flat on his back, his eyes closed. He was breathing with difficulty, and sweat ran off his face, soaking the pillow.

Olin snapped, "Get that intern up here, and tell him to hurry."

Dallas shook Baird's shoulder.

"Hey, you! Wake up!"

Baird opened his eyes.

"Did Hater tell you where the stuff is?" Dallas demanded. "Come on, spill it! It's not going to be of any use to you now."

Baird shook his head.

"I forgot to ask him," he said, in a voice that was scarcely audible. "Too bad, isn't it, copper?" His eyes moved from Dallas to Olin. "I holed up in this room after I knocked off those two in the drugstore," he said, speaking with difficulty. "I told her if she didn't hide me Rico would get her. She didn't want to do it. Do you understand? I made her. You're not going to hold it against her, are you?"

"Getting soft?" Olin said with a sneer. "You know as well as I do she covered you, and that makes her an accessory to murder!"

"She thought Rico would rub her out if she didn't cover me." Baird made an effort to sit up, but he couldn't make it.

"Quit lying!" Olin said. "Why should you want to shield her? She took your gun. If it hadn't been for her we wouldn't have found you. Now, come on: she hid you willingly, didn't she?"

Baird looked at Dallas.

"You fix it," he gasped. "She's a good kid. I made her do what she did. Put it in writing. I'll sign it."

"Listen," Dallas said to Olin, "if she hadn't got his gun, you'd have had a battle on your hands. What do you want to pick on her for?"

Olin made an impatient gesture.

"Oh, the hell with it! I don't want her. She can go for all I care. Where's that damned intern?"

Baird relaxed limply back on the pillow. His eyes closed.

Dallas said, "Can I tell your man to let her go?"

"Sure," Olin said impatiently. "Do what you damn well like."

As Dallas went into the passage, the intern came up the stairs.

Olin called to him, "Give this guy a shot of something. I want him to make a statement."

Dallas ran down the stairs.

Anita and a patrolman were waiting in the lobby. Dallas stepped past them and shut himself in the pay booth at the end of the passage. He put a call through to Purvis. Rapidly he brought Purvis up to date on the night's happenings.

"Looks like we're sunk," he concluded. "With Hater dead, our last chance of finding the stuff goes with him."

"How about the girl?" Purvis said. "Maybe she knows."

"Do you want me to ask her?"

"Certainly," Purvis said. "Tell her I'll give her ten grand if she can tell us where he hid the stuff."

"Getting pretty generous all of a sudden, aren't you?"

"Go and tell her!"

"Now wait a minute, if she knows where the stuff is hidden, and she tells us, what's to stop Olin nabbing her as an accessory?" Dallas pointed out.

"What do I care?" Purvis barked. "Let her worry about that. And listen, don't go putting ideas into her head. The chances are she won't think of that angle. Ten grand's a lot of money."

"Would you cover her if Olin asked questions?" Dallas persisted.

"I'm not that crazy," Purvis said. "Just don't tell her. The chances are she won't figure that angle."

"Hold on," Dallas said. "I'll ask her."

He laid down the receiver, left the pay booth and walked over to where Anita and the patrolman were waiting.

"The Lieutenant says this woman can go," Dallas said to the patrolman. "He wants you upstairs."

"Okay," the patrolman said. "That lets you out," he went on to Anita. "You'd better take a walk until they've got him out of here."

As he went up the stairs, he gave Dallas a slow wink.

"Just a minute, Miss Jackson," Dallas said as Anita began to move away. "I'm Ed Dallas of the International Detective Agency. We've been trying to find the Chittabad collection since it was stolen. I've been authorized to pay you ten thousand dollars if you can give me any information that'll lead to the recovery of the jewels."

She looked up at him, her face expressionless.

"It's only fair to warn you," he went on, "that if you do know what's happened to them and you tell me, you run the risk of being prosecuted as an accessory."

"But you shouldn't tell me that, should you?" she said.

"Maybe not, but I don't like the way my boss is handling this case. All he thinks about is what he's going to get out of it. It's up to you. If you think ten grand is worth the risk, and you know something, now's the time to spill it."

She shook her head.

"I have no information to give you."

"Sure?"

"Yes, I'm sure."

"Is there anything I can do for you?"

She stiffened, and her eyes became hostile.

"No, thank you."

He took out his card and slipped it into her hand.

"You might change your mind. If you do, give me a call. It's not much fun being on your own after a thing like this. I might be able to help you."

"Thank you, but I'll manage."

She walked past him, down the passage to the street door. Dallas watched her until he lost sight of her in the crowd that stood either side of the entrance. He wondered if he would see her again, and hoped he would.

He went back to the pay booth.

"You there?" he asked, as he picked up the receiver.

"Of course I'm here," Purvis said. "What did she say?"

"She doesn't know. Hater never told her a thing. I'm not surprised. She was only five when he went inside."

"You're sure she isn't lying?"

"Not a chance. I can always tell when a woman's lying. If you ask me the collection never will be found."

"I'm not asking you!" Purvis snapped. "Come back to the office. Maybe we can figure an angle."

Dallas watched two white-coated attendants carrying the stretcher down the stairs. They had covered Baird's face with the blanket.

"You still there?" Purvis asked suspiciously.

"Yeah," Dallas said. "They're just carrying Baird out. The crowd's getting a big bang out of it." He opened the booth door so he could watch the stretcher being carried into the street. "Funny how people like to gape at a corpse. I believe he was really fond of that girl."

"Will you stop muttering to yourself," Purvis said angrily. "Come back here at once. I think I've got an angle already."

"How you love to kid yourself," Dallas said pityingly and hung up.

THE END

James Hadley Chase

An Ace Up My Sleeve

When three very different people come together, all out for the same thing and prepared to go to any lengths to get it, the stakes are likely to be high. But, for a wealthy middle-aged woman, an international lawyer and a young American, games of bluff and counter-bluff quickly develop into a dangerous and deadly battle. As the action hots up, Chase weaves a fast-moving story of blackmail, intrigue and extortion with a hair-raising climax.

The Guilty are Afraid

When Jack Sheppey ends up dead in a beach hut in a wealthy town on the Pacific coast, his former partner in their detective agency starts a desperate quest to find his killer. But as private investigator Lew Brandon soon learns, this becomes a non-stop, terrifying and deadly hunt which will take him right to the heart of gangster territory.

JAMES HADLEY CHASE

HAVE A CHANGE OF SCENE

Larry Carr is a diamond expert in need of a break. So when his psychiatrist suggests he has a change of scene, he jumps at the opportunity to move to Luceville, a struggling industrial town, and become a social worker. This, he thinks, will give him all the rest he needs...until he runs into Rhea Morgan, a ruthless, vicious thief who also happens to be extremely attractive. He falls headlong into the criminal world and embarks upon a thrilling, rapid and dastardly adventure in true Hadley Chase style.

JUST A MATTER OF TIME

An old lady's will seems to be causing quite a stir. Suddenly everyone wants to get in on the action, everyone that is, including a master forger, a hospital nurse, a young delinquent, a bank executive and, to make matters worse, a professional killer. With such ingredients, a showdown seems inevitable and James Hadley Chase adds enough suspense to keep you guessing right up to the very last page.

JAMES HADLEY CHASE

MY LAUGH COMES LAST

Farrell Brannigan, President of the National Californian Bank, is an extremely successful man. So when he builds another bank in an up-and-coming town on the Pacific coast, he is given worldwide publicity, and this new bank is hailed as 'the safest bank in the world'. But Brannigan's success came at a price and he made many enemies on his way up the ladder. It seems that one of them is now set on revenge and determined to destroy both the bank and Brannigan himself.

YOU'RE DEAD WITHOUT MONEY

Joey Luck and his daughter Cindy were small-time criminals going nowhere fast...until they joined forces with Vin Pinna, a hardened criminal on the run from Miami. They began to set their sights higher and turned their hands to kidnapping. But their hostage, ex-movie star Don Elliot, seemed to have different ideas. He wanted in so they formed a 'quartet in crime' and this time the stakes were higher still – eight Russian stamps worth a million dollars.

'realistic and suspenseful' – *Observer*

Printed in Great Britain
by Amazon